PRAISE FOR THE JONATHAN QUINN SERIES

"Brilliant and heart pounding"

JEFFERY DEAVER, *NEW YORK TIMES*
BESTSELLING AUTHOR

"Addictive."

JAMES ROLLINS, *NEW YORK TIMES*
BESTSELLING AUTHOR

"Unputdownable."

TESS GERRITSEN, *NEW YORK TIMES*
BESTSELLING AUTHOR

"The best elements of Lee Child, John le Carré, and Robert Ludlum."

SHELDON SIEGEL, *NEW YORK TIMES*
BESTSELLING AUTHOR

"Quinn is one part James Bond, one part Jason Bourne."

NASHVILLE BOOK WORM

"Welcome addition to the political thriller game."

PUBLISHERS WEEKLY

THE BURIED

ALSO BY BRETT BATTLES

THE JONATHAN QUINN THRILLERS

Novels

Becoming Quinn

The Cleaner

The Deceived

Shadow of Betrayal (U.S.)/The Unwanted (U.K.)

The Silenced

The Destroyed

The Collected

The Enraged

The Discarded

The Buried

The Unleashed

The Aggrieved

The Fractured

The Unknown

The Vanished

Novellas

Night Work

Short Stories

"Just Another Job"—A Jonathan Quinn Story

"Off the Clock"—A Jonathan Quinn Story

"The Assignment"—An Orlando Story

"Lesson Plan"—A Jonathan Quinn Story

"Quick Study"—An Orlando Story

Takedown

STANDALONES

Novels

The Pull of Gravity

No Return

Mine

Novellas

Mine: The Arrival

Short Stories

"Perfect Gentleman"

For Younger Readers

THE TROUBLE FAMILY CHRONICLES

Here Comes Mr. Trouble

THE BURIED

A JONATHAN QUINN THRILLER

BRETT BATTLES

To the memory of my friend and former colleague
Danielle Velarde.
A talented artist, a voracious reader, and an enthusiastic supporter.

You are truly missed

1

JUNE 24

A STINGING SLAP ripped Dani from unconsciousness.
"Wake up." The words were calm but demanding.
She lolled her head back, groaning softly.

"I said wake up."

A second slap sent her face flying in the other direction. She squinted, straining against the bright light. She was in a chair, nude but for the straps restraining her arms and legs. A short, balding man stood in front of her, and behind him a much larger, hairier one. Laurel and Hardy, she thought, if Hardy had spent more time in a gym.

"What's so funny?" the short one asked.

She must have grinned without realizing it. She opened her eyes the rest of the way but left his question unanswered.

The talker leaned forward and examined her. "I believe you have some information my client is interested in. If you're smart, you'll give it to me now so I can pass it along."

She gave him nothing.

The man chuckled through a toothy sneer as he stood up. "You will call me Mr. Black. My friend here"—he motioned to his partner—"is Mr. Red. You'll do everything we ask of you. Do you understand?"

When Dani didn't answer, he smacked her again.

"Understand?" he repeated.

She locked eyes with him, licked a drop of blood from the corner of her mouth, and shrugged.

He stepped away. "Mr. Red, if you will?"

The big guy circled her and disappeared from sight. She braced herself but was still startled when he grabbed her head—one of his hands squeezing her chin, the other pinching the base of her skull at her neck. She tried to wrench herself out of his grasp but to no avail.

Mr. Black walked over to a nearby table and picked up something. When he returned, he was wearing a sick smile.

"Maybe you have the information hidden somewhere," he said. "Shall we have a look?"

She heard a mechanical click, then a low, vibrating hum. With his empty hand, Mr. Black touched a strand of her dark auburn hair, fingering it for a moment before letting it go.

"Pity," he said. "Such nice volume. But then again, you have excellent genes."

The vibrating device in his other hand turned out to be a pair of electric clippers. He raised them to her hairline, and in quick but steady movements he sheared her entire head.

"You can release her now," Mr. Black told Mr. Red as he returned the clippers to the table.

Mr. Red gave her a squeeze and let go. Once he was out of the way, Mr. Black examined every inch of her skull. Of course, what he was seeking was not there.

He stepped in front of her again. "Is it inside your skull?" he asked, tapping her temple. "Is that where you're keeping it? There are ways to get it out of there, too, you know. You may think you can hold on to it, but you can't." He scanned her up and down. "Or perhaps it's somewhere else."

Without warning, he grabbed one of Dani's eyelids and turned it out so he could look underneath, then did the same with the other. The ordeal was more uncomfortable than painful, and though she wanted to blink, she resisted.

Mr. Black grabbed the stool that had been sitting near the table and set it in front of her. After taking a seat, he pulled on a pair of thin rubber gloves.

"This shouldn't hurt much." He placed his thumbs on either side of her mouth. "Open."

It took all her willpower not to let her composure crack.

"Come on, let's go. Show me that smile."

She parted her lips but left her teeth clenched.

As he examined them, he said, "Very nice. Did you have braces growing up?" He pulled a penlight out of his pocket. "I know this goes without saying but don't try anything. You won't enjoy the consequences."

He peeled back her upper lip and shined the light on the underside. He repeated the process with the lower lip. Next, he pinched the corners of her mouth and pulled outward so he could look at the inside of her cheeks.

"You obviously floss. Good for you. So many people avoid that these days." He tapped the light against her teeth. "All the way now."

She wanted to keep her teeth locked together, but then she heard Marianne's voice, reassuring her like it always did when Dani was scared.

Don't worry. He won't find it.

Dani lowered her jaw.

"Good," Mr. Black said.

He swept the light through her mouth and then leaned back.

"Mr. Red, I seem to have forgotten the mirror. Could you get it for me?"

"Uh-huh."

Mr. Red lumbered over to the table, returned with a dentist-style, rod-mounted mirror, and gave it to the smaller man.

"Thank you," Mr. Black said.

He slipped the rod into her mouth and shined the light in again.

After several seconds, he said, "Lift your tongue, please."

There it was. The request she prayed would never come.

It'll be all right.

Dani curled her tongue down and pulled it as far back as she could, hoping that would satisfy him. Initially, it appeared to do the trick. He stuck the mirror in again and checked her lower gums. When he pulled the instrument out, he handed it to his colleague and then grabbed her tongue with a thumb and finger.

She came within a millisecond of chomping down, but again, her sister's voice stopped her. *Calm down. He won't find it. No way.*

Mr. Black's gloved thumb rubbed against the scar on the underside of her tongue.

There is *no scar*, Marianne reminded her. *It's been gone for years.*

But Dani knew the skin there felt different.

Mr. Black lifted her tongue high, his gloved thumb remaining over the spot. Finally, after what felt like hours, he removed his hand from her mouth.

"This may be hard to understand, but I'm trying to do you a favor here," he said. "It'll go a lot easier for you if the information you have is passed on through us instead of letting my client get it out of you herself. The Wolf won't waste time waiting until you feel ready to talk."

Dani closed her mouth and stared at him. Inside she was a mix of elation and dread. The former because Mr. Black hadn't found it, even though his thumb had been right on what he was looking for. The latter because he had said he was working for The Wolf.

Mr. Black returned the mirror to the table and pulled off the rubber gloves one finger at a time. When he was done, he said, "Yours isn't the only business I have to attend to today. I think maybe we'll talk again tomorrow. No reason The Wolf needs to know we've found you just yet. Mr. Red, would you see our guest to her room?"

"With pleasure," Mr. Red replied.

There was a lustiness in the bigger man's voice that Dani didn't like at all.

Mr. Black must have heard it, too, because he said, "Not this one. Special case."

"I know," Mr. Red shot back, irritated.

"I mean it."

"I said I know." The big man opened a switchblade and cut the restraints holding Dani to the chair. "That way." He pointed at one of the two exits. "And feel free to try something. I'd be more than happy to carry you."

Dani denied him that pleasure.

2

THE BEDROOM, LIKE the house, was surprisingly modest for the amount of money Samuel Edmondson had likely made over the years.

Nice things, sure. The furniture top of the line, but nothing garish, every piece understated. Ananke didn't for a second believe the décor was some kind of aesthetic choice. Edmondson had picked out furnishings that made him look like nothing more than what the world thought he was—a typical, upper-middle-class drone. Perhaps he had a few more things than others in similar positions, but his single, no-kids status would have explained that away.

No, this had to be a cover home, she decided. His real oasis was probably located someplace else. But since the intel provided by her employer indicated this was where Edmondson would be, it was the only location included in her briefing.

So be it. Even if she was a bit curious, it was always better not to know all the details.

A low groan broke the steady rhythm of the man's breaths. In a predictable pattern, his eyes creaked open and then confusion set in as he wondered why he'd gone to sleep without turning off the light.

He hadn't.

More puzzlement came when he tried to sit up and found nothing below his neck would move.

There it is, she thought from her chair against the wall as he started to pant. *The panic.*

He tried again to will his body to follow directions, but only succeeded in straining the muscles in his face.

In a kind, gentle voice, Ananke said, "It won't work."

Edmondson whipped his head around, his eyes widening at the sight of her. "Who the hell are you? What are you doing here?"

"Good evening to you, too, Mr. Edmondson."

His surprised look turned angry. "I don't know what you think you're doing, but you obviously don't realize the size of the mistake you've made. I am *not* someone you want to mess with. I will come after you, and I will find you."

A smile. "I'd like to see you try."

He scanned the room, obviously looking for something he could use to free himself, but even if a gun lay next to his palm, he would be unable to grab it.

Here it comes, she thought as he started to turn back to her.

The blood had drained from his face and all of his bravado was gone. In a halting whisper, he asked, "Who sent you?"

She raised an eyebrow. "Does it matter?"

"Yes, goddammit, it matters. I can make a deal," he explained. "I know things."

"Let me stop you before you embarrass yourself anymore. There won't be any deal."

Voice rising, he said, "There's always time for a deal. Just take me to whoever you're working for. Let me show them what I can do for them."

She looked at him with pity. "My client was very specific about what I was to collect. And I never disappoint my clients."

"Collect? Collect what?" He scanned the room for a few

seconds, then froze. "You found it, didn't you? You went down there. Oh, God."

"Mr. Edmondson, please. Use your head. You *know* what I've taken." Denial always played a big part in these events, but she was tiring of his refusal to connect the dots. There was a schedule to keep, after all, and more to be done this night.

She could see the exact second he finally let the truth in. "No. No, you're lying. I'm a valuable asset."

"My orders would seem to contradict that."

"I've got money," he blurted out. "A lot! T-ten million. It's all yours if you let me go. You can say I wasn't here, or, or...or tell them you killed me and tossed my body in the ocean. I'll disappear. No one will ever know."

She said nothing.

"Fifteen million," he said. "It's all I have. We can transfer it right now."

She arched her eyebrow again but remained silent.

Nervously licking his lips, he said, "Okay, thirty million. That's everything. Just let me go. I swear you'll be the only one who knows."

She rose from the chair and glided to his bed. "You misunderstand the situation," she said, patting his unmoving arm with her gloved hand. "You're already dead."

"What?"

"Two shots while you were sleeping. The first paralyzed you, and the second has been working its away into your brain for the last ten minutes. Soon..." She looked at her watch. "Wow, time really *does* fly, doesn't it?" She smiled. "In less than five minutes, your brain will stop sending the signals that instructs your diaphragm to expand and contract and your heart to beat."

"Please, no! Y-y-you must have an antidote, right? Give it to me and the money's yours! Don't you understand? Thirty million dollars!"

She couldn't help but laugh. "Even if an antidote does exist, do you really think my client would have allowed me to bring it along? My apologies you weren't given more of a warning, but who really gets that anyway?" She turned toward the door. "I'm sure you'd rather spend your last couple minutes alone."

As she walked out, he called, "No! Please! Don't leave me! There's got to be something you can do! There's got to be—"

She shut the door.

She hadn't been exactly straight with Edmondson. Yes, he was going to die, and though it could be in the next five minutes, it could also take ten, or, if he was a particularly rare case, he might even last another fifteen. So she had a bit of time to kill before she could verify his termination.

She set the timer on her phone for a quarter hour and headed down to the kitchen to see if there was something to eat. As she descended the stairs, she couldn't help but recall his words as he was trying to figure out what she'd taken. "You found it, didn't you? You went down there."

That sure sounded like Edmonson was hiding something. His money, perhaps? Now *that* might be interesting. While ethically she couldn't allow him to bribe her, if she happened to stumble upon some cash lying around, that was a different story.

A quick tour of the place won't hurt.

She took a stroll through the first floor, assuming that's what he meant when he said "down there." Kitchen, living room, family room, pantry, laundry, and bathroom, but nothing in any of them shouted "hidden treasure." Then again, he probably wouldn't leave the key to his stolen fortune lying around for all to see. She checked closets and cabinets, looking for signs of false panels and concealed doorways, but came up empty. The only place left to look was the attached garage off the kitchen.

She checked her watch. She still had over five minutes. More than enough time for a quick peek.

As she opened the door, a hint of warm air drifted into the kitchen, the remnants of the earlier hot day. The space was dark, so she felt around until she found the light switch and flicked it on.

Edmondson's Volvo S80 sedan was parked on the side closest to the door. On the other side of it, she could see part of a motorcycle.

When she circled the Volvo, her eyes lit up. Not just any motorcycle, but a vintage BMW with attached sidecar. Her estimation of Edmondson's character ticked up a notch. She owned several bikes herself, two of which were at least as old as this one. None with sidecars, though. She preferred the freedom of racing down the road on her own but she could appreciate the beauty of Edmondson's combo.

As she moved in closer, the small amount of regard she'd begun to feel for Edmondson faded. If he'd really cared about the bike, it wouldn't be covered in a layer of dust. She knelt beside it for a closer look. While the bike appeared mechanically sound, it definitely needed maintenance. Yep, Edmondson was an asshole, all right. Hopefully, its next owner would treat the bike with respect.

She stood up, thinking maybe she should take possession of it herself. That's when she noticed the handlebar grips. There was dust on the ends, but the parts where hands would go were clean. The seat, however, was as dusty as the rest of the bike.

So Edmondson had...what? Just put his hands on the bike recently for kicks?

She looked down at the tires and noted they were sitting on a large sheet of cardboard. Crushed into the sheet and leading off from the tires was a pair of well-worn tracks. The bike and sidecar had apparently been rolled off and on several times. Given the size of the garage, Edmondson could have done so without opening the larger door to the outside.

Curious, Ananke wrapped her hands around the clean spots on the handles and rolled the bike back. Once it was clear, she lifted the cardboard off the floor and propped it against the Volvo.

Huh, she thought. The cardboard had been clean but the concrete underneath it was covered with dark oil stains. Stains that seemed a little too perfect.

Getting on her knees, she carefully scanned the floor.

There, she thought a few seconds later.

A crack, one too straight to have been caused naturally.

She followed the line until it met another. That one led to a third that connected with a fourth that ran all the way back to number one. All together, they created a nice and tidy rectangle.

"Sorry, Mr. Edmondson," she whispered. "But I think I just found your 'down there.'"

The handle for the rectangle was hidden in the blackest patch of oil, under an oval chip of concrete that popped out when she pushed it. She slipped her fingers inside, found a lever, and flipped it.

The door was heavy enough to take both hands to pull it open. Once it was out of the way, she retrieved her pocket flashlight and shined it into the hole beneath the door. The beam revealed a steep staircase going down about fifteen feet.

Before she could decide what she would do next, the alarm on her phone went off. She cursed under her breath. As much as she wanted to see what was below, she had a job to do.

She thought for a moment. Perhaps there was still a way to get a peek.

Leaving the trapdoor open, she headed back upstairs to the master bedroom, where she found Edmondson staring dead-eyed at the ceiling. She checked his pulse, then pulled out her phone and made the call.

When the line was answered, she said, "All yours."

3

J ONATHAN QUINN ENTERED the house through the back
door, his partner Nate following a few steps behind. The
quiet Seattle suburb was not exactly Quinn's favorite type of
job site. Places like this were too friendly, neighbors knowing
neighbors, neighbors watching neighbors, neighbors sticking their
noses in neighbors' business—all raising the risk of him and his
team being noticed.

The late hour—about thirty minutes before midnight—helped,
but didn't guarantee anything. Every street had its night owls,
many of whom would sit in darkened rooms and stare out their
windows at the street.

Quinn and Nate headed up the stairs, the tools of their trade
packed in the duffel bags each carried. They were cleaners of the
highest order, the people you called when you had a body that
needed to disappear.

On rare occasions, however, a client would request that things
be arranged so that the body would be found and the death
attributed to something other than what had actually happened.
Such was the case with the Edmondson assignment.

Per the pre-mission brief, Ananke—the assassin—was to have
performed the deed in the target's bedroom, located on the second

floor. She had assured Quinn it would be a bloodless takedown. Having worked with her a few times in the past, he trusted she would deliver as promised, making the body removal and the cleanup of the termination scene the easy part of his and Nate's night. The part Quinn wasn't looking forward to would come after that. It too was a special request.

The target, Samuel Edmondson, posed as a small-time financial services broker in his civilian job, but made his real money as an information broker for less than reputable individuals and organizations. Among his clients were several terrorist cells and other groups that were considered enemies of the United States, hence the reason Helen Cho's group was involved. She was the client who had hired Quinn, Nate, and Ananke.

After Quinn and his partner finished prepping the body for travel, they were supposed to do a quick but thorough check of the house for anything that might provide information on Edmondson's clients before heading out to set up the target's alternate death scenario. Quinn could count on one hand the number of times he'd been asked to do the same kind of search. Though he didn't like it, he knew it wouldn't be a big deal. Grab whatever computers and files the guy had and move on.

While the upper hallway was dark, light leaked out the partially opened door at the far end. From the blueprints, Quinn knew it led to the master bedroom where the body should be. He pushed the door open but only took a single step inside before stopping.

"What are you still doing here?" he asked.

Ananke was sitting on a chair near the bed. Her part of the assignment complete, she should have left as soon as she'd notified Quinn.

"I had a little free time. Thought I'd watch you guys work. It's been a while." She smiled. "You don't mind, do you?"

He moved over to the bed. The target was lying on his back, under the covers. Quinn scanned the rest of the space. Nothing seemed out of order.

When he looked back at Ananke, he said, "You're in the way."

With an ease few people could match, she rose out of her chair and slinked by them. A stray finger traced the muscles on Nate's arm as she passed.

"You've been working out," she said.

He grinned. "A little."

"Nate," Quinn snapped.

Looking the innocent, Quinn's former apprentice said, "What?"

Though Ananke was a highly respected assassin, she could also be a distraction. She was as tall as Quinn, nearly six feet, with smooth dark brown skin and matching eyes that could be piercing or alluring or both at the same time. Her hair, black as the stocking cap it was currently tucked under, fell several inches below her shoulders when she wore it down. She was, Quinn knew, a lethal combination of danger and intelligence.

He had hoped she would leave, but instead she stopped in the doorway and leaned against the jamb. Doing his best to ignore her, he examined the bedcover to make sure she hadn't left any stray hairs behind. When he was sure it was clean, he folded the comforter onto the unused half of the bed and then went through the same routine with the sheets.

Edmondson was dressed in a pair of maroon silk pajamas, his monogram stitched on the breast in yellow. If not for the fact that his chest wasn't moving, he looked as if he were asleep. Quinn turned the body on its side, checking for any injuries that might have bloodied the bed, but, as promised, there was none.

"Ready," he said to Nate.

His partner unfurled a pre-cut roll of plastic sheeting onto the floor between the bed and the wall, and then they laid the body on it. Quinn grabbed a set of clothes out of the closet to dress Edmondson in later, and tossed it on top of the body. They then wrapped everything up and secured the bundle with duct tape.

Quinn examined the empty bed and found a single dark hair. He plucked it up and held it in the air toward Ananke. "Sloppy."

"Wrong color," she said.

She was right. Now that he was holding it in the light, he could see it had an auburn hint to it.

"No one else was here tonight?" he asked her.

She shook her head. "Only me and Sammy."

The hair might have been there for days. Quinn used a small piece of duct tape to secure it to the bundle, thinking he might as well get rid of it.

While Nate remade the bed to make it look as if Edmondson hadn't used it, Quinn began looking through drawers for the evidence their client was seeking.

"You're not going to find anything up here," Ananke said.

Quinn searched the closet before moving to the nightstand on the far side of the bed.

"I'm telling you, you're wasting time," she said.

"Hey, instead of the running critique, why don't you make yourself useful and help me carry Mr. Edmondson downstairs," Nate suggested.

"Sorry," she said. "My union frowns on crossing lines."

"Of course it does," Nate said.

Since Edmondson wasn't a large man, Nate was able to hoist him over his shoulder in a fireman's hold and carry him out of the room on his own.

"That assistant of yours is coming along nicely," Ananke told Quinn.

"I heard that," Nate said from the hallway. "I'm not his assistant anymore. We're partners."

"Oh, right. I'd forgotten," she called to him, then whispered to Quinn, "You're just stringing him along, aren't you? He's far too young to be on his own."

Quinn finished checking under the bed and rose back to his feet. "He's older than he looks."

Ananke glanced back at the hallway with new appreciation. "Is that right? Is he attached?"

"He is," Quinn said. Nate was dating Quinn's sister, though

Quinn would have answered the question the same way whether or not Nate had been attached. As skilled and savvy as Nate had become over the last few years, Ananke would eat him alive.

"Too bad. But maybe I could change his mind."

"Don't even think about it."

"So demanding," she said. "Maybe I should set my sights on you."

"I'm sure Orlando would like to see you try."

There was no love lost between Ananke and Orlando, Quinn's partner and girlfriend. He didn't know why, other than it had to do with something in their past that Orlando never talked about.

"Tempting," Ananke said. "But I wouldn't want to intrude on another girl's territory."

"Why do I have a hard time believing that?"

"Well, Orlando's territory, anyway."

"Now you're getting smart."

"Been there, done that."

He looked at her for a moment, not understanding what she meant. After deciding to ignore the comment, he packed up the duffels and did a visual check of the room to make sure everything was in order. Satisfied, he joined Nate and the late Samuel Edmondson downstairs in the kitchen.

The plan was to put the body in the trunk of the man's Volvo. Quinn would then drive it out, with Nate hiding in the backseat until Quinn transferred to their vehicle parked a few blocks away. Before sunrise, the Volvo would be involved in a single-car accident along a stretch of road near the Canadian border patrolled by an understaffed sheriff's department. The authorities would find only Edmondson's torched remains and enough evidence to point toward a crash caused by driving under the influence. Quinn had already arranged for the results of any lab tests to support this conclusion.

Everything nice and neat with no problematic questions asked.

"Are you ready for your surprise?" Ananke asked as she strolled into the room.

Quinn tensed, his hand hovering on the bag that held his SIG SAUER P226 pistol.

"Loosen up," she said. "Do you really think I would accept an order to terminate *you*? The last thing I want is your stupid girlfriend chasing me for the rest of my life."

Nate, who'd had his back to her when she entered, twisted around. "Wait. Who's getting terminated?"

"No one," Ananke said, her flirty demeanor faltering. "I want to…ugh. Never mind. Just follow me."

She marched past them into the garage.

Nate looked at Quinn. "What was that all about?"

Quinn shrugged. "You're asking me?"

"So…do we follow her?"

"If we don't, she'll never leave."

They crossed to the open door and looked into the garage.

Ananke was on the other side of Edmondson's Volvo.

"What are you waiting for?" she asked. "You need to come over here."

Sensing no immediate threat, they entered the garage.

As the two men came around the front end of the car, Ananke dramatically swept her arms forward, pointed at a hole in the middle of the garage floor, and said, "Ta-da."

"What in the name of…?" Nate said, moving in for a better look.

Stepping in beside him, Quinn peered down the hole. The only thing visible was the top riser of a set of stairs. The rest was in darkness. He turned to Ananke. "What's down there?"

"If I knew that, I wouldn't still be here," she said. "I'm hoping money. How about you?" When no one responded, she sighed and explained how she'd discovered the trapdoor.

"And you didn't go down why?" Nate asked.

"Because it was time to call you jackasses in. Figured you'd need to take a look anyway, so why not join you?"

Quinn lit up the hole with his penlight, but there wasn't much more to see other than the floor at the bottom.

"Stay here," he said to Nate.

"Seriously?" Nate said. "I want to see, too."

"And what happens if someone shows up and closes the door on top of us?"

"We push it open?"

"Not if they lock it and roll the bike back on top."

"What are the odds of that happening?"

"What's the number one rule?" Quinn asked.

"Depends. You have, like, thirty of them."

"Safety first."

Nate narrowed his eyes. "That's not even in your top ten number ones."

"It's implied."

Nate growled his displeasure, but said, "Fine."

"Are you two done?" Ananke asked. "Because I'm starting to regret I *wasn't* given orders to take you out."

"Hold on," Quinn said.

He jogged back into the kitchen and fetched his pistol and sound suppressor from his duffel bag.

When he rejoined the others, he said to Ananke, "Down there, I'm in charge. Everything I say goes. Understand?"

She bowed her head a few inches. "I hear and obey."

"See that you do," he said. "I'm going first. Wait here until I give you the okay."

At the bottom, he found a switch where the stairwell met a dark hallway. When he flipped it, overhead fluorescents flickered on, bathing an underground passage in sickly blue-green light.

The hall ran back under the main part of the house for about twenty feet before opening into a darkened space. Quinn moved cautiously forward a few steps, and then stopped and listened. All was graveyard quiet. Even the air seemed not to be moving.

"Come on down," he said.

A few seconds later, Ananke appeared at the bottom, also carrying a SIG, though hers was a P232.

As Quinn moved down the hall, he noted the faint but unmistakable smell of human waste. When he reached the end, he again motioned for Ananke to wait, and then swung his light through the dark room beyond. Linoleum tiled floor, a couple of metal tables in the middle, and floor-to-ceiling cabinets along the far wall.

There was another light switch just inside. When he turned it on, more fluorescents began to buzz and flicker, each tube illuminating at its own speed.

In addition to the cabinets along the back, more covered the walls on each side, breaking only for a door on the left. Along with the tables he'd already noted, there were two gurneys and a chair that seemed fixed to the floor.

"So?" Ananke whispered from down the hall.

Quinn continued scanning the room, not letting her question rush him. The only place anyone could be hiding would be in the cabinets or behind the other door, both safer to check with help.

"All right," he said, and moved into the room.

Ananke paused as soon as she entered. "Creepy."

A hard plastic box was sitting on one of the tables. Quinn headed over and opened it. Photos, four-by-six inch, stacked like papers in a file and separated into plastic sleeves. He leafed through them. There were at least thirty packets, featuring different women.

He called Ananke over and showed her.

"None of them look too happy," she said. "Trophy shots?"

The possibility had occurred to Quinn but he wasn't ready to speculate. "Let's check the cabinets."

They started at opposite ends of the room. The cabinets Quinn checked each contained female clothing in different sizes and styles. All the items looked as if they'd never been worn, most still with tags on them. Six cabinets were dedicated to shoes in boxes, a dozen different styles in a wide range of sizes.

Every door he opened added to Quinn's sense of unease. About the only good thing was that he hadn't come across any children's sizes. He knew he wouldn't take that well at all, especially given the new direction his own life was going.

"Check this out," Ananke said.

She was on the other side of the room, looking inside a cabinet. When he walked over, he saw that instead of clothes, the space contained three side-by-side lockers, the long kind you could hang a suit in. Each was locked with a padlock. He opened the next cabinet and found more lockers. There were ten of these cabinets, thirty lockers total. Seven of the lockers, those farthest from the first Ananke found, had no padlocks. When Quinn opened them, he found them empty.

Ananke pulled a lock-pick kit from her jacket and grabbed one of the padlocks.

Quinn said, "That can wait. Let's finish clearing this place first."

He nodded toward the closed door.

4

A S QUINN OPENED the door, lights on the other side blinked on automatically.

Fluorescents again. Edmondson must have gotten a deal on them.

The harsh glow lit up a ten-foot-wide hallway with three doorways on each side, offset so that none sat directly across from another. The doors were metal and had square plates at eye level that could be slid to the side. Where the handles should have been was only a keyhole.

A private prison. Apparently passing secrets on to terrorists wasn't the only illegal activity Edmondson was into.

"I don't hear anything," Ananke said. "Maybe the rooms are empty."

Quinn stepped over to the nearest door and pulled the viewing plate open. The stink of human waste from inside was many times stronger than what he'd noticed earlier, forcing him to back away for a few seconds. As soon as he could bear it, he looked inside.

The room wasn't large, maybe five feet across and six deep, just big enough for the mattress on the floor and the five-gallon paint bucket in the corner. The source of the smell.

The room appeared unoccupied. He scanned it again, and then lifted up on his toes to look downward through the hole. This allowed him just enough of an angle to see the sliver of a person's head. The hair was buzzed short so that barely a quarter inch remained.

The head shook with fear as the person tried to hide from sight.

"Hey. Are you okay?" When Quinn received no response, he said, "Just sit tight. Everything's going to be fine. We're going to get you out of there."

No reaction, not even a flinch.

He let Ananke take a look. When she pulled back, anger had usurped her usual sardonic façade.

By silent agreement, they moved to the next cell. The layout was identical but the smell was missing, and as far as Quinn could tell, no one was inside.

He slid the plate open on cell three, and immediately jerked back. A face was looking out, only inches away on the other side.

"Please, I'll, I'll do whatever you want," the prisoner said, the voice female. "Just let me go home. Please."

"No one's going to hurt you," Quinn said. "We'll get you out in a minute."

Her brow creased, and then she took a step away from the door, revealing not only that her hair was cut short but that she wasn't wearing anything. "Who are you?" She sounded even more scared than she had a moment before. "Where's Mr. Black? I want to talk to Mr. Black." She moved deeper into her room, her terror growing. "Where is he?"

"We're going to help you," Quinn said.

"Where's Mr. Black?"

Quinn's words were doing nothing to calm her, so he moved on.

"Jesus," Ananke whispered. "What the hell did he do to them?"

Cell four held another prisoner, also a woman, shorn and unclothed. But instead of hiding or begging, she sat on her mattress staring at Quinn. While there was a hint of fear in her eyes, she looked mostly defiant.

He decided not to engage her just yet and moved on to number five. Like cell number two, it was empty.

The occupant of the final cell was lying on her bed under a blanket. She looked asleep, but intertwined with the ever-present odor of waste was another smell that told Quinn otherwise. Tangy and metallic—blood, and lots of it. If she wasn't dead yet, she was well on her way.

He dropped quickly to a knee and examined the lock. It was a specialized piece that required a key that could move through a serpentine set of tumblers. He'd seen a few similar to it and knew it was impossible to pick with the tools they had at hand.

A bit of explosive would take care of it, but that would risk further injury to the captive.

"Did you see any keys when you were looking through the lockers?" he asked Ananke.

"No."

He hadn't, either.

"Wait here." He sprinted through the secret basement and up the stairs into the garage.

"So?" Nate asked. "Any hidden treasure?"

Quinn said, "Did you see any keys?"

Nate had worked with Quinn long enough to know when things were serious. "The dresser. Top drawer."

Quinn raced up to the second floor and found a ring with a couple dozen keys right where his partner said they'd be. They were all from the same manufacturer of the padlocks on the lockers. None, however, would work on the cell doors.

He stuffed them in his pocket and hunted through the other drawers, not worrying about the mess he was making, but he found nothing.

Back downstairs, he ran into the kitchen and was about to shout for Nate to help him search when he noticed the rack next to the garage door. It had vertical slots for mail, and at the bottom a tray with several keys in it.

He rifled through them, pushing aside keys for the car and the motorcycle and a set he guessed was for the house, until he spotted a key caged in a metal frame. When pushed into the right kind of lock, the key would emerge from the frame in tiny sections so that it could bend through a set of curving tumblers, exactly like the cell locks.

He snatched it and ran into the garage. As he hurried onto the stairs, he said to Nate, "Come with me. We're going to need your help."

Ananke was looking through the viewing hole of cell number six, but moved out of the way the moment she saw them.

Quinn unlocked the door, and then used the viewing hole as a handle to swing it out.

He rushed in, yanked the blanket off the woman, and rolled her onto her back, but he was too late. By an hour, if not more.

The portion of the mattress she'd been lying on was soaked with blood from two jagged cuts on her wrists. The tool she had used lay near where her right hand had been before they'd moved her. It was an inch-and-a-half-long chunk of concrete sharpened to a dull point. Scratches next to the cuts indicated it had taken the woman several tries to do the job.

"God, if she could have just waited a little longer," Ananke said, her voice a pained whisper.

A million different emotions churned through Quinn, but he kept them all in check and headed out of the cell.

"Do...do I get the plastic?" Nate asked.

"No," Quinn grunted.

He opened cell one next. The woman inside jumped back, confused and frightened, as the door swung wide.

Quinn touched Ananke on the arm and motioned with his eyes for her to take the lead.

"This isn't my kind of thing," she whispered.

"It's not like it's ours, either," Quinn said.

"I wouldn't even know what to say."

He frowned. "If you're not going to help, then go into the other room and make sure no one comes down."

"Just what I was thinking." Ananke left the hallway.

Quinn turned his attention back to the cell. He made a quick examination of the woman for any weapons, but her hands were empty and she was wearing no clothes to hide anything in. "You can come out."

The woman pressed herself against the back wall. "You're the ones who've come to take us away, aren't you? The ones Mr. Black told us about."

"Tell me, is Mr. Black a short, skinny guy, losing his hair?" Quinn asked.

The look in her eyes confirmed that Mr. Black was Edmondson.

"I don't work for *or* with Mr. Black," he told her. "But I can tell you he's not going to be bothering you anymore. The only place you'll be going from here is home."

She didn't move.

"How about this?" he said. "We'll leave the door open. Come out when you're ready. No one's going to force you to do anything."

He nodded for Nate to follow him to cell three.

As he opened that door, the woman inside rushed out. He braced himself, thinking she would try to tackle him, but instead she dropped to her knees and threw her arms around his waist.

"Please! I'll do anything. Please just—"

He peeled her arms off and pulled her to her feet. "No one's going to do anything to you. Whatever was going on here is over. You won't be seeing Mr. Black again."

In her eyes, he could see she was having a hard time processing this.

"Get her some clothes," he said to Nate.

"From where?"

Quinn nodded back toward the large room. "Ask Ananke. She'll show you where to find them."

As Nate escorted the woman into the other room, the captive in cell one yelled, "Don't listen to them! They're going to take you away like the others."

Quinn headed over to cell four and looked through the window. The prisoner was still sitting on the mattress. Instead of glaring at him, though, she was now staring at the opposite wall. He unlocked the door and opened it.

Without looking at him, she said, "What do you want?"

"I don't want anything. I'm just letting you out."

"I heard what you told the others. I know you're lying. You're not here to rescue us."

Technically, she was right. They were here to deal with Edmondson's termination, not to act as liberators of the man's... whatever this was.

"We have zero interest in harming you," he said. "We didn't even know you were here until a few minutes ago."

She looked at him and sneered. "So I just follow you out?"

"That's up to you."

"Like I really have a choice." She pushed to her feet and started to cover her chest, but then dropped her arm as if she wasn't going to let her nakedness embarrass her.

She wasn't like the other two. She still had fight in her. Either she was a new arrival and hadn't been beaten down yet or was stronger than her prison mates.

When she reached the door, she held her wrists out, hands clasped together. Quinn didn't move.

"No cuffs?" she asked.

"I told you, we're here to free you."

Another grunt. "All right, then. What now?"

"Now we get you something to wear."

He purposefully went first so that his back was to her, putting her in a position of control and hoping it would gain him a little trust. When they reached the larger room, he saw that the other woman was already wearing a shirt and was pulling on a pair of pants.

"What size are you?" Quinn asked the woman from cell four.

She looked over at the open cabinets full of clothes. "I don't want any of those. I want mine."

"I have no idea where yours are."

She nodded toward the other end of the room. "In the lockers. Mine's number seventeen."

Quinn pulled out the keys and opened the indicated locker. Inside were a pair of jeans, a long-sleeve dark brown T-shirt, a maroon hoodie, panties, bra, ankle socks, and a pair of sneakers. Sitting at the bottom was an empty messenger bag, the few items that had apparently been inside sealed in a clear plastic bag lying next to it.

"Yours?" he asked the woman.

She nodded.

"Are the other lockers the same?"

"How should I know?" she said. A pause. "Can I get dressed now? Or are you still enjoying the view?"

"Sorry." He'd been lost in thought, wondering about the other lockers.

He moved to the one next to hers and opened it. A single set of clothes and some personal items. He tried another. Same.

Like trophy cases, he thought, sickened.

Twenty-three of the thirty lockers were secured. If four belonged to the women he and Ananke found, that left nineteen unclaimed. He tried not to think what that meant, but failed.

This was way beyond his contractual obligation.

Wanting to have as much information as he could before contacting Helen, he took cell four's wallet from her personal items while she had her back to him, and then hunted through the next few lockers for more intel.

As he opened another one, the girl from cell three said, "That's my shirt!"

Quinn pulled her clothes out and tossed them to her, and then added her ID to the others he'd taken. He had five now and decided that was enough.

"Please help these ladies with anything they might need," he said to Nate and Ananke. "I'll be right back."

"What *I* need is to go home," the woman from cell three said.

"That's what I'm working on," Quinn told her.

He went up to the garage and pulled out his phone, but hesitated before dialing. He needed guidance from Helen, but he also needed to let Orlando know what was going on. In fact, it would be best to have her on the line when he talked to their client.

The phone rang five times before Orlando answered. "What?" she asked in a whisper. He could hear other noises—music and amplified voices.

"Where are you?" he asked.

"Hold on," she said.

For the next several seconds, he could hear the muffled sound of movement.

When she spoke again, the music and other voices were gone and she was no longer whispering. "Okay, I can talk now."

"Where are you?" he asked again.

"I'm at the movies."

"It's almost midnight. You should be in bed," he said.

"I couldn't sleep, all right? We need to get a new mattress. Our bed is horrible. I can't get comfortable."

"The mattress is fine."

"Well, then, you get fat and sleep on it."

"You're not fat."

"You obviously haven't looked at me in a while. But who could blame you?"

Pregnancy was getting in the way of Orlando's usually active life. Thankfully, it would be over soon.

"Why are you calling?" she asked. "Is something wrong?"

"You might say that."

"Dammit. It was Ananke, wasn't it? She screwed something up."

"The termination went fine. The body's wrapped and ready to go."

"Then what is it?"

"We, uh, found, I don't know, a dungeon, I guess."

"Excuse me?"

He described Edmondson's secret basement and the women they had found down there.

"Holy crap."

"Yeah, I know."

"Do you know who they are?"

"I grabbed a few IDs." He started to read off the names but Orlando stopped him.

"Let's get Helen on the line first. She's going to love this. Hold on."

Thirty seconds later, the night officer at Helen's office transferred their call to his boss's home.

"I've got Quinn on with me," Orlando said when Helen came on.

"Problems?" their client asked.

"Yes, but not what you think," Quinn said.

He explained how the mission had gone, what they had found, and then read off the names on the IDs: Laurie Wright, Vanessa Holland, Kelly Blackwood, Marsha Venton, and Danielle Chad. The last two were the women from cells three and four, respectively. "I need to know how you want us to handle this," he said when he finished.

Helen was silent for a moment before saying, "Give me ten minutes. I'd like to know a little about who you've found before making any decision. Can you shoot me photos from the IDs so I can check them against official records?"

"No problem."

"Thanks. I'll get back to you as quickly as I can," Helen said and hung up.

"Copy me on the photos and I'll see what I can find out on my end," Orlando said to Quinn. "If Helen calls you back directly, make sure you get me on the line."

5

SAN FRANCISCO, CALIFORNIA

THE MOMENT THE photos arrived, Helen logged into her agency's system and navigated to the information interface. The module would not only search her group's database, but also cull information from other US intelligence and law enforcement organizations.

She typed in the five names Quinn had given her, set the parameters for a basic search so that it would be quicker, and clicked the ENTER button.

She received the results for the first four women within minutes. Wright, Holland, Blackwood, and Venton all matched the IDs Quinn had obtained. Each had been reported missing within the last month from different locations, all within a three-hundred-mile radius of Seattle.

None of the cases were getting much attention, however. The four women were recovering addicts of one type or another, and law enforcement officials in charge of each case seemed to think the person they were looking for had probably fallen back into her addiction and would turn up eventually, either stoned or dead. Because of this and the distances between the cases, no connections had been made to reveal a pattern.

Helen had started to assume Danielle Chad was a similar case that just hadn't been reported yet when her computer spit out a response:

DANIELLE CHAD: A&D/Alpha One

A&D—apprehend and detain, in this case with the highest priority. It had been routed through the NSA, but could have originated from any of a dozen or more other agencies. Usually some basic information about the individual would come with such an order, even an alpha one, but the only other item was a link to a contact. When she clicked on it, she was presented with a screen telling her that remote access to the requested information was restricted.

She spent several minutes searching other databases for anything she could find about Danielle Chad but came up with nothing.

It looked like she wouldn't learn anything until she went into the office.

But that could wait for now. She was already late getting back to Quinn.

THE MOMENT ORLANDO hung up with Quinn, she arranged through an app service for a car to pick her up right away. By the time she reached the street and removed her laptop from her backpack, her ride pulled to the curb. She gave the driver her address and settled into the backseat.

Using the information from the IDs, she conducted a similar search to the one Helen was doing on the other side of town. Her results for the first four women were basically the same. When it came to Danielle Chad, all her normal sources returned nothing.

Orlando then did a general search on the woman's name. She received several hits but none matched the age and description of the woman Quinn had found.

There was only one other thing she could do. After cropping the woman's photo out of the ID, she uploaded it into her web-based facial recognition interface and hit START. There was no telling when, or if, it would kick back any results, so she closed her computer and put it away.

She squirmed in her seat, trying to alleviate some of the aches she was feeling. When that didn't work, she twisted to the side so she could rub the base of her spine. She couldn't remember having this much back pain when she'd been pregnant with her son Garrett twelve years before.

Barely five feet tall, Orlando's pre-baby weight had always hovered around ninety-four pounds. Her little passenger had added over twenty percent to that, rocketing her to—at last check —what she considered a hefty one hundred and fourteen.

Being pregnant again wasn't all annoying, though. She was having a baby with Quinn. Thinking about that always brought a smile to her face. Okay, perhaps they hadn't planned it this way, but damn if it wasn't cool. She could already tell Quinn was going to be one of those overly involved, pain-in-the-ass dads, and she loved him even more for that.

As the baby nudged against her belly, Orlando sucked in a breath, the movement catching her off guard. She rubbed the spot and said, "Sweetheart, come on out anytime you're ready."

"Excuse me?" the driver said.

She looked up. "Sorry. I was—hey! There!" She leaned forward and pointed down the street to where a small crowd had gathered next to several food trucks. "Pull over."

"But this isn't where—"

"Just pull over."

"Okay, okay. No problem."

She opened the door as soon as he stopped. "Wait for me. I won't be long." She started to get out but then asked, "You want anything?"

"No, I'm good."

"You sure? My treat."

"A Coke, I guess," he said. "And a taco. I mean, if that's okay."

Orlando climbed awkwardly out of the car and waddled over to the end of the line in front of the Mexican food truck.

Barely half a minute later, her phone rang, the caller ID reading HELEN CHO.

6

COLUMBIA CITY

QUINN REMAINED IN the garage, expecting Helen to get right back to him. When several minutes passed without his phone ringing, he began to pace.

What was taking her so long?

He and Nate should have already finished the job and been on their way home. Remaining in the house with the body lying in the kitchen was taxing his patience.

"Quinn?" Nate called from the bottom of the stairway.

Quinn walked over to the trapdoor.

"Our friends are getting a little anxious," his partner said.

Join the club, Quinn thought. "Tell everyone to relax. I'll be there soon."

He started pacing again, wishing he could step outside for some fresh air, but the way things were going this night, some idiot would see him and call 911. A full twenty minutes passed before his phone finally rang.

"I've got Helen," Orlando said.

"Sorry for the delay," Helen told them. "This is a...delicate situation."

"I don't care what kind of situation it is," Quinn said, not hiding his frustration. "You can't leave us hanging like this. This is a crime scene. We need to get out of here."

"And that's exactly what you're going to do," Helen told him. "Just with a slightly revised mission."

"What does that mean?"

"Two tacos *pollo* and two *carnitas*," Orlando said. "Extra hot sauce, please. Oh, and two Cokes."

"Excuse me?" Helen said.

In the background someone repeated what Orlando had said.

Quinn said, "I thought you were at the movies."

"Um, sorry. Picking up something to eat on my way home. Helen, go on. Don't mind me."

Helen laid out the new plan.

"I don't think so," Quinn said when she was through. "I deal with the dead, not the living."

"If there was someone close by to do this for me, I'd send them. But it would be hours before they could get there and I don't think you want to wait that long."

"According to you, we're going to be waiting anyway."

"Yes, but not there," she said. "I *need* you to do this. Please."

He cursed to himself and then grunted, "Do I have a choice?"

For several seconds no one said a word.

"This will, of course, increase the fee," Orlando informed Helen.

"Naturally," Helen replied.

"Ananke will probably want some extra, too," Quinn added.

"Ananke?" Orlando and Helen said in unison.

"She's still here," he told them. "Been helping us out."

"Well, I'm not negotiating for her," Orlando said.

"She can call me directly," Helen said. "So, is that a yes?"

"Like I said before, do I have a choice?"

"Order seventeen," a distant voice announced.

"Oh, that's me!" Orlando yelled.

EVERYONE WAS IN the central room when Quinn returned to the basement, even the woman from cell one. She still looked as if she expected to be tied up at any moment, but at least she was dressed now. Unfortunately, what he was about to say would do nothing to dispel her suspicions.

"Can we go now?" the woman from cell three asked.

"Just a second," Quinn said, and then motioned for Nate and Ananke to join him. Once they were huddled, he quickly explained Helen's new plan.

"Are you kidding me?" Nate whispered. "We can't do that to them."

"It won't be for long," Quinn said. "The sooner we do this, the sooner we're out of here."

Ananke shook her head. "This is your thing now. I think it's time for me to leave."

"Helen knows you're helping us, and said she'd be open to adjusting the terms of your employment."

"It's not all about the cash, sweetie," she said.

"We could really use your help," he said. "If you don't want to do it for the money, do it because I'm asking you."

She looked uncomfortable but said nothing.

"It won't take that long," he added. "I promise."

"Well, since you put it so nicely. But once we go up those stairs, I'm gone. And I'm not putting anyone anywhere."

"That's fine," he said. "You can watch Danielle and make sure she doesn't bolt. Nate and I will do the hard work."

"Lucky me," she said.

Quinn turned to Nate. "I'll deal with the woman from cell one. You take cell three."

The woman from cell one backed against a cabinet as Quinn walked over.

"It's okay," he said. "I just need you to do something for me."

"What?"

Before he could answer, the woman from cell three yelled behind them, "No!"

Quinn looked over and saw that Nate had lifted her over his shoulder and was headed toward the cells. As Quinn turned back, the woman from cell one rushed him, her eyes wild.

"I knew you were lying!" she screamed as she tried to claw his face.

He batted her arms away and leaned forward so he could lift her like Nate had done, but she threw a punch and tried to slip around him.

"No one is going to hurt you," he said.

He grabbed her wrists as gently as he could and jerked her to a stop.

As she screamed, "You're a liar!" he lowered his shoulder again and this time was able to lift her up at the waist.

Her hands free again, she pounded his back, but her strikes were feeble at best, probably weakened by her time as Edmondson's guest. He carried her back into cell one, where he set her down on the mattress.

She immediately scrambled to her feet but he rushed out of the room and shut the door.

"No! You can't do this to me! You can't put me back here!" She hit her fists against the door. "Let me out! Let me out!"

"I promise it won't be for long," he said through the viewing hole. "The police will be here soon."

"Liar!"

Down at cell three, Nate was receiving similar treatment.

What they were doing felt so wrong, but it was needed to sell the story Helen had concocted.

"I'll tell everyone about you and how you left us here!" the woman yelled. "I'll tell them. I'll tell them everything."

Quinn waved for Nate to follow him back into the other room.

"I will *never* do anything like that again," Nate said, his voice low. "I don't care how much I'm being paid."

"Agreed," Quinn said.

Danielle Chad was standing in the middle of the room with Ananke between her and the exit.

"Any problems?" Quinn asked the assassin.

"Not a one."

Danielle looked at Quinn and asked calmly, "My turn?"

"You're not going back in," Quinn told her.

She laughed humorlessly. "Of course I'm not." After a pause, she said, "Might as well not put off the inevitable. Shall we go?"

Quinn nodded for Nate to take the lead, and then extended his arm toward the hallway. "After you," he said to the woman.

Quinn and Ananke walked up together last. "She's kind of an odd one," Ananke whispered. "Makes me almost want to hang around for a little longer to see what happens."

"We'll be fine."

"I said almost. I wasn't really suggesting it."

From the garage, they proceeded into the kitchen, where Danielle's controlled demeanor finally cracked at the sight of Edmondson's plastic wrapped corpse.

She looked at Quinn. "Is that...?"

"I believe you all called him Mr. Black," Quinn said.

"Who *are* you?"

"This is probably a good time for me to make my exit," Ananke said. She extended a hand to Quinn. "Be safe."

He shook with her. "That's always the plan."

She said good-bye to Nate and nodded to Danielle. "Don't let their tough talk fool you. They're really softies." With that, she left.

Quinn walked over to the duffel bags and pulled out his med kit. From inside he selected the appropriate, pre-filled syringe and held it out of sight as he rejoined Nate and Danielle.

"Unfortunately, we still have a little bit of work to do and can't waste manpower to watch you," he told the woman.

"I've been tied up before," she said, some of her previous confidence returning. "Where would you like me?"

Before she could react, he plunged the needle into her arm and injected her with the sedative.

"Hey, what are you doing?" she said, trying to pull away.

Nate had moved in, however, and held her in place until Quinn was done.

"What was that?" she asked angrily.

"Nothing that will hurt you," Quinn replied.

She blinked, and blinked again, more slowly. After a third blink, it was difficult for her to keep her lids open.

"Son of a bitch," she slurred.

They helped her to the living room couch.

"You assholes," she said as they laid her down.

"Don't blame me," Nate said, nodding at Quinn. "He's the one who did it."

"You..." She passed out.

Their previous plan of making it look like Edmondson died in a car accident had been scrubbed. The nice part of the new narrative was that it removed the risk of transporting the body.

"Where do you want to do this?" Nate asked as they returned to the kitchen.

"No need to get fancy. Right here will be fine."

While Quinn grabbed one of the dining room chairs, Nate cut open the plastic they had wrapped Edmondson in and folded it so they could take it with them.

"Pajamas or dress him?" Nate asked.

"Just leave him as is and take the clothes back upstairs."

As Nate was pulling a hank of rope out of his duffel, Quinn said, "No. I saw some in the garage. Use his."

After Nate retrieved the rope, they propped Edmondson in the chair and tied him in place. Quinn had briefly considered making it look like a suicide, but no matter how realistic he and Nate staged it, they wouldn't be able to remove Ananke's drug from the man's system. He had made no accommodations with the local police lab, which would see right through their ruse. So they made it look exactly like it was. A murder.

Once the scene was set and the unneeded clothes were back upstairs, Nate make a quick trip to pick up their car and parked it in the driveway. Instead of using the front door to get Danielle out, they exited through the back and circled the garage to the car. Within seconds of laying the woman in the backseat, they headed out, Nate behind the wheel.

Quinn waited until they were safely out of the neighborhood before he called 911.

"Someone's been killed," he said, and gave Edmondson's address. "You'll find him in the kitchen, but you'll be even more interested in what you discover in the garage. They're still alive there."

"Sir, can I get your—"

"Hurry," he said, and hung up.

HELEN HAD ARRANGED for them to use a safe house across the lake in Bellevue, but Quinn was always more comfortable when Orlando took care of logistics. She found them a quiet house in Tacoma, at the edge of town.

Nate pulled in as close as he could to the front door and they hustled Danielle inside. There were several bedrooms upstairs, including one that could be locked from the outside. Quinn didn't like the idea of putting her in what amounted to another cell but he couldn't risk her running off.

"You can take the room at the end of the hall," Quinn told Nate. "I'll take the one across from her. Let's try to get a little sleep." He looked at his watch. It was nearly two a.m. "No more than four hours."

Nate said, "The way you say it sounds so luxurious."

7

SAN FRANCISCO

HELEN CHO LEFT her Pacific Heights home at ten minutes after one a.m., and headed for her office in the financial district so she could report to the mysterious contact that Danielle Chad had been found.

Tonight's mission outside Seattle wasn't even close to being the first job Helen had supervised that had gone off the rails, but there was no denying it had taken one of the strangest turns. She periodically checked her mirrors for anything unusual, but the cars behind her were an ever-changing mix and nothing stood out. Soon she was turning down the street where her office was located.

During the day, the street-level entrance was usually open, allowing people to drive down a ramp before reaching the main gate, but at this time of night, a metal curtain cut it off. She pulled up close to the control box and pushed the button to lower her window so she could flash her pass in front of the reader.

As the glass moved down, she heard the roar of an engine and started to turn toward it. Before she could see anything, she was rocked sideways, the air filling with the groan of twisting metal and the screech of rubber.

She swayed in her seat, momentarily dazed, before her

training kicked in. Fumbling open the central console, she grabbed for the pistol she thought she'd never have to use, but the muzzle hadn't even cleared the container when she heard the muffled *thup* and felt something hit her neck.

Her hand shot up to the wound. She expected to find blood and a bullet hole, but instead her fingers touched a small metal tube.

The world suddenly pulled away, everything growing distant and muted and unreal. The metal tube fell from her neck into her hand, its sharp tip pricking her palm. It was like she knew what it was, but didn't at the same time.

Within seconds, dark clouds began to move in, narrowing her vision to a point of light, and then nothing.

IT WAS THE job of the security officer on duty in the monitoring room to alert his supervisor and the overnight director of anything unusual.

Which is exactly what that evening's officer would have done if he'd been in the room to witness the takedown of Director Cho via the cameras mounted outside the garage. But the drops that had been put in his coffee fifteen minutes earlier by one of the very men he reported to had resulted in an emergency trip to the toilet, leaving the monitoring room temporarily unattended.

By the time he returned and saw Cho's smashed sedan abandoned in the street, the director was already crossing the Golden Gate Bridge toward Mill Valley.

BELLEVUE, WASHINGTON

THE SQUAD ASSEMBLED at 4:20 a.m. in the parking lot behind St. Luke's Lutheran Church in the Clyde Hill section of Bellevue, a few blocks away from the target house.

They were eight in number—four each from offices in Los Angeles and San Francisco. The Bay Area team had arrived first, their jet touching down at 3:42. From there, they transferred to a helicopter that flew them to the eighteenth fairway of the Glendale Country Club, where a black Suburban waited for them by the clubhouse.

The L.A. crew landed ten minutes later and followed the same route.

Though the two groups did not share a home base, they had worked together many times and were familiar with each other's strengths. Stevens, as senior officer, was squad leader.

He held up the tablet computer that displayed the diagram of the safe house each man had memorized on the trip north. He pointed at the sliding glass back door. "Red one and red two, here." Red was their team designation, with Stevens as red seven and the man assigned to remain at the vehicles as red eight. Stevens pointed at the garage. "Red three and red four." And then moved his finger to the front door. "Red five and red six. Questions?"

No one spoke up.

Stevens looked at his watch. "Transit time to site is three minutes. Once everyone's in position, wait for my mark and then we go. I want this done and us out of there by 4:35 latest." He paused, then said, "Mic check."

Comm gear was switched on, and in team order, each man said, "Check, check." They then piled into the Suburban and headed to the safe house.

According to the info packet Stevens had read on the flight up, the house had been seized years ago in a criminal investigation by some forgotten government agency. Control of the building had eventually shifted to the NSA, who loaned it out to other US intelligence divisions on an as-needed basis. It seemed odd to be raiding one of their own locations—it certainly was a first for him and his team—but orders were orders.

They approached via the backyard of the house directly behind the target.

Upon reaching the rear fence, Stevens raised his night scope and examined the other side. He picked up no heat signatures in the backyard, and also none near the windows, all of which had their shades drawn.

"Go," he whispered into his mic.

One by one, the team scaled the fence and crept across the open grass, each man to his assigned location. Stevens went last, joining the two men covering the sliding door at the back.

A click over the comm signaled red three and red four were in position. A few seconds later a double click confirmed the same for red five and red six.

Stevens clicked his mic button three times, signaling everyone to move in.

Safe houses were modified to make them difficult to enter—unless you had ties to the agency overseeing it. Master keys had been waiting for them in the Suburban, keys that not only freed the locks but also contained micro-transponders that disabled the home's security system. After the glass door slid open, everything remained nice and quiet.

Red one entered first, pausing just inside for a quick look around before motioning to Stevens and red two that it was clear. Silently, they made their way through the family room into the kitchen and the dining room. There they linked up with red five and red six, who indicated the front of the house was also clear.

On the other side of the first floor was a hallway that led to a guest room, a bathroom, and the garage. Stevens looked down it as red three and red four emerged from the guest room. They informed him no one was in that part of the house.

So far things were going even better than Stevens had hoped. No one on watch meant the targets were likely sound asleep in the second-floor bedrooms.

He silently instructed red five and red six to remain at the base of the stairs before he headed up with the others.

Another hallway ran the length of the second floor. To the left was the massive master suite, and to the right four more bedrooms, a bathroom, and a linen closet. Leaving red three and red four to hold at the top of the stairs, Stevens went left with the other two.

At the master suite, red one did the honors of opening the door and pushing it inward. When they heard no response from inside, they slipped through the gap, but within seconds all three lowered their weapons.

The bed wasn't just empty, it had no sheets on it, only two pillows and a folded blanket stacked at the foot of the mattress, waiting for the room's next occupant.

Stevens directed red one to check the bathroom and red two to check the walk-in closet, but both returned shaking their heads.

Apparently the targets didn't feel the need to use the best room in the house. That made a certain amount of sense given that Stevens had been told one of the targets was a hostage. Her captors must have felt it necessary to stay in the same room as she. It's what Stevens would have done.

They moved back into the hall and headed to the other end, taking red three and red four with them.

The first bedroom was exactly like the master—stacked blankets and pillows, no sheets.

The same was true of bedroom two.

And three.

The bathroom was also clear.

Stevens felt both confused and irritated as they approached the door to the final bedroom. As red one moved to open it, Stevens tapped him on the shoulder and signaled that he would do it. He turned the knob and pushed the door inward.

The room was empty.

Cursing, he pulled out his phone.

8

TACOMA

THE ALARM ON Quinn's cell went off exactly four hours after he'd laid his head down. He tapped the screen, killing the noise, and swung his legs off the bed.

Caffeine would be nice, he thought as he stood up. Two or three gallons' worth should do the trick.

Nate was already in the kitchen when Quinn entered.

"I see you slept like a baby, too," his partner said.

Quinn grunted as he set his phone on the counter and poured himself a mug of coffee from the pot Nate had brewed.

"I take it Helen didn't call with new instructions," Nate said.

Quinn shook his head. With the exception of his alarm, his phone had remained silent since their arrival at the safe house.

He took a sip and began to feel a bit more alive. After another, he asked, "Any noise from our guest?"

"Not a peep."

Quinn cocked his head. "Please tell me she's not gone."

"I took a look in before coming down. She's still there."

Sipping from their cups, they shared a long silence.

"Did you check the news?" Quinn asked.

Nate looked at him, not quite understanding, then his eyes widened. "Oh, right."

He disappeared into the living room, where the only television in the house was located. Quinn refilled his cup and followed, arriving just as Nate tuned in to a local morning news show.

On the screen was a helicopter shot looking down on a neighborhood, the focus on a familiar house.

"Looks like they sent someone to check out your call," Nate said.

Dozens of police officers roamed the yards surrounding Samuel Edmondson's home, their cars jamming the street. Even at this early hour, a crowd of looky-loos had gathered, but could only get as close as a barricade two houses away.

At the bottom of the screen, a graphic read:

2 ALIVE/2 DEAD IN COLUMBIA CITY HOME

"Turn it up," Quinn said.

As Nate increased the volume, an anchor was saying, "… found on the premises. Let's bring back in Tom Markewicz, who's on the scene. Tom, what's the latest?"

The image switched to a ground-level shot of a reporter standing just inside the barricade. The camera was angled to capture Edmondson's front door in the distance.

"Carol, while the police have not yet released any names, neighbors say the home is owned by a man named Samuel Edmondson. One woman told me Mr. Edmondson seemed friendly but tended to keep to himself." He went on for a while longer, sharing no real information.

The screen then split into graphic boxes, with the female anchor in the left box. "Any word yet if Mr. Edmondson was one of those discovered inside?"

"Not yet. All we know at this point is that one of the deceased is a woman and one a man. I'll report back as soon as I have more."

"Thanks, Tom." The shot of the anchor then took over the whole screen. "Rita Meyers is standing by at Swedish Medical

Center with an update on the two people found alive inside the house.

Another switch, this time to a reporter with the hospital in the background. "Just a few minutes ago a hospital spokesman told us that the two women are in fair condition. From what I understand, neither woman is—"

Nate turned it off. "It's kind of weird seeing our handiwork on TV."

Weird wasn't strong enough a word as far as Quinn was concerned. Though he was relieved to have confirmation that the women were no longer in their cells, he had an intense desire to quickly get as far away from the area as possible.

As he took another sip of coffee, a thump on the floorboards overhead signaled that their guest had woken. This was followed a moment later by the doorknob rattling and a fist slamming against the door.

"Hey!" Danielle yelled. "Let me out! I need to go to the bathroom!"

Nate held out his fist. "Rock paper scissors?"

Frowning, Quinn said, "I'll do it." He handed his cup to Nate and headed upstairs.

"You guys *are* just like Mr. Black!" Danielle yelled as she continued to hit the door. "New room, different prison!"

Raising his voice to be heard above the racket, Quinn said, "Hold on, I'm coming."

He might as well have kept his mouth shut because she continued pounding on the door until he unlocked it.

"Stand back," he ordered. His gun was in his room, but he knew he could handle her without it.

He waited until he heard her move away from the door before he pushed it open. As soon as it was wide enough, though, she sprinted at him, her hand restraints surprisingly missing.

Quinn pivoted, intending to knock her arms away, but before he could do so, she whipped them down and brought them up again between his arms and shoved him in the chest.

He staggered backward a few steps. Danielle was far stronger than the woman who'd been in cell one. But Quinn was not one to be fooled twice. As she attempted to hit him again, he moved with her and wrapped an arm around her.

"Stop it!" he ordered.

From downstairs he heard his phone ring.

At the same moment that Nate yelled, "I'll get it," Danielle kicked backward.

Quinn detected the move at the last second, and was able to twist enough to reduce the speed of her foot as it traveled up between his legs, but he couldn't stop it.

It was a miracle he didn't let her go as pain rocketed out from his groin. When she kicked again, he lunged sideways so that she hit only thigh.

"Quinn!" Nate called. "Get down here!"

Before she could take another shot, Quinn wrestled her to the ground and pinned her arms and legs to the carpet.

"Let me go!" she yelled as she tried to wiggle out from under him.

"Calm down," he ordered.

"Let me *go!*"

Quinn heard Nate heading up the stairs. "Quinn! Did you hear —oh. Um, hold on."

A moment later, Nate was beside Quinn, zip ties in hand.

"Behind her back this time," Quinn said.

"No!" Danielle screamed as they rolled her over.

Nate double tied her wrists. "Ankles?"

Quinn turned the woman back over. "Are you going to be good? Or do we need to restrain your feet, too?"

She huffed several times as if she could breathe fire, her gaze darting back and forth between the two men.

"Well?" Quinn asked.

She spat at him, her saliva hitting him below the eye.

He nodded to Nate. "Ankles, too."

"I've still gotta pee," she said before Nate could tie up her feet.

"Hold on," Quinn told his partner. He looked at Danielle. "If you try anything, we won't just bind your ankles, we'll tie you to the bed, too. Got it?"

"Yeah, yeah. Just hurry up."

They helped her into the bathroom, where she stood next to the toilet, looking at them expectantly.

"What?" Nate asked.

"I can't very well pull my pants down like this, can I?"

"You're going to have to figure out a way," Quinn told her.

"Come on. What does it matter? You've both seen me naked."

Reluctantly, Quinn undid her pants and pulled them and her underwear down while Nate held her shoulders to prevent her from getting any ideas.

After she sat, she looked at them again.

"What now?" Quinn asked.

"It creeps me out a little to have you watch me pee."

Nate said, "It's okay for us to take your clothes off, but you don't want—"

"Nate," Quinn said, quieting him.

They turned enough to give Danielle some privacy while still being able to watch for any sudden movements.

"What were you yelling at me about?" Quinn whispered to his partner.

"Oh, um…someone needs to talk to you." He formed the letter O with his mouth.

"God, I feel like I'm in high school," Danielle said. "Just say what you're going to say. What am I going to do about it? I can't even pee without your help."

Despite her request, they remained silent. When she finished, Quinn helped her get her pants back up and they returned her to the bedroom.

Nate pulled out some ties to strap her ankles but Quinn signaled for him to wait.

"If you promise to cooperate," Quinn said to Danielle, "we'll leave your feet free."

She studied him for a moment before saying, "Sure. I can be a good little girl."

"That's not the answer I'm looking for."

She rolled her eyes. "I *will* be a good little girl, okay?"

"Okay. No ankles, but the door stays locked," he told her. "For your own protection."

"Bullshit," she scoffed.

"Believe what you want." He followed Nate toward the exit but stopped in the doorway. "If you need anything, knock twice on the floor. You don't need to go all psycho. We'll hear you."

"Oh, that's real nice," she said. "Psycho? Is that what you think—"

He stepped into the hall and shut the door.

When he got downstairs, Nate was saying into the phone, "Sorry. We had an…incident….I'll let him explain."

He gave the phone to Quinn.

"Good morning," Quinn said.

"Are you sure?" Orlando said. "I heard screaming and banging."

"Danielle needed to go to the bathroom."

"It sounded like you guys were performing an exorcism."

"That might have been more pleasant," he said. "I haven't heard from Helen, have you?"

"That's why I'm calling. She's missing."

Orlando's words were so unexpected it took a second before Quinn could say, "What?"

"I expected to hear from her a while ago, so when I didn't, I called in to nudge her. Instead, I was put through to this guy who starts questioning me about why I wanted to talk to her."

"Did they actually say she was missing?"

"Of course not, but it wasn't hard to figure out. I checked. Turns out someone rammed her car in front of her office early this morning and grabbed her."

"So what did you tell her people?"

"I just said we had finished up a job for her and I was reporting in. That was it."

"Did they ask you what the job was?"

"Of course they did. But I told them I was uncomfortable talking to someone I didn't know on the phone. I offered to come and give a full report. I'm supposed to be there at nine thirty. Figured that might delay them showing up at my door."

"They may still come. You need to get out of there."

"They already did."

"What? Are you—"

"Relax. We weren't home. The first thing I did after talking to them was to grab Garrett and the Vos and get out. We're on the way to where Mr. Vo stores his RV, then we'll head out of the city. The house is a mess, though. They got there about ten minutes after we left. Watched the whole thing on my computer."

"I'm glad you guys are all right," he said. "We can deal with the house later."

"Oh, don't worry, we will. They're going to get a big repair bill."

"Were you at least able to figure out why Danielle's so important?"

Orlando snorted. "The only thing I can tell you for sure is that her name isn't Danielle Chad. But don't worry. I'll find something."

"I know you will." What a screwed-up few hours, he thought. "I don't like the idea of you being alone."

"I'm not alone," she said.

"You know what I mean. I'd feel better if Daeng were with you."

"It annoys me how much we think alike sometimes."

"You already called him?"

"No, but he's next on my list," she said. "You all should get out of there, too. They might figure out where you are."

"We will."

"Give me a little bit of time and I'll find you someplace to go."

"No. Don't worry about us. I'll take care of it. Just focus on staying safe," he said.

"You sure?"

"Absolutely. You concentrate on taking care of our family," he told her. "How are you feeling?"

"Pissed off."

"You know what I mean."

"I'm fine. *We're* fine."

"Stay that way, okay?"

"I will, if you will."

9

CALIFORNIA

THEY PICKED UP Mr. Vo's RV from a vehicle storage facility in San Mateo. It was one of the smaller recreational vehicles made, a twenty-footer with a sleeping area above the driving cabin. It had been a gift from Orlando, in thanks for the years the Vos had spent helping her with Garrett and around her home. Her hope was that it would encourage the Vietnamese couple to get to know a bit of the States when they weren't needed at the house.

At first, they only used it to visit a cousin in San Jose, a mere fifty miles from San Francisco. When Orlando had insisted they take a longer trip, they'd reluctantly headed off for a four-day tour of Yosemite National Park. The trip had been a success, and since then, the Vos had been to Death Valley, San Diego, Las Vegas, twice to the Grand Canyon, and had joined three RV clubs.

To avoid connecting Orlando's car to the RV, they had dropped it off at the Amtrak station in San Jose before heading out. Orlando would have much preferred to be behind the wheel but Mr. Vo insisted on driving. She instructed him to head to Oakland.

Once they were on their way, she moved to the back where her son and Mrs. Vo were sitting at the dining table. Garrett's eyes were droopy. He wasn't used to getting up anywhere near this early, especially during summer vacation. Mrs. Vo, however, was bright and alert.

"How's everyone doing?" Orlando asked.

"All okay," Mrs. Vo said. While there was a hint of concern in the woman's eyes, it wasn't nearly as much as most people would have under similar circumstances. Mrs. Vo was used to Orlando's crazy life, and this wasn't the first time they'd had to leave someplace in a hurry.

Garrett, however, said nothing.

"Scooch," Orlando told him.

He moved over so she could join him on the bench seat.

"Where are we going?" he asked.

"I don't know yet."

"I'm going to miss swim practice."

"We'll look for a campground with a pool."

"That's not the same."

She rubbed his hair. "I realize that, sweetie. It won't be for long."

He'd joined a swim team two years earlier and was already winning medals. Backstroke was his main thing, though he was more than decent at freestyle and butterfly, too. Breaststroke, well, he hadn't quite figured that one out yet, and more times than not his awkward kick got him disqualified.

He leaned against her. "It's your work, isn't it?"

"Uh-huh."

He didn't know specifically what she did, but he was aware she worked in a world far different from the ones his friends' parents occupied.

"Why isn't Quinn here?"

"He's busy. But he knows what's going on."

"Is he hiding, too?"

She squeezed his shoulder. "You're a little too smart for your own good, you know that?"

The baby chose that moment to adjust itself. Garrett jerked

away from Orlando's stomach, and then put his hand over the spot where his shoulder had been.

"Did you feel that?" he asked.

"Yeah. I felt it."

"I wonder what he's thinking," he said, still touching the spot.

"Or she." They had purposely decided not to know the baby's sex ahead of time. Her son had told her he didn't care which one the baby was, but she had a feeling he was hoping for a little brother.

"Yeah. Or she," Garrett said. "Do you think *she* dreams?"

"I'm sure she does."

"What about?"

"Us, probably."

He wrinkled his brow. "She doesn't know us yet."

"Of course she does. She hears us talking all the time."

That seemed to make him think. He leaned against her again, his head resting on her arm. A few minutes later he was asleep.

Orlando acted as his pillow until they neared Oakland. After she returned to the front, she guided Mr. Vo to an industrial park on the eastern edge of the city, and had him park in front of unit number twenty-four.

"We'll be here at least fifteen minutes, if not longer," Orlando told everyone. "Might be a good time for some breakfast."

"Do you need help?" Garrett asked.

She smiled. "If I do, I'll let you know."

She exited the RV.

The entrances to all the other units led either into a small front office or directly into the unit's main space. Her entrance, however, opened into a five-foot-long, three-foot-wide steel box. At the other end was another door that would only open when either Orlando or Quinn placed their right palm on the biometric scanner beside it. If anyone else tried, the metal box would seal shut and Orlando would receive notification of an intruder.

She pressed her hand against the glass, waited for the click, and entered. The unit was Quinn's and her private warehouse.

Secured cabinets full of weapons and ammunition and explosive devices lined the back wall. Through the center of the room ran three rows of heavy-duty shelves, holding a wide variety of other items that might be needed, such as communication gear, bugging equipment, and tracking devices. Many of the items had been created for specific one-time uses, but had been retained in case similar needs arose in the future.

Along the entire left side of the room was a workbench with drawers built underneath, holding a myriad of parts both mechanical and electrical. A pegboard covered with several hundred different kinds of tools hung on the wall above the bench.

She unlocked one of the back cabinets, removed several customized bags and a large plastic crate, and set them on the workbench.

She had no idea how long she would be away, or what she and the team might need, but given Helen's disappearance, she knew the smart move was to prepare for the worst.

She started with the weapons, selecting handguns based on the preferences of Quinn, Nate, Daeng, and herself, and loaded them into the bag designed to carry them. She added an ample number of suppressors and four night scopes. In a second bag, she packed enough ammo to hold off a small army.

Next up was explosives. As tempted as she was to bring along some of the big stuff, she stuck only to small devices that could be used to blow open locks and windows. That finished off the soft-sided bags, and she moved all three over to the door.

Into the plastic crate went the electronics. She ended up going a little overboard and had to get a second box, but she'd rather have extras than end up cursing herself for what she didn't bring.

Leaving the bags and the crates in the unit, she returned to the RV and borrowed the keys from Mr. Vo. The camper had plenty of storage cabinets accessible from the outside, but only the two at the back could also be reached from inside the vehicle, via hatches under the dining-area bench seats.

The Vos had stored a pair of folding chairs, a portable awning, and some blankets and pillows in Orlando's desired spaces. She removed them and began the back and forth trips to bring all her things out.

One by one, she slid them into the compartments, pushing them as far back as possible. When that was done, she measured the height and width of the space, and retrieved the appropriately sized metal dividers from the unit. They were a near perfect fit, making the storage areas look smaller than they actually were and completely hiding her equipment from view. She repacked the Vos' items in front of the dividers, and then made sure the shop was secured before climbing back into the RV.

Total elapsed time: twenty-three minutes.

"Breakfast," Mrs. Vo said as Orlando closed the RV door. She was holding a plate with a thick omelet and a sliced banana.

"I don't know if I can eat all that," Orlando said.

"Not for you, for baby. You eat."

"Okay, okay. But after we get going."

Mrs. Vo frowned but held on to the plate.

Orlando looked past her to where Mr. Vo was sitting with Garrett. "Mr. Vo, do you need a little more time?"

The man stood. "No, no. Wait only for you. Where you want to go?"

Orlando had given that considerable thought as she'd loaded up the RV. Quinn might not need her help, but she wanted to be close enough to provide it if it turned out he did.

"North," she said.

LOCATION UNKNOWN

HELEN WOKE TO the smell of sweat and bleach.

As she opened her eyes, her lashes batted against the fabric of a bag that had been pulled over her head.

When did that happen?

The last thing she recalled was reaching for her gun.

Wait. There'd been a stinging sensation, on her...on her...

Where, she couldn't remember.

Though it had been years since she'd done any fieldwork, she hadn't forgotten the lessons she'd learned. Keeping her breaths even and her body still, she mentally checked for any injuries. She didn't feel any pain beyond a dull headache, but she did discover she was restrained to a chair, unable to move her arms and legs.

Focusing outward, she tried to get a sense of her surroundings. Light did seep through the bag, but the fibers were woven tight together, keeping her from seeing anything. The light, though, was telling. It was neither particularly bright nor dim. If the room was small, a few lamps at most. If larger, maybe scattered overheads.

She listened for the sound of people, but all she could hear was her own pulse racing. She took a few deep, quiet breaths to slow her heart rate and tried again. This time she heard nothing but an empty space.

She wanted to scrape her foot on the ground and listen to how the sound reacted to the room. That would give her a better idea of its size, but doing so might alert her captors that she was awake. It turned out it wasn't long before she learned the answer without even moving a toe. A door opened, ahead and to her right, the sound a good forty feet away. She was in a big room, then.

Heels clicking on concrete, or perhaps stone. A woman's.

The door closed again, and the footsteps headed toward Helen at a relaxed pace. Ten feet away, they stopped for a couple seconds, and then something dragged across the floor and came to rest directly in front of Helen. A chair, she realized, as it creaked when the person sat.

In the silence that followed, a faint odor drifted off the visitor. A clean smell, more scented soap than bleach.

"I know you're awake." The woman had a French accent. "You have been for the last seven minutes."

They must be monitoring my vitals, Helen thought. Perhaps a few of the restraints she'd detected weren't restraints at all. With no reason to keep up the charade, she adjusted herself into a more comfortable position but did not say anything.

"Thank you," the woman said. "I hate it when people try to play unnecessary games. It's such a waste of time." She paused. "So, Director Cho, where are they?"

Helen remained silent.

"The safe house you arranged for them to use was a ruse, was it not? Where did they really go?"

If Helen had any doubts this was about Danielle Chad, they were gone now. The only safe house she'd arranged recently was for Quinn, though she was surprised to learn he hadn't gone there.

The chair groaned, and when the woman spoke again she was no more than a foot in front of Helen's face. "Where are they?"

Though Helen's extremities were tied down, her chest and shoulders were not, giving her room to move. The moment the last word left the woman's mouth, Helen thrust forward with all her strength. Her aim was a bit off. Instead of smacking her forehead into the woman's nose, she caught her interrogator on the cheek, but it was still a good, solid hit.

The woman grunted as she knocked against her chair.

Helen braced herself for her interrogator's retaliation.

But she heard the woman stand. "Perhaps a little time will make you more cooperative."

Helen heard the click, click, click of the woman's heels heading across the room.

A few seconds later, she was once more alone.

10

NEW YORK CITY, NEW YORK

L YLE CLARK STUDIED his appearance in the full-length
mirror before grabbing the knot of his tie and nudging it
ever so slightly to the right.

There. That was better. Everything symmetrical.

He was dressed in a dark gray suit handcrafted by his favorite
tailor in Milan. His shirt and tie were from London, also specially
made for him. His shoes, Spanish, constructed by a master cobbler
in Barcelona.

A light, double tap on his bedroom door.

"Yes?" he said, his eyes still on the mirror.

The door opened.

"Sorry to disturb, Mr. Clark," his butler William said. The man
was English, naturally. It wouldn't do to have a butler from
anywhere else. "A phone call, sir."

"Who is it?"

"Mr. Morse, sir."

"I'll be right there."

"Very good, sir," William said and left.

Clark spotted a tiny bit of lint on his left sleeve and plucked it off.
Now he was ready.

He took the call in the study of his twenty-second-floor Manhattan apartment.

"Good morning, Mr. Morse," he said, looking out his window at Central Park. "I assume this is important."

"I have news," Morse said. As always, the man's voice sounded strained, his long damaged vocal cords doing their best to get his words out.

"Concerning?"

"The Hayes matter."

Clark turned away from the window, the outside world no longer of interest. "What about it?"

"The girl's been found."

Clark did his best to hold back the wave of excitement building in his chest. "Is that so?"

"She was discovered during an unrelated operation."

"By us?"

"No. Helen Cho's agency."

Another government intelligence organization. That could complicate things.

"What has she done with the girl?" Clark asked.

"That's unclear at the moment. What I know is that an operation in Seattle turned up more than expected. While it was still ongoing, Cho initiated a search on several names. One was Danielle Chad."

One on a list of possible aliases. "Are we sure it's *our* Danielle Chad?"

"Cho had a copy of the girl's ID on her computer. It's definitely the one we're looking for."

"There must be something you can use to pressure Cho to hand the girl over."

"Cho is missing."

A pause. "Missing as in presumed dead?"

"Kidnapped."

"By who?"

"Also unclear. She was ambushed on her way to the office not long after she got the copy of the ID."

"Someone else interested in the girl."

"Yes, sir. That would be my assumption, too."

"Can I assume you're doing something to find Danielle?"

"I've sent a group of my best men to the area where she was last seen. Unfortunately the safe house Cho's people were supposed to be using turned out to be a dead end. My team continues to look, though. What I need to know is if we run into resistance, how far do we take this?"

"If Danielle Chad is really Danielle Hayes and they have her, all the way," Clark said without hesitation. "Just remember, we need her unharmed. Anyone who gets in the way is expendable."

WASHINGTON, DC

IT WAS ONE of those political breakfasts where everyone was smiling and glad-handing and saying nothing of real importance.

Scott Bennett did at least three of them every week. Add on the even more frequent cocktail parties in the evenings, the multiple getting-to-know-you lunch meetings, and the inevitable weekend special events and he almost never saw his office or his home anymore. Such was the life of a top-tier lobbyist.

"Senator, it would be my pleasure," Bennett was saying. "Have him call me and I'll take care of it."

Often it was the little things that served Bennett's needs the best, such as obtaining box seats to a Washington Nationals baseball game for a senator's friend. The senator would receive nothing on paper, but in the invisible ledger called What Have You Done For Me, another would appear in Bennett's column.

"I appreciate that, Scott. I really do," the senator said. "Harry can't wait to take his son to a game when they're out here."

"I'll personally see to everything. Don't give it another

thought." By everything, Bennett meant flying the senator's friend and son to the district, putting them up in the best hotel, providing the car that would take them to and from the game, and supplying the guide who would see them to their seats and handle the procuring of any food or drinks or souvenirs they wanted. They would do more than enjoy their evening. They would never forget it. And the friend would be sure to let the senator know.

Bennett spoke to the man for a few more moments, and then left before the conversation could turn stale.

The affair was informal. There were places to sit but most people stood, making it easy to see who was still new at this. They would be the ones balancing plates of muffins and fruit and sausages and eggs as they attempted to remain relevant to whatever conversation they were participating in.

Bennett, ever the professional, never touched the food at this type of event so he could move from lawmaker to lawmaker hands free. He was heading toward Representative Loggins when someone tapped him on the shoulder. Turning, he found Ryan Barkley, his assistant, holding an envelope.

"This just came for you," Barkley said.

"From who?" Bennett asked as he took the envelope.

"A man in the lobby. I've never seen him before, but—"

Bennett was about to rake his assistant over the coals when he turned the envelope over and caught sight of the single word printed in the upper left corner.

Valor

"Thank you," he said. Barkley had only been following instructions. Anything marked VALOR should immediately be brought to Bennett. "You can head back to the office. We're done here."

Barkley looked confused. "There's still another—"

"We are done," Bennett said firmly.

"Yes, sir. I understand. Don't forget the meeting at noon with General McFadden."

"Reschedule it."

Barkley still looked unsure, but this time he only said, "Yes, sir," and left.

Bennett made his way to a quiet alcove and opened the envelope.

The Hayes girl has surfaced. Current alias: Danielle Chad. Obtain.

Below this was a series of numbers that, once he entered them in his computer, would take him to a secured web page with additional information.

How about that? he thought.

He pulled out his phone.

BERLIN, GERMANY

THE ASSISTANT TRADE attaché at the Russian embassy answered the phone on the second ring. "Komarov."

"Good afternoon, Herr Komarov. This is Karl Schwartz, Schwartz Engineering. I believe you were expecting my call."

Komarov froze. At one time perhaps, he had been expecting it, but that had been years ago. "Of course, Herr Schwartz," he said. "I am happy to hear from you."

"I hope I am not catching you at a bad time."

"Not at all. It is always a pleasure to speak to someone of your business experience."

"That's kind of you to say. I am calling concerning the project we are working on outside Moscow."

"The Dishinki Hotel?"

"Yes. Exactly."

The conversation continued in the same boring fashion, the whole time Komarov writing down the key words. After they said good-bye, the attaché rose from his desk, made sure his door was locked, and retrieved the book that served as the code key from the secret compartment at the back of his filing cabinet.

After he deciphered the message, he composed an e-mail, similarly encoded, and sent it to the address he had memorized before being sent to Germany.

He then settled back in his chair and picked up working where he'd left off, hoping his involvement in the matter was now done.

CHICAGO, ILLINIOS

RICKY ORBITS—NOT his real name, but his favorite—leaned back on his sofa, wearing only an open silk robe. He picked up the TV remote and began hopping through the channels.

SportsCenter. Nope.

He actually loved the show, but couldn't stand watching it on days after his beloved White Sox lost. It was especially bad today since last night it had been to those damn Detroit Tigers.

He clicked again. *Pawn Stars*. Another show he loved, but he'd seen the episode multiple times so he kept going.

Bones reruns. Okay, he could get into that. That girl was seriously smart but whacked, man. And that Angela chick was hot.

One of the doctors was pulling a skeleton out of a barrel of congealed crude when Ricky's phone vibrated twice on the glass coffee table. A text.

He waited until a commercial and then reached for the phone, but before he even got his hand on it, a second text came in.

Someone's anxious, he thought.

He was wrong. The two texts had been sent by two different numbers. The first was from a regular client based in Washington, DC, and read:

Assignment: find and obtain
Last known loc.: Seattle, WA

Usual fee plus bonus if completed within 24 hrs.
Details upon acceptance

As he read the second text, he let out a surprised "huh."

It was from a client in Moscow he'd done a couple jobs for the previous year. The weird thing was, the Russians wanted to hire him for what appeared to be the exact same job as the DC client's. But the Russians were offering double fee plus bonus.

Well, this is a first, he thought. *If there was a way to accept both, that would be awesome.*

He spent a few minutes considering the possibility, but in the end, he knew he'd have to give the package to someone, meaning one of the clients would not be happy. That could turn ugly.

He had nothing currently booked so it wasn't a question of whether he would take the job or not, just who he would take it from. While the second was offering more cash, number one had been a much more reliable employer.

Wanting to see if his first choice would come around to more agreeable terms, he sent a reply:

Double fee, w/bonus up to 48 hours
and I'm yours.

The answer came back within seconds.

Done.

Ricky smiled. After he sent his regrets to the Russians, he pushed off the couch and looked toward his bed on the other side of the loft.

"Babe, you gotta get out of here. I got things to do."

The woman, lying naked on top of the sheets, barely moved.

He tried to remember her name but it wasn't coming to him. Hell, he couldn't even remember what her face looked like, but knew she was a looker. Even as drunk as he'd been, he wouldn't have brought her up otherwise.

He walked over to the bed and slapped her ass. "Honey, snap to it. The hunter's been activated. Time for you to go."

He laughed as he headed into the bathroom to take a shower. That was a good one. He'd have to remember that.

"The hunter's been activated. Time for you to go," he whispered at the mirror and laughed again.

11

TACOMA

W HILE QUINN WOULD have liked to leave the Seattle area immediately, he knew if they didn't first get a handle on their situation, they could run themselves right into trouble.

The logical place to start was with Danielle.

He stationed Nate in the hallway in case she tried to run, and then unlocked her door.

She looked at him as he walked in, disappointed. "I thought maybe you were bringing me something to eat. At least Mr. Black fed us."

"When we eat, you eat. I promise." He stopped a few feet from the bed. "I'm hoping you can help us."

"Oh, really. In what way?" she asked, her tone dismissive.

"This doesn't need to be a confrontation."

"Whatever you say."

"Look, we don't want to be here any more than you do. We were supposed to be done last night after we dealt with your Mr. Black. Rescuing anyone was not part of the plan."

"You didn't rescue anyone. You're holding me, and you left the others behind."

"The police were at the house within twenty minutes after we left. Your cellmates are being cared for in a hospital right now."

"Why should I believe you?"

"You don't have to," he said. "Follow me."

He walked into the hallway and waited.

A few seconds passed before Danielle stepped through the doorway. "Is this another trick?"

"No trick," Quinn said. "We're going downstairs."

He motioned for Nate to go first and then he followed. The girl took her time, but eventually made her way down.

Quinn picked up the remote control and switched on the TV. Like before, the news was all about the events at Edmondson's house. The girl watched, rapt, inching closer and closer until she was standing next to Quinn. After another update from the reporter at the hospital, he hit the mute button.

Danielle blinked and looked at him. "All right. So you did let them go. You still have me, though."

"We do."

"Why?"

"There's the big question. Why don't you tell me?"

"I don't know what you mean."

"Why would our client tell us to free the others but hold on to you?"

She shrugged. "Why don't you ask him?"

"Her. And she's gone MIA."

A hint of surprise in her eyes. "Then, then…you should probably let me go, too."

"I wish it was that easy. Until I know why she wanted you, I can't do anything."

She straightened, reasserting her defiance. "Sorry. Can't help you."

"It would make things easier if you told us."

"If you're looking for the *easy* method, why don't you beat it out of me?"

"No one's going to do that."

"Right. You're going to be all polite and nice and respectful.

And then you'll hand me over to your missing client when you find her. What do you think *she'll* do?" She stared at him. "Torture me now or later, it's the same damn thing."

"You're not going to be tortured."

Her eyes narrowed. "Don't promise something you can't guarantee."

She was right, of course. He had no idea what Helen's intentions were. That bothered him. He liked the girl's spirit, and his intuition was telling him she wasn't an enemy.

"If you don't want to talk, I'm not going to push," he said.

"Prefer to leave it to them, huh?"

He turned to Nate. "Take her back to her room."

As she was led away, Quinn lowered himself onto the couch. There had to be some other way to learn what was going on. He ran everything that had happened through his mind again.

What about Samuel Edmondson?

Sure, the creep was dead, but he couldn't have been acting alone. The girl from cell one had mentioned others coming for them. If Quinn found one of Edmondson's associates, he might find his answers.

Usually he'd set Orlando to the task of tracking people down, but until Daeng joined her, he'd rather she focus on her own survival. Luckily she wasn't the only one he could turn to for help.

The Mole answered in his typical, oddly patterned monotone. "It's a little…early."

"Sorry. Didn't mean to get you out of bed," Quinn said.

"I did not say I…was out of…bed."

It would take a while for Quinn to get that image out of his head. "I need your help."

"Of course you…do. What…is it you need?"

There had been a time when the Mole was a pain in the ass to deal with, but since Quinn had helped rid him of someone who'd been taking advantage of the Mole for years, things had changed.

Now the Mole's monotone didn't come with quite the same amount of contempt as it had before.

"Are you familiar with what's going on in Seattle?"

"I...am familiar with many...things...going...on in Seattle."

"I'm talking about the women who were missing."

"The Edmondson matter."

"Yes."

"It was only a...matter of time."

"What do you mean? Do you know something about it?"

"Not...exactly."

"That's not a no."

"You're right."

"For God's sake, can we not play twenty questions and you just tell me what you do know?"

"Not on the news...yet, but my private channels...tell me...he had several...holding cells in his...basement."

"Six," Quinn said.

A pause. "Maybe...you know...more than I."

"We're the ones who found the place and tipped off the police."

"Interesting."

"You are now the only one besides those involved who's aware of that, so if you decide to share it with anyone, I'll know it came from you."

"Your...secret's safe...with me, Batman. I assume there...is a... reason you are...telling me this."

Quinn described what they had discovered in Edmondson's hidden lair.

"It sounds like...a way station. There...have been rumors of... a human smuggling...operation running...in the Northwest. And given...that the news has been reporting that the three...girls who were found...had all been...missing, I...would speculate that the rumors...are true."

"There were actually four," Quinn told him.

"I'm sorry?"

"Four women. We have one of them."

Even for the Mole, the pause that followed was a long one. "Why?"

"Not something you need to know."

"If you…say so. You…still have not…told me what you want."

"There's no way Edmondson was operating alone. Others had to have known about his setup. I need to talk to one of them."

"Why…are you asking…me? Is something wrong…with Orlando?"

If the Mole could be said to have any true friends, Orlando would top that list.

"Don't worry," Quinn said. "You're not treading on her territory. She's just otherwise occupied. If it helps, I'd like you to concentrate on anyone within fifty miles of Seattle."

"You're still…there," the Mole guessed.

"In the area, but not for long. Two hours. That's all I can give you."

"That…may not be…enough time."

"It'll have to be."

AN HOUR AND forty minutes later, the Mole called back.

"One name," he said. "Roger Platt."

"Who is he?" Quinn asked.

"Shift foreman…at Roland-McNeil Aeronautics."

"A shift foreman?"

"On the…horizontal stabilizer assembly…line. RMA does contract…work for…larger aircraft…companies."

"I'm not seeing the connection here."

"Platt and Edmondson were best…friends in high…school."

"Oh, really? I take it they've remained in contact."

"Daily."

"Do you happen to know if Mr. Platt is at work right now?"

"He works…the graveyard shift."

"So he's home?"

"Satellite data shows him…arriving home…at 7:41 a.m. Would…you like his…address?"

LEAVING NATE AND Danielle at the safe house was not an option. They'd been at the location far too long already. Unfortunately, Quinn also knew they couldn't count on the woman's cooperation once they were on the move, so as much as it pained him, the only real choice they had was to drug her again.

She spotted the needle in Quinn's hand the moment he and Nate entered the room. But instead of fighting, she rolled up her sleeve and stared into the distance, expressionless.

Quinn was under no illusion that the cooperation was a sign of anything permanent, and knew she would run if given the opportunity. So while Nate went out to obtain a new vehicle, Quinn inserted a tracking chip in one of her shoes.

Nate returned with a khaki green Jeep Grand Cherokee and pulled it into the garage, where they transferred the unconscious Danielle into the backseat. Nate then drove off again, tasked with staying on the move until Quinn contacted him.

Using the sedan they'd first arrived in, Quinn headed north.

Roger Platt lived in a working-class neighborhood of single-family homes east of Sea-Tac International Airport. Some of the houses had undergone extensive renovations, while others looked like they hadn't been touched in the decades since they'd been built, all signs of slow but steady gentrification.

Platt's house fell somewhere in the middle of old and new. It had no obvious addition to the outside, but it had been repainted recently, and the roof couldn't have been more than a year or two old.

Quinn drove past, looking for the best way to approach the man's place, and hit pay dirt five houses down. Plunked in the middle of the front yard was a FOR SALE sign. From the lack of curtains in the windows, he could see the house was empty. Better yet, there was a lockbox on the front door that would contain the house key, meaning neighbors would be used to seeing people going in and out.

He pulled into the driveway like he was a Realtor, and then used his phone's camera to zoom in on the lockbox. It was one of the new versions. Instead of operating with one specific combination, it was wireless enabled and could accept individual Realtor codes. This served two purposes: preventing Realtors from having to hunt down different numbers for each property, and allowing the selling agent to know who had visited.

A quick text to the Mole garnered a usable code. Quinn pulled on his gloves, climbed out of the car, and, less than thirty seconds later, was through the house and into the backyard. He sneaked across the neighboring yards until he reached Platt's.

After easing onto the deck that protruded from the back of the house, he crept up to the set of French doors leading inside, and looked in. A family room, dim and unoccupied.

Using his detection app, he discovered that the house was protected by a surprisingly high-end security system. Fortunately, it was still civilian grade, so the software Orlando had created was able to rapidly disable it. Quinn then picked the lock and let himself in.

A quick search revealed that Platt was sound asleep in the master bedroom. Before waking him, Quinn took a look around.

No woman's touch here, just a house-sized man cave for a rabid Seattle sports fan. Leather seemed to be the covering of choice when it came to furniture, and no expense was spared on the seventy-five-inch TV and accompanying sound system. The kitchen, however, had not seen the same infusion of cash, and was filled with appliances that looked to have been there for decades. In light of the trash can full of takeout containers, Quinn concluded cooking was not one of Platt's talents.

Wondering if the man's garage was equipped with its own

secret basement, Quinn checked it but found only a vintage Ford Mustang, dozens of storage boxes, and a solid concrete floor.

Back in the house, he searched a closet near the front door and then the one in the hallway right outside the man's bedroom. In the latter, he found a hidden compartment in the back, a space more than large enough for the three photo albums it contained.

Quinn pulled out the top album, opened it, and tensed. There was no question now of Platt's involvement with his high-school buddy.

The album was full of pictures of women, all unclothed and lying on the same mattresses Quinn had seen in Edmondson's cells. A few of the shots were closer, taken by someone on top of the subject, and in several the photographer's hand was visible—strong and callused. Not Edmondson's hand.

It was only Quinn's years of experience that kept the rage boiling in his chest from taking over as he put the album back and reentered Platt's bedroom.

The man hadn't moved since Quinn had first seen him. His hair was cropped short, military style, though his graying goatee was definitely not regulation. One of his arms lay atop the blankets, bearing the muscles of someone who'd seen a lifetime of physical work. And then there was the hand on the blanket, the same hand from the pictures.

Platt would likely put up a good fight if given the chance, but Quinn was in no mood to let him try. He placed the muzzle of his suppressor against Platt's hip, grabbed the spare pillow with his free hand, and said, "Hey, asshole."

Groaning, Platt's eyes slowly fluttered open. As soon as he realized he wasn't alone, he tried to push himself up, but he'd barely raised his head before Quinn pulled the trigger. As Platt started to scream, Quinn shoved the pillow in his face, muffling the sound, and pressed his gun against Platt's groin.

"If you don't shut up, the next shot goes here."

Platt continued to cry out as if he hadn't heard the threat, one hand on his wound, the other trying but failing to push the pillow away.

"One...two...thr—"

"Okay, okay," Platt yelled, his voice distorted. "I'll stop!"

Quinn kept the pillow in place for a few more seconds before moving it to the side.

"You son of a bitch! What the fuck, man?"

Quinn switched his aim to the man's forehead. "Samuel Edmondson."

A split second of confusion, then fear. "I don't know who you're talking about." He closed his eyes, wincing. "Oh, man. Call an ambulance."

"Samuel Edmondson," Quinn repeated.

"Yeah, all right, I know him. So what?"

"Samuel Edmondson."

"We went to school together, that's all. What do you want?"

Platt may have thought himself subtle, but he was far from it. When the guy's arm swung out, Quinn was already moving out of the way, allowing it to catch only air.

"Bad call." Quinn jammed the gun against the man's offending shoulder and pulled the trigger.

Another scream brought a return of the pillow. Platt was a quick learner, however, and when his cries became whimpers, Quinn removed the pillow.

"Samuel Edmondson."

"I didn't know it was going to turn out like this, okay?" Platt said, tears rolling down his cheeks. "He just asked for my help, that's all. I didn't realize what he was into until it was too late."

Lies, of course, but ones that Quinn could work with. "And what was he into?"

"If you're asking about him, you already know the answer, man. Come on. I need help!"

Quinn moved the gun to the man's other shoulder.

"No! No!" Platt yelled.

"What was he into?"

"Girls, all right?"

"For himself?"

Platt shook his head. "Orders would come in."

"And how would the girls get to him?"

"Some kind of…ne-ne-network he set up," he said, his strength diminishing. "I don't…know the details."

Another lie. "And your job?"

"I just…I just helped him get them in and out."

"That's all?"

"Yes," he pleaded, as if doing only that wasn't already reprehensible.

"And when they were in their cells?"

"What? I never, um, dealt with them in their cells."

Quinn was tempted to shoot him again, but knew that would put an end to their talk.

"How did the orders come in? By body type or…?"

"Yeah. Type. Skin color. Weight. Eyes. That kind of thing."

"Always that way? Never by, say, name?"

"Name? Um, um, no."

"I'm really tired of being lied to, Roger."

"I'm not ly—"

Quinn shoved his gun against the man's wounded shoulder. "Sometimes there were women requested specifically by name, weren't there?"

Platt cried out.

Quinn pressed again. "Answer the question."

"Yes! Every once in a while, he would get a name."

Quinn pulled his gun back. "Did these requests come from the same clients who wanted the other girls?"

"No. Someone different."

"Who?"

"I don't know who! I swear."

"Who?"

"Different times, different people."

"What about the last time?"

Platt stared at him but said nothing.

"Danielle Chad. She was one of the special requests, wasn't she?"

"I've never…heard that name—"

"Don't. She was a request?"

Another swallow, this one followed by a weak yes.

"By who?"

Platt clenched his teeth as another wave of pain washed over him.

"You know who, don't you?"

A small nod. "Sam…sometimes refers to her as…as The Wolf. That's all I know."

The name meant nothing to Quinn.

"How long did Edmondson have the girl?"

"We picked her up three…wait, no, four days ago."

"From whom?"

Platt didn't know the contact's name, and could only tell Quinn where the pickup had occurred.

"When were you supposed to give her to this Wolf?"

"We hadn't set a drop-off yet."

Quinn ground his weapon into the wound again. "You're lying."

"I'm not! Sam hadn't told The Wolf we had the girl yet."

"Why not?"

"He, um, he wanted to get something from her first."

"What?"

"A…uh, uh…location."

"What location?"

"Hell if I know. That's what he called it. I swear, he never told me. Oh, God, please call an ambulance."

"Did he get the location from her?"

"Not as far as I know. He would have set up a drop-off if he had."

"How did he contact The Wolf?"

"I have no idea. The business side was all Sam."

Quinn thought for a moment, making sure he'd asked every-thing, and then said, "Thank you. I appreciate your time."

He pulled his gun back and took a step away.

"Wait," Platt said, his voice drifting. "I need...a doctor."

"I have bad news for you. A doctor's not going to do you any good."

"You can't let me die! You need to do something!"

The man continued to plead as Quinn left the room.

Before leaving, he removed Platt's trophy albums from the closet and set them on the floor of the entryway, opened to partic-ularly damning pages. He then unlocked the front door so that when the police showed up after he called them, they'd have no problem getting in.

12

SOUTHERN OREGON

"I'M GOING TO suck at this," Quinn said.

Orlando smiled. "Hardly."

"Yes, I am. It's not like I had a great role model."

"If you even come close to sucking, I promise I'll kill you. Does that help?"

"You should. Look what a mess *I* am. I don't want to do that to our kid."

She grabbed his face with both hands. "You're not going to be anything like your stepfather. You're going to be a great dad." She touched his chest. "You have a good heart. And you're one of the smartest people I know."

His features softened a bit. "Not as smart as you."

"That goes without saying," she said. "Our baby is going to be lucky to have you as a father."

"How can you know that?" he asked.

"I can, and I do."

He laid his head in her lap, his ear against her belly. "I think I hear something."

"Just my lunch."

"No, really. I think the baby's moving."

Orlando's eyes snapped open. For a few seconds she didn't

know where she was, but then the drone of an engine brought everything back. She was in Mr. Vo's RV, lying on one of the dining table bench seats.

She assumed a bump in the road had caused the jolt that woke her, but as she struggled to sit up, she felt a tightening of muscles in her lower abdomen.

A contraction? *Hey, I know I said you could come at any time, but let's put a hold on that for a little while, okay?*

She took a couple deep breaths. Up front, she could see that Garrett had moved into the passenger seat next to Mr. Vo, and that Mrs. Vo was lounging on the built-in recliner near the side door. None of them had noticed Orlando was awake.

With each breath the cramp lost strength. To distract herself, she thought about the dream. She'd been having a conversation with Quinn about...she couldn't remember. The baby, most likely. It was always the baby these days.

When she'd been a teenager, she couldn't even fathom the idea of having a kid, much less two. Garrett was turning out all right, though, despite everything. And at least this second child would have the advantage of having two parents around.

The pain finally gone, she decided it had been a false contraction. She'd had them with Garrett, too.

She maneuvered off the seat—something that was much harder to do than it should have been—and headed up front, her hands on the walls to steady herself.

When she passed Mrs. Vo, she saw that the woman was asleep, so she took extra care not to disturb her. Up front, she held on to a side panel and attempted to kneel, but her balance was off. Her right arm flailed out and snagged the back of Garrett's chair.

Her son turned quickly. "Mom?"

He reached out to grab her but his seat belt held him back. By the time he got it unbuckled, she'd managed to lower herself ungracefully to the floor without any permanent damage.

"Are you all right?" he asked.

"I'm fine," she said.

"Sorry, sorry," Mr. Vo said, looking at her through the rearview mirror. "I not see you come."

"It's okay. I'm fine."

Looking unsure, Garrett let go of her arm.

"Where are we?" she asked.

"Oregon," he told her.

"Cross border forty minute ago," Mr. Vo said.

"What time is it?" she asked.

"Twelve-twenty," he told her.

"Twelve-twenty-two," Garrett corrected him. He was at that age when time was an exact thing. None of this "rounding off" stuff. Give or take the two minutes, she'd been asleep for over four hours, far longer than she'd planned.

"Looks like you guys have everything under control," she said as she pushed herself up.

She reached into her pocket, pulled out her phone, and called Quinn. The call went straight to voice mail.

"Checking in," she said after the tone. "Call when you have time."

She called Daeng next.

"*Sawadee, khrap,*" he said, greeting her in his native Thai.

"*Sawadee, ka,*" she replied in kind. "Where are you?"

"Eugene, Oregon."

"I thought you were flying to Portland."

"I did, and then I drove here. You're about two hours south of me, near a place called Grants Pass."

"Oh, you're tracking me, are you?"

"I'm merely using the software you provided," he said. "Shall we meet in the middle? Say, Roseburg?"

TACOMA

NATE PICKED QUINN up in a parking lot just off the interstate, south of the airport.

After Quinn shared what he'd learned, Nate asked, "The Wolf? Any idea who she is?"

"I've been thinking about it. I think there was someone years ago who used that name. I don't remember the context. At most it was something I heard in passing. Next time we talk to Orlando, we'll see if she remembers."

"So what now?"

"Now we leave town."

Nate hesitated. "You know, there *is* one other thing we can check before we get out of here."

Quinn looked at him.

"The safe house Helen set up for us," Nate explained. "If someone went there looking for us, wouldn't it confirm her disappearance is tied to our mission?"

Though Quinn was already convinced the connection existed, it would be better to have proof. But was checking worth the risk?

He mulled it over and consulted the map. "I-90's up that way. We can at least do a drive-by, and then take the interstate east when we're done."

Looking pleased with himself, Nate shifted into drive and headed for the freeway.

———

DANI HEARD VOICES, close, but the words were lost to her, the drug still clouding her ability to understand. She tried to part her eyelids, but each felt as if it were sealed in place.

Her thoughts seemed to drift this way and that, until she couldn't even remember what she was trying to figure out.

A continuous hum, either heard or imagined, underlined everything. That, and the voices—*right, the voices*—were the only sounds.

She fought through the fog. The voices, she realized, belonged to the two men. Nate, the younger one had been called. And... and...Quinn? That was it, right?

She felt oddly relieved that they hadn't handed her off yet. She wasn't sure why, but she had a sense that the longer she could stay with them, the better her chance of protecting the secret.

Her thoughts began to scramble again and slowly scatter.

The voices faded.

And there was only the hum.

Then that faded, too.

THE BELLEVUE SAFE house was much larger than the one in Tacoma.

As they drove slowly past the place, Quinn noted that it looked exactly as it should have—deserted.

Maybe no one had been here at all, he thought.

"Pull over," he told Nate as they neared the end of the block.

When they were stopped, Quinn retrieved two sets of comm gear from one of the duffels and tossed one packet to Nate.

"If you can't reach me for any reason," he said, "get out of here right away."

"Got it."

His senses on alert, Quinn headed down the sidewalk, but made it all the way to the safe house's driveway without any warnings flashing in his head.

He paused there and pulled out his phone, looking as if he'd received a text.

Quiet. Not the tense quiet of men lying in wait. Just…quiet.

Deciding it was safe enough for a closer look, he headed up the driveway, ready to grab his weapon at the first sign of trouble. He took in the roofline and the bushes and the windows and the door, but spotted no unexpected movements anywhere.

An attached garage sat at the end of the driveway. Quinn headed for the small section of fence between it and the edge of the property, and hopped over. No longer in view of anyone on the street, he pulled out his SIG and made his way into the backyard.

Trees lined the rear half of the property, with a large grass area taking up much of the rest of the space. As for the house, a sliding glass door at the back was closed, vertical blinds pulled across it. Shades were also drawn across the rest of the windows.

Quinn returned his attention to the yard, giving it a longer look this time. The grass ended three feet from the fence, leaving a strip of land covered in dark bark chips acting as buffer between the two.

Sticking to the grass, he moved along the strip and studied the chips. About a third of the way down the side opposite the garage, he stopped. Several chips had been disturbed in a way unlike anywhere else. A few were broken. Someone had come through this way, but it could as easily have been a week ago as an hour.

He found the proof he was looking for several feet farther down, in a spot where the chips petered out, leaving a three-inch patch of soft soil. On the dirt was the partial print of a boot. Quinn had examined thousands of prints since becoming a cleaner, so it wasn't difficult to determine this one was no more than twelve hours old.

With this in mind, he studied the grass again. Though the blades were already in the process of returning to their normal state, he could now pick out several points where they had recently been bent down.

He keyed his mic. "Nate."

"Go for Nate."

"You were right."

RICKY ORBITS NEVER checked luggage onto a plane. Waiting at baggage claim was his definition of hell. Besides, the most important items he usually needed would never pass inspection. So when he landed at Sea-Tac International at 12:10 p.m., he walked straight out to the parking area where the car he'd ordered was waiting for him, complete with a loaded suitcase in the trunk filled with the rest of his requests.

The client had provided him with the address where the girl had originally been found, and a list of possible locations she'd been taken to afterward. Orbits had sent out some feelers before he boarded the plane at O'Hare, and had received several responses by the time he landed. Most had no information other than what was on the news. Seems the girl wasn't the only one being kept at the Columbia City address. Why she was more important than the others, he didn't know, nor did he care.

One of the responses, however, reported that an elite team from a California-based security agency had arrived in the area early that morning and gone to a house in Bellevue—a house that was at the top of the list of possible hiding locations Orbits had been given.

His client had informed him that other interested parties would likely also be looking for the girl, so it was a good bet the California team was one of his competitors. He was sure they hadn't located the girl yet, though. If they had, he would have already received a text thanking him for his time and releasing him.

He thought for a moment. It wouldn't hurt to have a look around the Bellevue house. If the Californians had gone in hard and heavy, they might have missed some clues that could put Orbits on the right path.

He plugged the address into his GPS and hit the road. Thanks to a bit of traffic, the eighteen-mile drive took over thirty minutes.

The house was located in a nice neighborhood where most of the homes were set back from the road, with lawns of deep green grass running right up to the sidewalk.

"Your destination is one hundred feet ahead, on the right," the female GPS voice informed him.

Right before he reached the property, he noticed a man

walking along the sidewalk in front of the house. The guy hadn't been there a moment before. Either some of the bushes near the end of the driveway had blocked him from view, or he'd been up at the house.

Another hunter?

Orbits grabbed his phone and switched on the camera. Draping his arm across the other seat and holding the device next to the headrest, he snapped off several pics as he passed the man.

Maybe the guy was no one, but it wouldn't hurt to have him checked out.

Fifteen minutes later, he had finished his examination of the house and was sitting in his car again. He had seen signs that others had recently been there, but a look inside revealed no one had used the place for some time.

He smiled. The Californians had definitely not found the target here.

He sympathized with the others, he really did. Catching that first scent of a prey was always the hardest part of the job, but for him, it was also the most enjoyable. He was damn good at it. He was Ricky Orbits, after all. The number one hunter in the world.

The brief had mentioned that the woman had been helped in her escape by unknown individuals. Find them and he'd find her.

He pulled out his phone.

"It's me," Orbits said.

"What's up, boss?" Donnie said.

"Got a few things I need you to look into."

13

LOCATION UNKNOWN

THE DOOR OPENED again, and heavy footsteps crossed to where Helen sat. As her new visitor stopped in front of her, Helen caught the distinct odor of cigarettes.

A deep breath was followed by a loud expulsion of air. A second later a stream of smoke hit the cloth bag. The material filtered out much of the cloud, but plenty still got through. Helen tried not to cough but failed.

Her visitor took a step closer. Helen held her breath but there was no second cloud. Instead, the person circled her slowly to the point directly behind the chair.

"We can kill you whenever we want." A male voice, rough from his cigarette habit. "Is your life really worth protecting someone you've never met before?" The steps completed the circle and came to rest back in front of Helen. "You are a foolish woman, Ms. Cho. You have an opportunity to help yourself and yet you act the hero. There is no such thing as heroes."

Suddenly hands grabbed both sides of her head and tilted her face up. Though she couldn't see him through the bag, she could taste his sour breath as he squeezed her skull like he was going to cave it in.

He laughed as he finally let go. "This could have been so easy for you. Know that what comes next was chosen by you alone."

When he walked out of the room, three new pairs of steps entered, accompanied by the sound of rattling wheels. The procession came to a halt a few feet to Helen's left. There was the clinking and jangling of items being placed on a metal surface. Then silence.

She was about to make a smartass remark when someone grabbed her arm. Though she was already strapped to the chair, the trio wrapped two new restraints around her chest and shoulder, further limiting her ability to move.

After this was done, they left.

The silence lasted less than a minute before Helen heard the familiar clicking of heels.

The woman.

She approached in the same casual manner as she had on her first visit, stopping at the same place the man had.

"My associate pointed out to me that I forgot to introduce myself. I am Nanou Deschamps."

Helen knew she had heard the name before, but her mind was still muddled and she couldn't place it. "Good for you."

A hum whirred to life, followed by the sizzle and pop of an electric arc.

"People in my home country call me Le Loup."

Oh, God, Helen thought, making the connection. *It couldn't be.*

"In English it means—"

"I know what it means," Helen said.

The Wolf.

14

WASHINGTON STATE

DANI WOKE AGAIN, the clouds that had jammed her mind all but gone.

She opened her eyes and saw she was lying in the backseat of a vehicle, her head to the driver's side of the car. Quinn was sitting in the front passenger seat, so she assumed the one called Nate was behind the wheel.

She tried to gauge the time from the sunlight, but the best she could do was rule out dawn or dusk. She could see an expanse of trees out the window so they probably weren't in a city.

Glancing down, she saw her wrists and ankles were restrained, but at least they'd left her arms in front. She tried to lift her hands so she could rub her eyes, but could only move them a few inches before they tugged to a stop due to two additional zip ties connecting those around her wrists with belt loops on her jeans.

"You're up. Welcome back."

Quinn was looking at her.

"I bet you're hungry," he said.

"Sure. Let's pull into the next restaurant. We can go in, have a nice sit-down meal."

"No need." He reached down by his feet and pulled up a bag that said Arby's on the side.

"Awesome," she said coolly.

A silent message passed between the two men. Within moments, the vehicle slowed as it descended a short hill, then turned a couple times before traveling several minutes down a bumpy road.

When they finally stopped, Nate climbed out, opened the door behind Dani's head, and helped her into a sitting position. She could now see they were on a narrow dirt road, with trees close in on both sides, removing any chance she could flag someone down for help.

They were obviously in a forest, but which one she had no idea. Somewhere in North America, though in light of all the sedatives she'd been given, she could be wrong.

She'd thought she'd waited long enough. Marianne had said not to come back for at least five years. She'd waited ten. Still, she had somehow been recognized. Her passport picture when she came through Immigration in Los Angeles? Maybe. Her alias? Maybe that, too. She should have never kept her real first name, but it had been *so* long, and she'd been afraid if she were called by a different name, she'd forget to respond and instantly expose the lie.

They had seized her in a rundown motel just off the strip in Las Vegas. She mistakenly thought she could hide among the mobs of tourists while she worked up the courage to go to her final destination. Since then, she'd always either been blindfolded, kept in spaces without windows, or drugged. In a way, Mr. Black's prison cell had been a relief after what had seemed like days on the road. What she hadn't realized until these new creeps came onto the scene was that the cells had been in the basement of a house.

Quinn handed the bag of food to his buddy and got out.

"We weren't sure what you'd like," Nate said. "So we got you a roast beef sandwich and a chicken sandwich. Fries, too. The curly kind." He touched the side of the bag and smiled. "Still a little warm."

"Are you going to feed me, too?"

He gave her another one of his winning smiles before pulling out a pocketknife and cutting the ties holding her wrists to her belt. He did not, however, remove the bindings holding her wrists together.

After putting a sandwich between her fingers, he said, "You should be able to manage from here."

"Did you get me anything to drink?"

"Wow, you are demanding, aren't you?"

He pulled out a bottle of water from the bag.

Once she started eating, she couldn't stop. As she finished off the sandwich, Nate asked, "You want the other one?"

Instead of answering, she picked up the water bottle and held it toward him. "I can't open it."

He took care of it and handed it back. "Sit tight. We'll be leaving soon."

He climbed out and shut the door.

Dani twisted around and watched the two men walk down the road behind the SUV for about twenty feet before stopping to talk.

Thinking this might be her only chance, she leaned between the front seats and looked for anything that could help her get away.

The vehicle employed a button to start the engine, so there were no keys dangling from the ignition. She did, however, spot a black bag in the passenger footwell and reached for it.

Beep-beep-beep-beep-beep.

She looked around for the source, but before she could find it, the passenger door opened and Nate leaned in.

"Sorry about that." He touched a black square affixed to the armrest and the noise stopped. "Motion detector. Why don't you settle back in your seat while I reset this."

"SHE THINKS WE'RE just like Edmondson," Nate said as he joined Quinn behind the SUV.

"Well, wouldn't you?" Quinn said.

Nate sighed. "Probably. What are we going to do if Helen doesn't turn up? We can't drive around with Danielle forever."

Quinn looked out at the woods. "I don't know. It's something we'll have to—"

Beep-beep-beep-beep-beep.

They turned toward the SUV. Quinn had mounted the motion detector before he climbed out, on the off chance the woman tried anything. Well, more an on chance than off, apparently.

"I got it," Nate said, already moving toward the vehicle.

Quinn looked back out at the woods. They needed a plan, or at least a partial one that included more than getting out of Seattle.

One option would be to find someplace around here to hide out in and think things through. There had to be dozens of isolated cabins in the area, and at least a few should be unoccupied. But while that idea had a certain appeal, Quinn felt they were still way too close to the city to stop.

If they continued the way they were going, they would cross into Idaho. They could get lost in the backcountry up in the panhandle. He liked that idea a lot better.

As much as he wanted to avoid using Orlando, she could probably arrange things a lot faster than he could. He pulled out his phone, saw the cell signal was down to one bar, and switched it to satellite mode.

"How far have you gotten?" he asked Orlando.

"Almost to Portland. We'll cut east from there."

After Quinn and Nate had left Bellevue, Quinn realized she'd left him a voice mail. When he called her back, she'd sprung her idea of shadowing them. He wasn't keen on it, but he couldn't fault the logic that it would be smarter for her and Daeng to be nearby.

"I was thinking Idaho," he told her. "Maybe someplace

isolated up north. If you have time, you think you could look into it for us?"

"It's not like anyone needs me here. Daeng's driving and Mr. Vo's telling him what he's doing wrong. Garrett's on the bunk playing video games, and Mrs. Vo is pretending to watch one of her *telenovelas* but is really just napping. Time, I've got."

"Thanks. Any progress on Danielle?"

She'd filled him in on what she'd been doing to find out more about the girl, but ultimately the answer was no.

WEST TEXAS

UNENDING STRINGS OF data streamed skyward and earthbound, as they had since the satellite had come online.

At various points in the orbiter's history, the monitoring equipment housed in a western Texas facility had experienced undetected augmentations to its operating software. Some of these new modules had built-in self-destruct codes that activated after a specified period of time had passed. Others continued to run long after their initial purpose had been fulfilled. The instigators of these intruders were varied, but they all came from the same family tree—United States intelligence.

The latest module had been integrated into the software at 5:17 a.m. Central time, and immediately began its task of scouring incoming information. The process continued throughout the morning and into the early afternoon without kicking back a single result.

That changed at 2:21 p.m.

The coordinates of the call's originator pinpointed a spot along an unused access road 1.6 miles off the I-90, on the eastern side of the Cascades Mountain Range. The recipient's location was not so easily identified. For some reason, the satellite received multiple coordinates for it throughout North America and Europe.

The call would have been flagged for this alone, but another, more telling marker had also been ticked. The conversation had been entirely encrypted.

The module was not designed to decode anything, but it did contain a subroutine that snagged a recorded copy of the conversation, which was then sent along with the notification.

NSA MONITORING STATION
ARLINGTON, VIRGINIA

AT THE SAME moment a *ding* rang out from the computer's speaker, a dialogue box appeared on the screen.

COMMUNICATION ALERT

Sat. 6 G2

Below this were two buttons: VIEW and IGNORE. The attendant clicked the first and then read the details of the alert. After determining it wasn't an anomaly, he consulted the instructions for this particular hunt.

Adhering to the stated procedures, he created a map of the location and e-mailed the message, the file that had accompanied it, and his map to the listed contact. In addition, he sent a text to the contact's phone alerting the man of the incoming information.

Then, much like the illegal software had done, he returned to his previous task.

NEW YORK CITY, NEW YORK

MATTHEW MORSE SET down his fork and leveled his gaze at the man across from him. "I don't care what they're saying in Hong Kong," he said, his words straining to escape his damaged vocal cords. "We know the threat exists, and we know it starts there."

Ketterman, one of Morse's assistant directors, smiled uncomfortably. "I understand that, sir. I've seen the data myself. But our team in country has been unable to locate Tsu anywhere. There's no indication that he's in the territory."

"You just said you read the data yourself. Then you know there is *every* indication."

"Gold team is one of our best, sir. If they can't find him, then—"

"Then they're not looking hard enough. I suggest you encourage them to do so."

Morse picked up his fork again, signaling that the meeting was over.

"Of course, sir. Right away." Ketterman left quickly.

Morse finished off his salmon, dabbed the corner of his mouth with his napkin, and touched the intercom button.

"Mr. Carter, I'm finished."

A moment later, his assistant came in, collected the used dishes, and exited without a word.

Morse was getting ready to head to his 2:30 meeting when the special cell phone in his left pocket buzzed. He removed it and read the text.

HIT RECEIVED. INFO SENT.

He checked his e-mail and clicked on the message from the NSA.

He ran the recording of the call through his agency's decoding software. Though the encryption was impossible to fully break, a few words leaked through—Seattle, Cho, photo, and a garbled word that sounded to him like Danielle—leaving no doubt that the scrambled satellite call was related to the woman.

He consulted a map. From where the call was made, the originator could go in only two directions—either east or west along the interstate. If, as Morse suspected, the caller was one of those involved in extracting the girl from Edmondson's house, he would have come from the west and logically would continue east. This presented an excellent intercept opportunity.

He grabbed the main phone.

"Stevens," the leader of the field team in Seattle answered.

"It's Morse. How quickly can you get to your helicopter?"

15

COLUMBIA CITY, WASHINGTON

"HIS NAME IS Jonathan Quinn," Donnie said over the phone.

"Why does that sound familiar?" Orbits asked.

He was sitting in his car, two blocks away from the Columbia City home where the missing girls had been found, close enough to see the frenzy of police and media and looky-loos, but far enough away not to draw any attention.

"He's a cleaner," Donnie said. "Pretty highly regarded from what I understand. I haven't been able to confirm it, but one source heard he was on a job at the Edmondson house last night."

So he hadn't just been some random guy walking down the street.

"He was there, all right," Orbits said. And if Quinn had been at Edmondson's, then he either had the girl or knew where she was. "Quinn...didn't he used to work for the Office?"

"He did," Donnie said. "Right up until they folded."

Orbits nodded to himself. He knew exactly who the guy was. Orbits had never directly crossed paths with him but had snooped around a few jobs Quinn did.

Excellent work each time. Quinn clearly knew how to handle the dead.

"Where is he now?" Orbits asked.

"Been trying to figure that out but got nothing so far. Except…" Donnie hesitated.

"Except what?"

"I heard Edmondson was a termination. Which makes sense if Quinn was there. The thing is, the doer was supposedly Ananke."

"Oh, really?" Orbits hadn't expected that.

"Again, not confirmed.

Ananke was an old…acquaintance. Orbits hadn't actually talked to her since she'd walked in on him having a little fun at Mardi Gras with a couple of forgettable college girls. But come on, how long could she stay mad at him? It was *Mardi Gras*, for God's sakes. You're supposed to have fun there.

"I'll touch base with her," he said. "What about the group from California? Are they still in the area?"

"They were a few hours ago."

"Check again and call me back."

After Orbits hung up, he scrolled through his contact list until he reached Ananke's newest number.

As he pressed SEND, his heart began to race. Maybe he wasn't quite as over her as he'd thought. He was saved from making a fool of himself, though, when his call went straight to voice mail.

"Hey, kitten, it's Ricky. Long time. Give me a shout back when you get this, okay? Later."

He hung up, sure she'd be excited to hear from him again.

BOULDER, COLORADO

ANANKE CAUGHT AN early morning flight out of Seattle to Denver, picked up her car from long-term parking, and drove home to Boulder.

Her house was along a dead-end road on the western edge of the city. Under most circumstances, the lack of alternate exit routes would have ruled the place out, but the views were spectacular—hills and trees and mountains on one side, and on the other a sky that seemed to move eastward forever.

She solved the escape-route problem by also purchasing the house on the next street over and creating a private drive between them. In all likelihood, she would never have to use it, but it was good to know it was there.

After a light snack, she stretched out on her king-sized bed and fell asleep. A call woke her, but by the time she was able to grab her cell, the call had gone to voice mail. The phone number looked vaguely familiar but she couldn't place it. She played back the message.

The second she heard, "Hey, kitten," she froze.

Ricky Orbits. That son of a bitch.

How did he get her number? She'd changed it multiple times since she left him specifically because she hadn't wanted to talk to the asshole again. And now he wanted her to call him back?

An image flashed in her mind, not just of Ricky on the phone but Ricky on the phone standing outside her driveway gate. He'd somehow gotten ahold of her number. Why not her address, too?

Before she realized it, she was hyperventilating. She raced to the sitting area that had the window overlooking her garage, and sighed in relief when she saw that the street beyond the gate was empty.

For someone so cool on the job, I sure lost it in a hurry.

It was that goddamn bastard. Orbits was the only one who had ever gotten so far under her skin. She had known he was a mistake from the beginning, but she couldn't help herself. And boy, how she'd emotionally paid for it after she'd found him in all his glory with his two new surgically enhanced friends. He'd even invited her to join in.

Just the memory of it made her shiver.

Three years of scar tissue that apparently could still be ripped off at will. She didn't want him back. God, no. She didn't want anything to do with him.

"No, Ricky. I will *not* be calling you."

After she deleted his message and his number in her missed calls list, she went to her safe, retrieved one of the many unused SIM cards she kept for emergencies, and traded it with the one in her phone. The card for her old number she cut in half and then burned in the kitchen.

COLUMBIA CITY, WASHINGTON

WHEN ORBITS'S PHONE rang, he hoped to see Ananke's name on the screen, but the caller ID read DONNIE.

"Yeah?" he answered, not bothering to keep the disappointment from his voice.

"Got something for you on the California team," Donnie said.

"What about them?"

"They just boarded a helicopter and headed east out of the city."

Orbits sat up, his funk forgotten. "Where are they going?"

"I have it on good authority they've got a location on Quinn and are on the way to intercept him."

If the team reached Quinn first and grabbed the girl—assuming the cleaner had her—then Ricky's bonus was gone.

"I need to follow them," he said.

"Already got you covered. I'm texting you an address. Get there quick. There's a chopper waiting. One of those *jet* kinds. Goes real fast."

Donnie could be a little weird but he was surprisingly efficient at times. "Thanks, buddy," Orbits said. "You rock."

The helicopter was revved and waiting when Orbits arrived.

As Orbits climbed aboard, the pilot, a thirtysomething guy in a dark green jumpsuit, pointed at a set of headphones hanging next to the passenger seat.

"Afternoon, Mr. Orbits," the man said. "I'm Marv Sutter. I'll be your pilot."

Orbits shook his hand. "Call me Ricky."

"All right, Ricky, where are we off to?"

Orbits pulled out his phone. On the drive over, Donnie had been texting every minute or so with updated GPS coordinates of the other helicopter's position. Orbits used these to track the aircraft's route on a map. At last report, it was southeast of Bellevue, paralleling the only major road in the area.

"Follow the I-90 east as fast as you can."

"How far we going?"

"You'll know when I know."

ORBITS WASN'T THE only hunter to arrive in the Emerald City looking for Danielle Chad. Four others touched down at Sea-Tac International Airport on separate flights that morning.

Each represented a different interested party. Three had the singular goal of finding the woman. The fourth, however, was operating under slightly different instructions.

The first of the other three landed at 10:45 a.m. on a flight from Las Vegas, took possession of a waiting car, and drove straight to Edmondson's neighborhood. The second and third arrived right before and right after 11:00 a.m. They, too, had vehicles standing by. While the second took the same route as the first, the third chose to start his search with the Bellevue safe house. All three had been briefed that others might be interested in the woman, but each was sure he would be the one to find her.

Bianca Zorn—hunter number four—arrived on the same Las Vegas flight as number one. Unlike the other three, she knew for a fact she wasn't the only one searching for the asset. As she had waited for her flight north, she had received an e-mail with pictures of six men potentially in or on their way to Seattle for that express purpose. It turned out that one, Drew Evans, was seated two rows in front of her.

Upon arrival, she followed him through the airport. In the crowd as they neared baggage claim, she moved in close enough to slip a tracking node under the bottom of his suit jacket. She then let him move ahead, and waited until he exited to the street before doing so herself.

She, too, had arranged for transport. In her case, it was not a car but a KTM 1290 Super Duke R motorcycle—an extremely agile, high-performance bike. Hanging from the seat, locked in place, was a helmet.

She donned the black leather jacket she'd brought with her, then detached the helmet and set it on the ground. Reaching under the seat, she felt around until she found the hidden latch and clicked it into the open position. A portion of the seat flipped up, revealing a Heckler & Koch VP9 pistol, two spare magazines, a suppressor, and a small kit bag containing the other items she thought she might need. She placed the magazines in her backpack, attached the suppressor to the gun, and slipped them into a custom-made slot inside her jacket.

Next, she retrieved the mounting kit she'd brought with her and affixed her phone near the midpoint of the handlebars so she could see it while she drove. After pulling on the helmet, she synched its comm to her phone via Bluetooth and climbed on the bike.

She followed Evans at a distance of a quarter mile, down I-405 and into Columbia City. She had no idea what he expected to find at the Edmondson house. The woman was long gone and the police would still be crawling all over the place.

Another one of those sense-driven hunters, she guessed. They like to "feel" where their target had been, saying it gave them valuable insight. It was all bullshit, sideshow stuff. She relied on a combination of actual clues and logic-based intuition, not some invisible vapor memory that didn't exist.

She parked the bike around the corner from where Evans had stopped. Leaving her sunglasses on, she exchanged her helmet for a blue baseball cap from her bag. She pulled her long blonde hair through the back and created a loose ponytail, making her look nothing like she had at the airport.

According to the tracking dot, Evans hadn't moved for the last three minutes. She confirmed this as she rounded the corner and spotted him sitting in his car, parked at the curb. The chaotic scene in front of Edmondson's house started about a block farther down. Evans seemed to be staring at it, "sensing" all he needed to know to find the girl.

Bianca had other tasks to deal with so there was no reason to prolong this. As she walked down the sidewalk, she unzipped her jacket halfway. Right before she reached the man's car, she moved into the street, stopped near his closed driver's-side window, and stared off toward the police activity.

After a few seconds, she looked at the car and asked, "Hey, do you know what's going on?"

Evans acted like he didn't hear her so she tapped on the glass.

"What's with all the police?"

Reluctantly he glanced in her direction. "Sorry, don't know."

"Was there a fire or something?"

He looked at her again, clearly annoyed. "I *don't* know."

She saw him reach for the ignition button. She'd been hoping to get him to open his window but you couldn't have everything.

Keeping the gun tight to her chest, she slipped it out of its slot and pulled the trigger, her aim instinctive and dead on. Because the window was made of laminated safety glass, it crunched instead of shattered as the bullet pierced it. A quick look around revealed that no one seemed to have noticed.

Instead of slumping onto the passenger side as she would have liked, Evans had been wearing his seat belt and remained mostly sitting up with his head lolled onto his shoulder.

Moving quickly, she put her gun away and folded the fractured glass inside the car. She then removed the shoulder strap holding Evans in place and shoved him below dash level.

Upon returning to her bike, she pulled out her phone and called The Wolf. As usual, she was greeted with a single beep.

"Bianca checking in," she said. "One down. Daniel Evans."

She stuffed the phone in her pocket and climbed on the bike.

As she was pulling the helmet over her head, a car drove past and turned down the same street Evans was parked on. Though the glimpse she got of the driver had been brief, she'd seen enough to know it was Kimball Norris, another one of the hunters whose photos she'd received.

She took the helmet back off.

16

THE FOREST-COVERED mountains finally gave way to wide swaths of grassy, rolling land. Soon homes began appearing, scattered here and there, signaling the approaching town of Ellensburg.

"We need to fill up," Nate said.

Quinn glanced back at Danielle. "Find someplace to pull over for a minute first."

Once they were stopped, Quinn hopped out and opened the back passenger door. Danielle was lying on the seat, with seat belts strapped over her.

"I know this isn't going to help you trust us," he said, "but if I were you, I'd be doing whatever I could to draw attention and get some help." He could see in her eyes she'd been thinking exactly that. "We can't have that. I'm sorry."

"For what?"

He leaned over the seat and, from one of the duffels in the back, pulled out two unused rags and the leftover plastic sheeting.

Holding one of the rags, he said, "I'll take this off right after we fill up."

He moved it toward her mouth.

"No, no, no," she protested, pulling her head back. "I won't say a word. I promise."

"I'd say the same thing if I were you, and I'd be lying."

"I won't! I swear!"

"I'm sorry."

She gritted her teeth, but he was able to pry her jaw apart enough to get the rag in. He then wrapped the second rag over the first and around the back of her head, where he tied it. "I promise as soon as we're on the road again, it comes off."

The look she gave him said she couldn't care less about his promises.

The last thing he did was drape the plastic over her in a way she couldn't easily shake off. Feeling slimy for what he'd done but knowing he had no choice, he climbed back into his seat. "Let's go."

They stopped at the first gas station they saw. While Nate filled the tank, Quinn went inside and purchased some drinks, pre-made sandwiches, and an assortment of snacks.

As soon as they pulled away from the pumps, Danielle began grunting. Quinn reached back and lifted the plastic enough to see her. She said something through her gag that he interpreted to mean, "Get this off!"

"As soon as we get on the freeway."

He dropped the plastic back down and glanced out the rear window.

A dot hung in the distant sky, moving at a fast pace paralleling the interstate. Not a bird. An aircraft, the first he'd seen since not long after leaving Seattle that wasn't flying at forty thousand feet. It was no more than fifteen hundred feet up.

Not a plane. A helicopter.

The California Highway Patrol had a whole fleet of aircraft to spy on highway traffic. Perhaps the state of Washington did, too. But in California, Quinn seldom saw CHP helicopters this far from a big city. Could be private, some ranch owner heading home, or maybe a corporate aircraft traveling to a factory.

Whatever the case, it made him uneasy.

"Stay with the traffic flow," Quinn told Nate as they pulled onto the freeway. "No sudden movements."

Nate flashed him a concerned sideways glance. "What is it?"

"Helicopter. May be nothing, but…"

Nate nodded as he merged the Jeep onto the interstate.

In the back, Danielle yelled in protest.

"Slight change of plans," Quinn said in her direction. "As soon as I can get to you, I will."

She continued to scream so he lifted the plastic again. "I'll move this off of you if you'll be quiet."

The shouting stopped. He folded the plastic away from her head, tucked it behind her shoulder, and turned back around.

"I don't see it," Nate said, his eyes flicking between the road and the mirrors.

Quinn looked at the mirror outside his window, and then moved down until the helicopter came into view. Its silhouette was clearly visible now, leaving no doubt as to the type of aircraft. It was a big one, the kind that could hold a dozen or more passengers.

"It's still there," he said.

He checked the map. A couple miles past Ellensburg, I-90 intersected with I-82. The latter headed south to Yakima and eventually into eastern Oregon. If they stayed on I-90 past the junction, there would be only a few alternate routes they could take in an emergency —all county roads of unknown quality. I-82 offered more options and went through the larger towns of Yakima, Richland, and Kennewick.

The decision was an easy one.

Quinn checked the mirror again.

"Crap," he muttered.

The helicopter was large behind them and would reach the junction of the two interstates before they did. From there, its occupants could monitor both the cars staying on 90 and those making the transition to the 82. The perfect observation spot.

As long as the aircraft kept going east, Quinn could relax, but if it stopped at the junction, he'd have to assume it had been sent after them.

He could hear the *whoop-whoop-whoop* of the helicopter's propellers as it flew overhead.

"What do you want me to do?" Nate asked, his voice mission calm.

A road sign was coming up.

Exit 109
Canyon Road
Ellensburg
1 Mile

Quinn consulted the map again. Maybe not the perfect observation spot after all. "Take that exit," he said. "Then go south."

He leaned forward and looked up through the windshield as the helicopter roared into view. Black with no identifying marks—neither local law enforcement nor civilian. It was the kind ops teams used.

He watched as it raced toward the junction, willing it to continue on, but right on cue, it slowed and dropped to the ground, out of sight.

Trouble for sure.

The off-ramp at Canyon Road was a wide, one-eighty turn, pointing them back in the direction they had come from before they could turn onto the new route. At the stop sign, Quinn noticed another silhouette flying toward them from the west.

"You seeing what I'm seeing?" Nate asked, his gaze also fixed on the new aircraft.

"Keep moving."

As Nate turned south, Quinn tracked the new helicopter. It was traveling faster than the other one had been and appeared to be smaller.

If they were working together, that would complicate matters. Two aircraft could follow both highways.

"So where am I going?" Nate asked.

"This bypasses the junction and still gets us to the 82."

"And then?" Nate asked.

"It's too early for 'and then.'"

STEVENS HAD HIS pilot set down on a grassy field north of the interstate, fifty yards west of where it met up with I-82. On the flight out, he had arranged for the Washington State Patrol to be notified of a military emergency preparedness exercise that would be taking place in the area. That should keep official attention at arm's length, and provide an easy answer for any curious civilians who called 911.

Stevens's men set up the camera equipment right outside the helicopter. He would have preferred a rig with multi-spectrum capabilities so they could view both visual and thermal images of the cars going by, but they had to use what gear they could get on short notice and were stuck with just the visual spectrum.

It would have been nice, too, if the area had some bushes and trees to shield them from the road, but no such luck. Again, you play the hand you were dealt. By the time their targets realized they were passing through a trap, it would be too late for them anyway.

"We're up," Manny Garcia announced. He was in the control seat behind the equipment. Taped to the sides of the monitor were photos of the three suspects.

"Find them," Stevens ordered.

ORBITS HAD FINALLY caught a glimpse of the Californians' aircraft ten minutes earlier, and had Sutter slow enough to not overtake them. He had watched through the pilot's high-powered binoculars as the other helicopter descended to the ground, near where the interstates met.

Had they spotted the vehicle the woman was in? If so, they were one up on him. He still didn't know what kind of car Quinn and his friends were using. Donnie was searching traffic camera footage in hopes of picking them out, but so far had not found anything.

"We'll fly by their position in about a minute," the pilot informed Orbits. "I'm guessing you don't want to do that."

"You're right. I don't." Orbits looked to the north. "Can you take us over the town, then circle around so that we're directly behind them?" He may not have wanted to fly past them but he did want to know what they were doing.

"No problem."

"Bring us to about a quarter mile away and hold there."

"Roger."

The helicopter banked hard to the left and buzzed over the town. When they reached the desired location, Sutter put them into a hover a thousand feet up.

Orbits focused the binoculars on the others. They had set up some equipment, and though he couldn't see the gear well enough to know what it was, it had to be something that scanned the passing vehicles. So *they* didn't know what kind of car Quinn was in, either.

Good news, but not great.

If the cleaner and his friends drove past the Californians' observation point, then it was game over. Which meant Orbits had to write off anything east of that point on the 90 or south on the 82, leaving him only the last few miles prior to the junction the targets were probably traveling down right now.

He looked at the map to confirm he was right. He wasn't.

For the last hundred miles or so, most of the roads leading off the I-90 were local streets going no more than a dozen miles before ending. But while the junction with I-82 provided the first real opportunity to change directions, the junction itself wasn't the only way to get to the new interstate. A few miles west of where the Californians had landed was a couple of cut-off roads that could get someone from the I-90 to the I-82 without the interchange. So the I-82 wasn't a write-off after all.

Whether Quinn and his friends would go that way or not was still an open question, but it was Orbits's only option.

"This way," he said, tracing the route he wanted Sutter to fly.

The pilot looked hesitant. "We're going to have to turn back pretty soon or we won't have enough fuel to get home."

Orbits reached into his bag and pulled out his wad of petty cash. After removing ten one-hundred-dollar bills, he held them toward the pilot. "For you, on top of the agreed upon fees, if we keep going and you find somewhere on our way to fuel up."

The pilot didn't even hesitate to take the bills and slip them into his pocket. "I'm sure I can make that happen."

17

LOCATION UNKNOWN

THE PLAYROOM WAS part of a private, unregistered club with a very discreet membership. Whips and racks and ropes were all in their places awaiting the next party. For the moment, though, the club was closed, the entire building bought out by The Wolf for entertaining her special guest.

She had Helen Cho tied to a suspended X, arms and legs stretched in different directions. She was still using electricity—small zaps never in the same place twice—to break her prisoner.

A knock on the door.

"*Oui?*" she called out.

Braun stuck his head in. "I have the hunter on the line."

The Wolf patted Helen on the thigh. "Don't go anywhere. I'll be right back."

As soon as she entered the hallway, Braun handed her a phone.

"Hello, Bianca," The Wolf said.

"My apologies, Madame Deschamps, for not answering when you called. I was…occupied."

"Understandable. And?"

"Three players out of the game now."

"Already? I'm impressed."

Bianca gave her a quick report.

"Where are you now?" The Wolf asked.

"I'm heading east, tracking two other hunters. I believe they may be following the target."

"Even better news. Well, I don't want to slow you down. Keep me posted."

"Of course."

Perhaps The Wolf wasn't going to need Helen after all. Still, no reason to stop the interrogation until she knew for sure.

She gave the phone back to Braun and returned to the playroom.

18

CENTRAL WASHINGTON

QUINN WATCHED THE sky behind them as they joined the I-82 and headed south.

A minute passed, then two. Just when he thought they were in the clear, he tensed. "We still have a follower."

"The smaller one," Nate guessed.

"Yeah."

Quinn kept an eye on the helicopter, fully expecting it to be joined by its larger companion, but it remained alone. Then, after only a few miles, its speed increased as it shot off to the west, away from the freeway.

Maybe he had been wrong. Maybe those inside the chopper weren't interested in them at all. Still, he couldn't shake the feeling that things were closing in on them.

"We need a new ride," he said.

Nate looked over. "Not a lot of choices out here."

They had entered an area of scrub-covered hills with no buildings or turnoffs for as far as the eye could see.

Quinn consulted the map. The next bit of civilization didn't crop up until they neared Yakima, about another twenty minutes away. He checked in with Orlando, telling her about the helicopters, and then spent the rest of the time scanning the skies for trouble, but neither of the aircraft reappeared.

They took the first exit after crossing the Naches River, entered the city under a sign proclaiming YAKIMA WELCOMES YOU, and then stopped in a lot next to a gas station.

Quinn looked back at Danielle. "If you stay quiet, we'll leave the plastic off. Yes or no?"

She nodded.

He reached for his door handle. "I'll get us a car," he said to Nate. "You're on plates."

From the back of the SUV, Quinn grabbed the tools he would need and put them and his gun into his backpack before heading to the street.

They had passed several motels on the drive in, all prime targets. A stranger getting into a car in one of their lots would likely not be looked at twice.

The first motel he passed had security cameras focused on its parking lot. He'd grabbed a signal jammer that would disrupt any broadcast device within a hundred feet but thought it better to check the other places first.

No cameras at the next two motels, but not much of a vehicle selection, either. Motel number four proved to be the best. No cameras and nearly twenty cars in its lot, including a year-old Audi A4—performance and comfort, the combination he preferred.

He called Nate. "Audi A4," he said.

"Can't you find something a little more common?" Nate asked.

"Blue."

"Oh, sure," Nate said. "A blue Audi A4. I'm sure there are *dozens* of them here."

"Last year's model."

Nate started to say something else but Quinn hung up.

He cut into the lot and headed straight for the Audi like it was his. As far as he could tell, no one noticed him.

He loved the age of the electronic locks. It meant he seldom had to use the hard-to-disguise slim jim to open a door. Instead, he pulled out a small, matchbook-sized box and placed it near the handle, where the box's magnet held it in place. He opened the app that Orlando had named Picker.

After it synched with the box, it worked out the code to open the door. Starting the engine utilized the same gear but took an additional ten seconds. When the motor fired up, he looked back toward the motel to make sure no one was running in his direction, and then drove on to First Street, nice and casual.

He headed to the other side of town, parked behind a fast-food place, and fired off a text to Nate telling him where he was. While he waited, he removed the existing plates and tossed them in the restaurant's Dumpster.

Nate drove up a few minutes later and backed the Jeep into the spot beside the Audi.

He climbed out and said, "Here," as he tossed Quinn a set of plates.

"Audi?" Quinn asked.

"Of course."

"A4?"

"Naturally."

"Blue?"

"Yeah, blue."

"One year old?"

Nate frowned. "Two. But, hey, you're lucky I even found that."

Quinn attached the plates. Now if the state patrol began looking for a stolen Audi and ran the license number of their car, there would be no red flags. It was the little details that kept one free.

Using the doors of the opposite facing vehicles to create a kind of tunnel between them, they moved Danielle into their new ride.

She said something once they had her situated.

Quinn asked, "What?"

She repeated herself, slowly this time, allowing him to make out, "I need to pee."

"We'll find someplace to stop as soon as possible. But you'll have to hold it for now."

She pleaded with her eyes.

"I'm sorry. It won't be long. I promise." He shut the door, feeling like an asshole for about the millionth time since they'd found her.

Nate transferred the duffels into the trunk, then wiped down the interior of the SUV.

"I'll drive," Quinn said.

He started to open the door, and stopped.

The sound was low, distant, but oh so familiar. He glanced at Nate and saw that his partner heard it, too.

The rhythmic *thump-thump-thump* of a helicopter.

———

WHILE THE HELICOPTER was refueling, Orbits purchased an energy drink from a vending machine in the lobby of the operations building in charge of the helipad in Yakima. As he headed out to the aircraft, his cell rang.

"Yeah?" he answered.

"I got 'em," Donnie said excitedly.

"Spill."

"They left Seattle in a khaki green Jeep Grand Cherokee."

"You sure?"

"Hell, yeah. Found a shot on one of the I-90 traffic cams twenty miles east of Bellevue, clear as day. Quinn's partner was driving and Quinn was in the passenger seat."

"So they're definitely headed this way."

"Well, at least east on the ninety."

"And the woman?"

A slight pause. "I could only see the two of them."

That didn't bother Orbits much. There was plenty of room in a

Cherokee for her to hide in. Besides, if Quinn and his partner had ditched the girl, they'd be on a plane headed home instead of driving around the countryside.

No, she was still with them. He could *feel* it.

"Any sightings of them after that?"

"I haven't had the chance to look yet. I just found them and wanted to let you know."

"Well, then, look, dammit."

Donnie said, "That'll take time."

"Do I have to tell you how to do your job? Start with the cameras closest to where the ninety and the eighty-two split."

"Right, yeah. That makes sense."

"Of course it makes sense! Now get to it."

Orbits hung up.

He was about to head over to the helicopter when he remembered he hadn't heard back from Ananke. He dialed her number again, but this time it didn't even ring before he was sent to voice mail.

He frowned, then left a message similar to his previous one, but couldn't help thinking she was avoiding him. He was sure she had information that would make his job easier.

This was not a problem without a solution, however. They shared a common friend, a job broker by the name of Marko Lutz.

"Ricky! How's it going, man?" Marko had one of those always-on personalities. Orbits liked that about him.

"Going well, Marko. How are things with you?"

"Same as always. *Outstanding.*"

"Good to hear," Orbits said. "Listen, I'm wondering if you can do me a favor."

"If it's in my power, I am at your service."

"Nothing big, just need you to get a message to someone for me."

"Sounds easy enough. Who to?"

BOULDER, COLORADO

"HE SAID TO tell you he needs to discuss Seattle with you," Marko told Ananke. "Something about a mutual friend. A Mr. Q? That make any sense?"

The only reply she could manage was, "Uh-huh."

"He also wanted me to pass along his number in case you lost it." Marko recited it to her.

"Thanks," she said, barely moving her lips.

"Anything you want me to tell him?"

"Nope."

"Cool. Hey, what's your schedule look like next month? I might have something right up your alley."

"I'm...pretty booked up."

"Tell you what, when things firm up, I'll call you anyway and see how your schedule's looking. Cool by you?"

"Sure, Marko. That's fine."

"Then I guess I'll talk to—"

Her thumb touched the disconnect button.

She stared out her window at the hills behind her house. Now she understood what was going on. Ricky was a hunter, and if he wanted to know about the job in Seattle then he had to be hunting the girl Quinn and Nate had taken from the basement.

This was not good.

As lame of a lover as Ricky had been, he was a good hunter. During the time she'd spent with him, he had never once failed to track down his prey.

Maybe if she hadn't gone down in that basement with Quinn, hadn't seen the women Edmondson had been holding there, hadn't talked to Danielle, maybe there might have been a miniscule chance she'd tell Ricky what he wanted to know.

But she *had* done all those things and there was no way she would talk to Ricky now.

If she needed to talk to anyone, it was Quinn.

When she called him, she was immediately prompted to leave

a message. She hung up before the beep. Who knew how long it would be before he listened to it? He needed to know about Orbits now. Since she didn't have Nate's number, she was left with only two other options, only one of which was good. She called Helen.

The first hint that something was wrong was the male voice answering the call. "Yes."

Helen had always picked up this line herself.

Ananke considered hanging up, but said, "I'm looking for Director Cho."

"She's unavailable at the moment, but I'd be happy to have her call you back. May I have your name, please?"

"Magenta twenty-two slash m," she said, using the emergency code that should immediately put her through to the director.

But the man said, "I apologize, but as I said before, the director is unavailable at the moment. Your name, please."

Ananke didn't even bother hanging up. She popped out the phone's battery, removed the SIM card, and broke it in half. It was the second card she'd destroyed that day—a record. But something was not right in San Francisco.

She retrieved a new card from her safe and reluctantly dialed her final option.

Given that her number would not be recognizable to the person on the other end, she expected to be sent to voice mail and was not disappointed.

She recited her new number, said, "Call me as soon as you get this," and hung up, knowing there would be no mistaking her voice.

The return call came within twenty seconds.

"What do you want?" Orlando asked.

"Always a pleasure to hear your voice," Ananke said.

"I don't have time to chat right now, Ananke. I'm a little tied up. So if you don't have a point…"

As much as Ananke knew she shouldn't, she couldn't help but

push the other woman's buttons. "Literally tied up? Because that would be interesting."

"I'm hanging up now."

"Wait, wait, sorry. I, um, I have something you need to know."

"What?"

"Quinn and Nate are in danger."

"That's not exactly news," Orlando said.

"Why? Did something happen?"

A beat, then, "Is that the extent of your information, or do you have anything useful?"

"I do," Ananke said. "They need to know that someone's chasing them."

"Also not news."

"Well, do you know *who* it is?"

"Are you saying you do?"

"You know what? Never mind. I'll just leave Quinn a message."

"Hold on," Orlando said. "If you know who it is, tell me."

Ananke fought the urge to hang up, and said, "A hunter named Ricky Orbits."

"Orbits? I've heard of him. How do you know he's after my team?"

"How I know isn't important."

"Like hell it isn't. I'm just supposed to believe you?"

Ananke closed her eyes and clenched her jaw, giving herself a second to get her growing anger under control. She had to remind herself that Orlando's hatred wasn't really Ananke's fault but it was still justified. "Look, I know you're not my biggest fan but I'm doing you a favor here. I'm not lying." She paused again. "Ricky called me, all right? He wanted to know what happened in Seattle."

"Why would he call *you*?"

"We used to be…friends, I guess."

"Oh, I get it. Another one of your side projects."

"If you don't want to believe me, then don't."

Silence.

"So what did you tell him?" Orlando asked, much of her confrontational tone gone.

"I didn't tell him anything. He left me a message that he wanted to talk, that's all. And to answer your next question, I have no intention of calling him back. I'm telling you because Ricky's...unconventional. He's not going to follow any set of rules to get what he's after. You need to tell Quinn."

"I...I will," Orlando said. "Thanks."

It was suddenly as if a whole new level of awkwardness had descended on the conversation.

"Yeah, uh, don't worry about it. Good luck, huh?"

Ananke was starting to pull the phone away from her ear when Orlando asked, "How many people does he usually work with?"

"What do you mean?"

"How big is his team?"

"Team? He doesn't work with a team."

"Not even on a temporary basis?"

"Maybe a specialist or two as needed but...why are you asking?"

Orlando took a breath, and then told her about the two helicopters Quinn had spotted following him, one large enough to carry a whole squad.

"I don't know," Ananke said. "I guess he could have hired some freelancers."

"It would be really nice to know for sure."

Ananke saw where this was going. "No way. I am not talking to that asshole."

"Ananke, you're the only one who can find out what he's up to. If he's in one of those helicopters, we need to know."

"I said no."

"I'm not asking you to do this for me, but I know you like Quinn and Nate. Are you going to let them hang out there blind?"

It was basically the same argument Quinn had used to get her assistance in Seattle, and it was just as effective now. "Dammit!"

"That's a yes?"

"I'll call you back."

CENTRAL WASHINGTON

DONNIE REPORTED TO Orbits that he'd spotted the SUV on an I-90 traffic cam just east of I-82, but when he checked the next camera after the junction, the SUV had not passed by when it should have. He then checked the first several cameras on I-82. Sure enough, the vehicle was heading south toward Yakima.

Orbits grinned. His instincts had been dead on.

Further cam checks showed the vehicle a few miles north of Yakima, but no sign of it in the group of cars it had been traveling in after the town.

"Find where they exited," Orbits said as he climbed into the helicopter. "I must be right on top of them."

Sutter was already in his seat. "Back to the highway?"

"No. Get me high enough so I can take a look at this damn town."

Sutter flew them out of the space around the airport and up five hundred feet.

"Hold here," Orbits said.

Through the binoculars, he scanned the roads leading from the highway, paying particular attention to the gas stations nearest the off-ramps. There were plenty of SUVs but no khaki green Jeep Grand Cherokees. Had they gone farther into the town, or slipped back onto the interstate when Donnie wasn't watching?

"Take us a quarter mile south," he ordered.

As the helicopter began to move, Orbits's phone vibrated. *Donnie had better have found something,* he thought as he pulled the cell out. Only it wasn't Donnie.

He pushed ACCEPT. "Hello?"

"Ricky?"

He grinned. "Kitty-kat."

"Do *not* call me that," Ananke said, "or I'll hang up right now."

"What's wrong? You still mad at me? Man, you really had it bad for me, didn't you?"

"Ricky, I swear to God…" she said, and fell silent.

"Hello?" he asked, wondering if she had followed through on her threat.

"I'm here. So?" she said.

"So…what?"

"Marko said you wanted to talk to me."

"Maybe I just wanted to say hi?"

"Then why did he tell me it had to do with Seattle?"

"Okay, okay. Guilty. Still, it's nice to hear your voice. I miss you, kit—"

"Last chance. Tell me what you want or I'm really hanging up and you will *never* hear from me again."

Like she could stay away from me forever, he thought. "Relax. I heard a rumor that you were part of that crazy thing that went down in Seattle last night."

"Is there a question?"

"Were you?"

"I wasn't anywhere near Seattle last night."

He laughed. "Like you'd say anything different."

"If I was there," she said, "what would it matter?"

"It ties in on a little something I'm working on. If you were there, thought maybe you could help me out a little. You know, for old times' sake."

"You know I can't talk about the details of a job."

"Sure, sure, but what would it hurt to tell me who you were working with?"

"I work alone."

"But someone always has to *clean* up after you."

"Was that your attempt at being subtle?"

"Jonathan Quinn was on the assignment with you, wasn't he?"

"Ricky…"

"He was your cleaner."

"I already told you—I wasn't there."

"Of course not. Neither was he, I suppose. He also didn't leave with a woman he found there, did he?"

The pause on the other end was short but undeniable. "What woman?"

Instead of answering, he said, "I'm curious if you might know where they were headed."

"Let's pretend this hypothetical job even happened," she said. "How would I know who he found and where they would be going? I'm always long gone by the time a cleaner comes on the scene."

"So you don't know where they were headed?"

"Sorry, Ricky, I have no idea where Quinn is."

Now it was Orbits's turn to pause. He was pretty sure she wasn't lying this time. She might have been aware of the woman but it was very possible that was the extent of her knowledge. Which meant she was of no use to him.

"Who are you hunting?" Ananke asked. "Quinn or this mythical woman?"

"You know I can't talk about the details of a job."

She snorted. "If you're going after Quinn, you'd better have some backup."

"That's funny. Since when have I ever needed backup?"

"No help at all? I don't know, Ricky."

"I've dealt with worse people than this Quinn without breaking a sweat. He won't be a problem. Look, baby, I'd love to continue chatting but I've got to run. Why don't we go out for dinner next week and catch up?"

The line went dead.

Orbits smiled and began scanning the streets again, sure he would get that dinner in the near future.

BOULDER, COLORADO

ANANKE SNAPPED THE SIM card in two, feeling like she needed a long, hot shower. After slipping the fourth card of the day into her phone, she called Orlando.

"He's definitely in a helicopter," Ananke said. "I could hear the propellers."

"Working alone?"

"That's what he told me."

"Do you believe him?" Orlando asked.

"It would be out of character for him to work otherwise, so yeah, I believe him."

19

LOCATION UNKNOWN

FIRST IT HAD been electric shock, and then an injection of God knew what into Helen's arm that had sent her world spinning.

The Wolf seemed to think Quinn was still following Helen's directions. Helen had so far held on tight and said nothing to encourage or dispel this belief. The longer she could keep the woman focused on her, the better the chance Quinn would have to disappear.

The Wolf. Helen and most of the intelligence world had thought the woman was out of the game. A broker of mercenaries and shady deals, she had disappeared from the scene several years earlier. The rumor was her business had suffered serious cash-flow problems that had forced her into hiding from those she owed. Apparently she had settled her debt.

"A little stimulant, I think," The Wolf said, her voice seeming to hover far above.

Within seconds after the needle punctured her arm, Helen felt as if a hand had grabbed her heart and squeezed as hard as it could. She sucked in a deep breath as she arched back in her chair, her body feeling like a pressure cooker ready to blow. If blood had started gushing out her ears or nose, she wouldn't have been surprised. But then the crest passed, and while adrenaline still rushed through her system, she no longer felt like she was about to be torn apart.

The Wolf smiled and regarded the syringe in her hand. "It's a rush, isn't it? An oldie but goodie from your early agency days, I believe." She set it down on the portable table next to the chair and picked up another. "This one's newer but I'm sure you've heard of it. Fire and Ice?"

Helen tried to keep her face blank. Fire and Ice was not the drug's official name, but that's what most in the know called it, and for good reason.

When The Wolf moved the syringe toward her, Helen couldn't help but flinch.

"Relax," the woman said. "It won't kill you."

She stuck the needle into Helen's arm.

For a few moments, nothing happened. Helen even started to think maybe the woman had been playing her, but then every vein and capillary in her body ignited.

All thought stopped, her brain unable to process anything but the blaze under her skin. Never in her life had she considered dying an option, until now.

Finally, the burn began to recede. She knew from reports she'd read that a subject's temperature remained unchanged throughout the drug's interaction. Yet the fire had felt real, as did the cold she sensed coming on now.

"If you're lucky, you'll black out before you reach the bottom," The Wolf said. "But don't count on it. Now tell me, where are they going?"

Helen kept her lips pressed together.

"Where are they going?"

The cold. Oh, God!

"Where?" The Wolf demanded.

Helen screamed.

20

SOUTHERN WASHINGTON

Q UINN SAW THE helicopter twice more as they continued south on I-82—the first time when they'd left Yakima, the aircraft hovering over the town, and the second time when they were almost to Richland as it raced by and disappeared to the southeast.

He decided a change of course was in order, and instructed Nate to exit the interstate when they reached Kennewick and take US 12 east to Walla Walla.

Once they were on the country highway, they had no more sightings of the helicopter. By no means did Quinn feel they were out of trouble yet, though. From Ananke, via Orlando, they had learned one of their pursuers was a hunter named Ricky Orbits. Quinn seldom dealt with hunters so he had no personal knowledge of the man, but Ananke had told Orlando that Orbits was more than competent at his job. The information Orlando had pulled together and e-mailed to Quinn seemed to back this up.

Walla Walla came into sight just after six p.m. Though they could still reach Idaho before dark, one look at Nate told Quinn his partner was as tired as he was. They needed rest, not all night but for a few hours at least, or else they were liable to make mistakes.

He checked the Internet and directed Nate to a motel near the airport on the east end of town. There, he arranged for a first-floor room on the backside as far from the office as possible. While Nate moved the car, Quinn walked through the building, listening for other guests. TVs were on in four of the rooms, but the rest, including those surrounding the one they'd be staying in, were quiet.

He went outside through the exit closest to their room, and studied the parking lot as Nate pulled into a nearby spot.

When Nate joined him on the sidewalk, Quinn said, "We've got three cameras." With subtle nods, he pointed out their locations. The cameras were mounted to the building, two at either end and the third above the door Quinn had come through.

They retrieved jammers from the Audi's trunk and placed them within twenty feet of each camera to scramble their signals.

"Our room's two doors down on the right," Quinn said, flipping Nate the room key. "Take the bags in, then come back and give me a hand."

While Nate took care of the luggage, Quinn opened the car's rear door and leaned in. "We're going to stop here for a bit. I could give you another shot but I'd rather not. And I don't think you want that, either."

The look in Danielle's eyes confirmed this.

"Can I trust you to be quiet?"

She nodded.

Quinn checked the lot to make sure no one had appeared, and then helped her into a sitting position. When Nate returned, they cut the ties around her ankles and helped her out. True to her promise, she made no attempt to try anything as they led her inside.

Their room was more than serviceable—two queen-size beds, a counter/desk that covered most of the opposite wall, a TV, and a couple of padded chairs.

They sat her on the bed farthest from the door.

"I'm going to take your gag off, but the same rule applies if you try anything," Quinn said. "Understand?"

Another nod.

He unwound the first rag and then removed the one lodged between her top and bottom teeth. As soon as this last was gone, she coughed. Nate handed her a bottle of water and she downed almost the whole thing.

"Are you okay?" Quinn asked when she was finished.

"Go to hell."

"I think she's all right," Nate said.

"I need to use the bathroom," she told them.

Quinn looked at Nate. "Check it."

His partner disappeared into the bathroom for a moment before coming back out. "No way out."

"Go ahead," Quinn said to Danielle. "But leave the door open."

She raised her cuffed hands and stared at him.

He knew he should leave them on, but he pulled out his knife and cut the ties. He didn't expect thanks, nor did he get any, as she walked into the bathroom.

"Maybe we should just let her go," Nate said.

"How long do you think she'll last out there? We know one hunter's looking for her, and there's probably more. With us, she at least has a chance."

"True," Nate said slowly. "And I know helping her is the right thing to do, but I feel I should point out that's not our job."

"You're right, and you don't have to stay," Quinn said. "I can do this on my own."

Nate snorted. "Right. Did you hear the part where I said it's the right thing to do? I was just making sure we were on the same page. I'm not going anywhere."

THOUGH DANI WAS acting all tough while she walked into the bathroom, what she really felt was exhausted and scared. She had been lying down the whole trip but hadn't been able to fall back to sleep since the sedative had worn off.

Initially, she'd been fueled by anger toward the one called Quinn for putting a gag in her mouth and then reneging on his promise to remove it, but that had soon turned to fear as she listened to talk of helicopters and hunters.

She heard a hushed voice from the other room. She pressed up against the doorjamb and listened as Nate and Quinn talked. Their words confused her. Sure, they could have been trying to trick her, knowing she would overhear them, but she didn't really believe that. Despite the fact they had tied her up and gagged her *and* drugged her—twice—they had not treated her unkindly. If she were honest with herself, she'd have to admit they had been very respectful, even concerned.

You can't trust anyone, her sister had often said. *People will tell you anything to get what they want.*

She knew she should heed Marianne's words, but something Quinn had just said replayed in her mind, too.

"With us, she at least has a chance."

WHEN DANIELLE EXITED the bathroom, Quinn pointed to the bed by the window.

"You can use that bed. My friend and I are going to take turns sleeping, so try to get some rest and don't waste your time thinking about making a run for it."

She mumbled something under her breath as she crossed over to the bed.

"I didn't catch that," he said.

She looked back at him. "I said, I won't run."

He'd expected her to be angry and uncooperative when she came out of the bathroom, but that wasn't the case at all.

"Look, Danielle, I know this—"

"Dani," she said. "Call me Dani."

"Okay, Dani." He paused. "I know this hasn't been easy. I know whatever secret you're holding you don't want to share. That's fine. I get it. But there are other people out there right now trying to find us...trying to find *you*. If there's anything you can tell us that might give us an idea of what's going on here, it would help us know what to do. We're kind of operating in the dark."

Her gaze turned to the floor and she seemed momentarily lost in thought. "You should have left me with the other women."

"That would have made it even easier for these people to find you."

She shrugged, her eyes still on the carpet.

"Let me ask you something. Have you ever heard of a woman called The Wolf?"

Dani became very still.

"Who is she?" he asked.

She shrugged again.

"Did Mr. Black tell you The Wolf was the one who hired him to grab you?"

She finally looked at him, her eyes narrowing slightly. "He did, but how did you know that?"

"His partner told me."

"His partner?" she asked. "Mr. Red?"

Quinn gave her a quick description of Platt.

"You talked to him?" she asked.

"I paid him a visit while you were...sleeping."

"Did you kill him?"

"He was still breathing when I left, but I doubt that lasted very long."

"Good. He was a son of a bitch."

"Did he hurt you?"

"He wanted to, but Mr. Black wouldn't let him. I could hear him with the others, though. Whatever you did to him, he deserved worse."

"He told me that Mr. Black was trying to get a location out of you."

Dani tensed.

"That's what this is all about, isn't it?"

She stared at him but said nothing.

"How long have you been in hiding?"

For a moment she didn't move, and then her lips parted. "A long time."

"Then you know the people looking for you aren't just going to give up."

"I know."

NORTHERN OREGON

THE BOUTS OF indigestion had started around the time they reached Portland, and had only increased in duration as they headed east. Orlando had taken an antacid but that hadn't done a thing.

She touched her stomach. "How about shifting a few inches to the right?" she said.

The baby was less than cooperative. Orlando hoped that wasn't an indication of future behavior.

She grabbed a couple more of the chewable antacid tablets and shoved them in her mouth before returning her attention to her computer.

Since she hadn't received any facial matches for Danielle, she had been concentrating on learning more about what had happened to Helen Cho. If she could identify the kidnappers, they might lead her to who had hired Ricky Orbits or perhaps another group looking for the girl.

It took her about forty-five minutes of hacking into security systems and spot checking cameras in the neighborhood around Helen's office, but she finally found a feed from two properties down that had captured the kidnapping.

Because of the distance and angle, the image detail wasn't the greatest, but the footage was sharp enough to show the gist of what had happened. The jackpot came when the getaway car drove right past the camera, giving Orlando an excellent view of not only the vehicle and its license plate, but also of the two men inside.

She grabbed images of each man, uploaded them to the facial recognition interface, and started the searches. Like with Danielle's picture, there was no telling how long it would be before she received any results.

Knowing it was a waste of time, she ran a trace on the license plate anyway. It was not a match for the car the men had been driving.

Leaning back, she rubbed her eyes with one hand, and her indigestion spot with the other.

"You work too hard. You need rest."

Mrs. Vo was twisted around in her chair, looking at Orlando.

"I'm okay," Orlando said.

"Not okay. Computer all the time not good for baby." Mrs. Vo pushed off her chair and moved over to the kitchen. "You need sleep. Food, too, I think. What you want to eat?"

"I'm fine. Really."

"Not say again. Not fine. You be mother again soon. You need take care." Nodding, she said, "I heat up pork chop, okay?"

Without waiting for a response, she opened the refrigerator.

Orlando would have told her she didn't need to do that, but in truth, one of Mrs. Vo's pork chops sounded great.

"You lie back on seat," Mrs. Vo said. "I wake you when ready."

Orlando closed her computer, thinking a little rest wouldn't be such a bad idea, but as soon as she lay down, her phone rang.

With a sigh, she started to push herself back up, but Mrs. Vo said, "No, no, no. Sleep!" and snatched the phone off the table.

Orlando thought she was only moving it out of reach, but Mrs. Vo said, "This Quinn?….No, cannot talk. She tired…she fine, she fine. Just need sleep. She pregnant....Yes, I know you know, but cannot—"

Orlando had shoved herself up. "Let me talk to him."

Mrs. Vo waved at her to lie back down and said into the phone, "I have her call you back."

"Mrs. Vo, give me the phone," Orlando said.

"I don't know how long," Mrs. Vo said to Quinn. "One hour. Two hour. Maybe morning. Okay?"

Struggling to her feet, Orlando said, "Mrs. Vo, please."

The woman huffed before handing over the cell. "You need sleep. Not talk long," she said. With another huff, she returned to preparing the food.

"Hey," Orlando said into the phone.

"What was that all about? Are you feeling all right?" Quinn asked.

"I'm fine. She's just being overprotective, that's all."

"Are you sure? Do you need to see a doctor?"

"Quinn, relax. Nothing's wrong." As if taunting her, her indigestion chose that moment to flare back up. She turned so Mrs. Vo wouldn't see her wince.

"What?" Quinn asked.

"What what?" she asked back.

"It sounds like you're in pain."

She hadn't realized she'd made any noise. She rubbed a hand across the same spot as before, willing the burning sensation to cease. "You're hearing things."

"Maybe you're in labor."

"I'm not in labor."

"You can't be sure."

"Of course I can be sure. Don't you think I'd know if I was in labor or not? This isn't my first time, remember?"

A second of silence. "You're sure?"

"I'm about to hang up on you."

"Okay, okay. Sorry."

She lowered herself back onto the bench seat, a loud exhale

escaping as she finished. Before Quinn could react, she said, "Not labor! Just sitting down. I'm fat. It isn't easy."

"I didn't say anything."

"But you were going to."

His non-response confirmed she was right.

"Where are you?" she asked.

"Walla Walla. And you?"

"Somewhere along the Columbia River. If you wait, we can meet up with you in a few hours."

"Absolutely not. I'm uncomfortable enough with you following us," he said. "In fact, I was thinking it would be a good idea for you to go back to Portland and wait there."

"No way. You may need help."

"And you're in perfect condition to give that to us, I suppose," he scoffed.

"I'm better than nothing. And I've got Daeng."

"I don't like you out on the road. Not right now. Maybe I should call Daeng. He'll do what I say."

"Quinn, stop. We're not turning around."

Mrs. Vo walked over to the table and set down a plate with two cut-up pork chops, a mound of rice, and some broccoli on it. "I get sauce."

"Thanks," Orlando said.

"You talk too long."

"Just a few more minutes." When Mrs. Vo left, Orlando asked Quinn, "Any more helicopters?"

"Not for a couple hours," Quinn said. "I did get our passenger to talk a little, though."

"You did? And?"

He told her about his conversation. He hadn't learned a lot but it was more than they'd had before.

"Dani, huh?" Orlando said when he finished.

"Still might not be her real name," he said. "I take it her ID photo hasn't brought back any hits."

"Not yet."

She became aware that Mrs. Vo was standing a few feet away, holding a bottle of fish sauce and impatiently staring at her.

"The plan still the same?" Orlando asked Quinn.

"I don't know what else to do," he said. "We'll get a few hours' rest here and then head for Idaho. Have you found someplace for us?"

"I have. Just east of Moscow. I'll e-mail you the details."

"Thanks."

"Food get cold," Mrs. Vo said.

Orlando glanced at her and said into the phone, "I need to go or I'm going to get grounded."

"Are you sure you're feeling okay?"

"I'm pregnant. What do *you* think? I'll talk to you later."

Mrs. Vo waited until Orlando put the phone away before handing over the sauce. "You eat, you sleep."

"Thank you, Mrs. Vo."

"No more phone."

"Okay."

"Also no computer."

"We'll see."

Mrs. Vo scowled.

21

CENTRAL WASHINGTON

S TEVENS AND HIS team stayed at the interstate junction outside Ellensburg for three hours. During the first two, Stevens had hoped they would spot the girl's abductors, but by the end of the third hour, he knew the targets hadn't come their way.

There were only three possibilities for what had happened. One, the targets had circled back and returned to Seattle. Two, they were holed up somewhere between Seattle and the junction. And three, they had turned off I-90 and gone in a new direction.

He could speculate all he wanted on which was the most likely, but what he needed were facts. And though he had hoped he and his team could wrap up this mission without any assistance, he reluctantly admitted that was no longer the case.

He called his bosses in Los Angeles and enlisted the tech department to see if they could track down the car the targets were using. At five p.m., he received word that the vehicle was a khaki green Jeep Grand Cherokee, last sighting two hours and twelve minutes earlier right outside Yakima.

Stevens and his team piled back into the helicopter and made the quick flight due south. It angered Stevens that somehow their targets had made the transition onto the I-82 without his team spotting them, but there would be time later to assess where the error was made.

They touched down at the airport and arranged for three vehicles so they could split into teams and search for the Cherokee more effectively.

It was nearly nine p.m. when the Jeep was located behind an A&W restaurant. One touch of the cold hood told Stevens all he needed to know. The SUV hadn't moved in hours. The targets were driving something else now.

The techs went back to work to identify the new vehicle. The task was tedious and time consuming, but at 11:14 they had it. A blue Audi A4 sedan. Fourteen minutes later, they'd traced it as far as Walla Walla, and Stevens and his men lifted into the air again.

THE FLYOVER OF Yakima had proved useless, so Orbits resorted to an old-fashioned ground search and finally discovered the Grand Cherokee in the A&W lot at 7:50 p.m.

Hoping to find out what vehicle Quinn and his friend were now using, he had Donnie hack into the local police department's system and search for cars stolen that afternoon. It had turned out to be a slow day crime-wise. Only two vehicles had been reported missing. One was a three-year-old Ford F-150 crew cab truck taken right out of the driveway of the owner's home. Not the kind of theft an operative would usually undertake. The second stolen vehicle was textbook tradecraft. An hour and a half earlier, a blue Audi A4 had been reported missing from a hotel parking lot not far from the freeway.

Using a time range of two hours prior to the report, Donnie hunted for the Audi. By 8:20, he spotted the car on archival footage, heading southeast on the interstate. He tracked it all the way to Kennewick and then east toward Walla Walla, where the trail once again stopped.

Orbits was already driving his rental car back to the airport when Donnie shared this news. As he pulled in, Orbits was momentarily surprised at the sight of the California team's helicopter sitting not far from his ride.

Its presence meant the team had identified the Jeep, but since no one seemed to be around, he assumed they were in town looking for it. He briefly considered sabotaging the aircraft, but he could neither risk the time it would take nor the chance of getting caught.

He hurried into the building where he'd left his pilot, only to find that the man wasn't there.

He looked around until someone pointed him in the direction of Security.

"You Orbits?" the night supervisor asked when he inquired about Sutter.

"Yeah."

"Operations sent your pilot to a motel to get some sleep. Apparently he was over his hours."

"You're kidding."

"I'm just telling you what I was told. He can't go up again until morning."

"Is there anybody else?"

"You mean like another pilot?"

"Yes. That's exactly what I mean," Orbits said, not hiding his frustration.

"Not my area, but I doubt it at this time of night."

Orbits stormed out of the building, fighting hard not to punch every wall he passed. The girl was right in his sights, but if he didn't catch up to her and her friends soon, the Californians would get her first.

"Goddammit!" he shouted into the darkness.

There was only one thing to do. Walla Walla was about a hundred and thirty miles away. He could drive that in less than two hours.

22

WALLA WALLA

QUINN'S EYES POPPED open when the phone under his pillow vibrated. He turned off the alarm and sat up.

In the dim light, he could see Dani asleep on the other bed in nearly the same position she'd been in when he lay down.

Quinn got up and walked over to Nate, who was sitting on the chair by the door, reading something on his phone.

"Right on time," Nate said.

"Go ahead and head out. I'll get things ready here."

Earlier, after he'd talked to Orlando, Quinn had driven the Audi into the heart of town and left it parked behind a strip mall where, hopefully, it would be at least a day before anyone took notice of it. They still needed another ride, though.

"Back in a flash," Nate said, and left.

Quinn took a quick shower, the hot water helping to stave off his desire to return to bed. When he was done and dressed, he turned on the bedroom lights and gently shook Dani's shoulder.

"Time to get up," he said.

She groaned. "Already?"

"You can sleep in the car. If you need to use the restroom, now's the time."

Reluctantly she climbed out of bed. "Do I have time for a shower?" she asked as she walked into the bathroom.

"If you make it fast."

She started to close the door, but then stopped. "Sorry, I forgot."

"No, it's all right," he said. "Close it."

She glanced at him like she thought he might change his mind, then gave him a thankful smile and shut the door.

As Quinn checked the duffel bags to make sure they were ready to go, he heard the shower come on. When the water went off again a few minutes later, he looked toward the main door.

Nate should have been back by now. Quinn waited another minute, and then sent his partner a text:

ETA?

NATE STROLLED OUT of the hotel, looking like a guest in search of a late-night snack or maybe a bar, and headed toward the heart of town. When he was out of sight of the building, he picked up his pace. Though he was too close to where they were staying to procure a vehicle, his practiced gaze took in each car he passed and assessed its potential.

He gave it another few minutes before he turned down a new street and began his search in earnest.

ORBITS ARRIVED IN Walla Walla at 10:57 p.m.

During the drive, he had checked in with Donnie every fifteen minutes, and was told each time that the Audi had not reappeared on the highway. This made Orbits cautiously optimistic, but there was still the very real possibility that his prey had switched to another car again and were miles away already.

Thankfully, Walla Walla was a third the size of Yakima. He divided it into sectors and began quickly working his way through the town, looking for the Audi. After a little more than an hour, he'd almost made it to the eastern end, with still no sign of the car.

He turned onto Wellington Avenue. The first two blocks were strictly residential, but after that, small businesses started cropping up—a couple motels, a tavern, a lumber store. He checked the lots of each but saw no sign of the car.

Not much farther up the street, he tensed involuntarily as he passed the offices for the Washington State Patrol. Doubting the Audi would be anywhere in its vicinity, he turned off Wellington, intending to pick up the search several blocks away. But as he rounded the corner, his headlights lit up a man walking down the sidewalk.

Orbits kept driving, making no indication that anything was amiss, but he recognized the walker. The guy had been in the photos of both the Jeep and the Audi.

Quinn's partner.

Watching through the rearview mirror, he saw the man cross the road and head down Wellington the way Orbits had come.

As soon as the guy was out of view, Orbits turned down a parallel road and doused his headlights.

Son of a bitch, he *had* them. All he needed to do was follow the guy back to wherever they were keeping the woman.

He worked his way back toward Wellington and parked half a block short of the intersection, next to the warehouse building of the lumber supply place. After making sure the dome light was off, he opened his door and climbed out.

Other than a few scattered security lamps, the area was dark enough that he was able to move unseen through the lumberyard parking lot until he was almost to Wellington. There, he hunkered down beside the front building.

He'd expected to hear footsteps, so when he didn't, he became concerned that the guy had already disappeared into the night.

But then he heard a crunch, faint, almost not there. Sand between shoe and concrete.

He waited, but there was no second step. He was pretty sure the noise had come from his right, which meant the guy had already passed the lumber place. He eased around the corner and worked his way along the front of the building, until he reached a short wooden fence dividing the lumber store's parking area from the tavern's next door. He tried to pick up the steps again, but too much noise was coming out of the tavern for him to hear anything else.

He noted a few people standing—smoking, it looked like—near three stacked wagon wheels under the tavern's sign, but none were the same shape as his target.

He figured the guy must be farther down the street than he thought. He was about to sneak over to the sidewalk to get a better look when he detected movement in the tavern's rear lot. He carefully scanned the couple dozen cars parked there. Halfway through the back row, he spotted Quinn's partner standing next to a sedan. For a second, it didn't look like he was doing anything, but then he yanked his arm up with a quick thrust and opened the door.

Orbits noted the make and model—a Nissan Altima—then turned and hustled back to his own vehicle. He went the long way around the block, avoiding Wellington altogether until he neared the other side of the tavern. There he slowed as he passed the parking entrance, and saw that the Altima was pulling out of its space.

Orbits continued through the intersection and stopped at the curb, quickly taking his foot off the brake so that the lights would go out.

Turning in his seat, he watched the Altima exit the lot and head in the opposite direction.

Grinning, Orbits executed a U-turn and took up pursuit, lights off.

WHEN NATE HAD started his cleaner apprenticeship, Quinn had made him learn many things that went beyond the specific means of dealing with death. At the time, Nate didn't always understand why he needed to perfect certain skills, but one thing he had recognized as important from the beginning was the ability to know when he was being followed.

As he pulled out of the tavern's parking area, he noticed the car parked at the curb on the other side of the intersection, and the silhouette of someone in the front seat. The vehicle had most definitely not been there when he'd walked into the lot.

Another customer arriving for a late-night drink?

Perhaps.

Just to be safe, he turned the other way. Two blocks on, as he was preparing to turn again, he checked his mirror. Enough light was spilling from the tavern for him to see the other car was no longer at the curb.

His senses went on alert. Instead of turning right on the new road toward the motel, he went left. Checking the mirror every few seconds, it wasn't long before he caught a glint off the windshield of a darkened vehicle turning the corner behind him.

He didn't have time to think about who it was or how the person had found him. Keeping his pace unchanged, he navigated a course that would take him to the western end of town, as far from the motel as he could get. He watched the mirror to make sure his new friend was tagging along.

He was.

23

ORBITS FROWNED.
The Altima had already driven halfway across Walla Walla and yet didn't seem to be nearing its destination. And the car thief had been on foot, which meant it was highly improbable the guy had walked this far.

Of course, Quinn's partner could have dumped the Audi in the area, but it would have been sloppy to abandon one car so close to where you stole your new ride. They had certainly taken better care when they'd exchanged the Cherokee for the Audi in Yakima.

At least Orbits had the guy in his sights. That was the important thing.

NATE'S PHONE BUZZED with a text. He glanced at the screen. Quinn, wondering how long he was going to be.

He tapped the Z key, hit SEND, and shoved the phone into his pocket.

Up to that point, he had kept to residential streets, none of which had any traffic at that hour. When he turned onto East Rose

Street, however, he entered a business district where he was no longer the only vehicle on the road.

He checked behind him again to make sure his tail hadn't gone away. Not only was it still following, but now that they were on a main street, the driver had turned on his lights to blend in.

Ninth Avenue seemed to be another major road, so Nate turned left onto it and drove southward for several blocks, taking him even farther from the motel.

When he sensed he'd soon be running out of city, he decided it was time.

A park on the left side of the road provided just the cover he was looking for. He turned left onto a street that went down the far side of it. As soon as the trees at the front of the park blocked him from the view of his follower, he slammed the accelerator to the floor.

Ahead another street headed off to the left, but Nate was still thirty feet short of it when the other guy swung onto the street behind him. Nate's tires squealed as he took the turn fast. There was another intersection, this one much closer than the last. He barreled around it long before the other guy got behind him again.

If he could do that a few more times, he'd shake him.

He sped ahead.

MUST BE GETTING *close*, Orbits thought as he saw the Altima turn off the main road.

The park he was passing suggested the other car was heading into a residential area. Maybe they had located a safe house Orbits didn't know about. Whatever the case, he would have to take extra care now. If he could keep them off guard, this would be a piece of cake, and by lunchtime tomorrow, he'd be home, his bank account balance satisfyingly increased.

He turned down the new road at the same even pace he'd been

going, expecting the Altima to be not much more than fifty yards ahead.

"Son of a bitch."

The car was one *hundred* and fifty yards ahead, racing away.

Orbits hit the gas, knowing he didn't need to remain subtle anymore.

"Son of a bitch."

"YOU DIDN'T HAPPEN to grab any extra clothes I could wear, did you?" Dani called out from the bathroom.

"Hold on," Quinn said.

He grabbed his backpack and pulled out an unused black T-shirt. When he rapped on the door, she opened it a few inches.

"This is the best I can do," he said, holding out the shirt.

His phone vibrated.

"This is great," she said. "Thanks."

As the door closed, Quinn pulled out his cell and checked the text.

Z

"We've got to go," he said, shoving the phone back into his pocket. "Now!"

Dani opened the door again. "What's wrong?"

He grabbed the duffels. "There's trouble. We need to leave."

His team had a shorthand for those times when longer messages were impossible. Z meant *get the hell out*.

Dani rushed out of the bathroom, buttoning the top of her jeans. She grabbed her shoes and pulled them on. When she rejoined Quinn, she held out her hands.

"What are you doing?" he asked.

"Cuffs."

He hesitated for a moment, then said, "No."

"What if I run?"

"Then you run. But it would be better if you didn't."

"Because you'll hurt me if I do?"

"No. Not me. But I can't say the same about the people looking for you."

She lowered her hands. "Thank you."

"I could use your help," he said, holding out Nate's backpack.

"Sure."

After she pulled it on, he gave her the lighter of the duffels, keeping the one with the firearms for himself. "We're going to go out the same way we came in. On the other side of the parking lot is a set of train tracks paralleling the highway. We'll follow those."

"How far?"

"Not sure yet. Stay behind me, but close. Clear?"

"Clear."

"Let's go."

Quinn led her through the hallway and out into the rear parking area.

The night was warm with only a slight breeze. Crossing the lot to a strip of bushes at the back of the motel property, they could hear cars driving by on the highway.

"There's a path," Dani said, pointing to a gap between bushes.

Quinn let her take point until they reached the train tracks.

"Easier to walk on the other side," he said.

They passed over the raised bed and then walked parallel to it, heading east. The highway was less than a hundred feet away, up a small embankment. Every few seconds another car would roar past, its headlights sweeping across the top edge of the incline.

"Can you go any faster?" Quinn asked.

Dani looked over her shoulder. "Is someone coming?"

"Not yet. But I'd rather not be in the open if they do."

She picked up her pace.

Not far ahead, Quinn spotted a large area of brush growing along a downward slope. As they neared, he realized what he'd thought was one large group of brush was really two patches separated by a dry wash.

"This way," Quinn said.

They crossed the tracks and stepped down into the space between the bushes. After finding the most level spot, Quinn set down his duffel and helped Dani do the same with hers.

"Stay low," he said, crouching.

As she hunched down next to him, she asked, "What now?

"We wait."

NATE TOOK EVERY turn he came to, randomly mixing lefts and rights, just the way Quinn had taught him.

Four times, he caught sight of his pursuer's headlights in the distance, but when the road in his rearview mirror finally stayed dark, he cautiously began working his way back to the east side of town.

Not far from the Super 8 motel, he pulled behind a grocery store, tucked into the loading dock, and grabbed his phone.

QUINN WAS HOLDING his cell when it vibrated.

"What happened?" he asked Nate.

"I picked up a tail."

"Who?"

"Don't know. Never got a look at him. Just the car." He explained what had happened.

"You sure you lost him?" Quinn asked.

"Yeah, but I'm also sure he's still looking for me."

Quinn told him where he and Dani were.

"The guy saw this car," Nate said. "So I'll grab a new one and then I'll be right there."

ORBITS POUNDED THE steering wheel again as he turned onto yet another deserted street.

Where was he?

He clenched his teeth and thought about the last few moments before the Altima made its getaway. Obviously, the driver had spotted him, but how and where? Orbits could think of nothing he'd done that would have spooked his target.

"Dammit," he mumbled. He must have been right earlier. The guy hadn't walked clear across Walla Walla to steal a car. He must have spotted Orbits early on and driven to this part of town as a ruse.

Orbits made a hard left, his car nearly flying onto the sidewalk before it swerved into the middle of the street. Shoving the accelerator down as far as it would go, he raced to Ninth Avenue and headed back to the east end of the city.

AFTER MOVING THE bags to the top end of the wash, Quinn motioned for Dani to join him.

"Where is he?" she asked.

Quinn gave her arm a gentle squeeze. "He'll be here soon."

Two minutes later, he spotted a car turning onto the highway about half a mile down.

As it reached the spot parallel with the motel, it slowed.

"Get ready," he said.

He waited until the vehicle eased onto the shoulder before raising his phone and turning the screen on for a couple of seconds. The moment he was sure Nate had spotted him, he turned it off again.

The car, a late model Lexus ES, stopped directly between their position and the road. As Quinn and Dani carried the bags over, the trunk popped open and Nate climbed out.

"You guys all right?" he asked.

"We're good," Quinn replied.

Quinn saw that Nate noticed the missing cuffs from Dani's hands, but his partner said nothing as they shoved the bags into the trunk.

Dani hopped into the back, but before Quinn climbed in, Nate said, "Do you hear that?"

Quinn cocked his head and listened. A noise in the distance. For a second, he thought it was a big rig heading their way, but then he realized that wasn't it at all.

A helicopter, and by the deep rumble of the motor, a big one.

"We need to go," Quinn said and jumped into the car.

ORBITS COULDN'T HEAR the helicopter over the noise of his own engine. He weaved in and out of neighborhoods, hoping to spot the Altima again. He finally found it ten minutes later, abandoned at the side of the road.

He fired off a string of curses, his head feeling like it was going to explode. He yanked out his phone.

"I need you to check the highway again," he told Donnie. "Start twenty minutes ago, both directions. I have no idea what kind of car they're in, but there can't be that many on the road right now so I expect to hear from you within ten minutes."

"I'll do what I—"

Orbits hung up, coming within a hair's width of throwing his phone against the dash.

The next time Quinn and company were in his sights, he vowed they would not escape.

USING THE SAME method they'd employed in Yakima, Stevens's team discovered the Audi in the parking area behind a strip mall. Like the Cherokee, it had been abandoned.

Stevens called his tech liaison. "They've either switched again or are hiding somewhere here in town," he said. "Check satellite feeds from the last seven hours and see if there's any useful traffic-cam footage."

BIANCA GLANCED UP at the sky as the helicopter flew overhead.

That would be Morse's people, a small, quasi-independent organization that was ultimately just another cog in the US intelligence machine. There could be only one place the helicopter was headed. The same place she was—Walla Walla. Her information contacts had identified the town as the last known location of the vehicle carrying the two men who, she'd been assured, would have the girl. Apparently Morse's people were on to them, too.

Unfortunately, the helicopter would get there soon, while she still had a good forty minutes of driving ahead of her. She didn't let this panic her, though. She didn't do panic.

Thirty minutes later, a buzz in her ear informed her of an incoming call.

"Zorn," she said.

"Status update," her contact reported. "New vehicle. Type: Lexus ES. Color: dark gray. Location: US 12 northeast of Walla Walla, approximately nine miles from your current position."

That was excellent news. Not only were they still on the run, they were within striking distance.

"Additional item," the liaison said. "Confirmed sighting of the woman in the car with them."

"Copy," Bianca said. Even better news.

"Good hunting."

The line went dead.

24

"MOM? MOM, WAKE up."

Orlando felt the tug on her leg and wondered if she'd knocked into something. In the dream she'd been having, she was in her house, trying to sneak up on the men who had broken in.

A tug again.

"Mom. Wake up."

She reached out to grab the guy's shoulder—

"Mom."

The dream disappeared.

She opened her eyes and saw Garrett standing at the other end of the bench seat, next to her feet. He helped her sit up.

"What time is it?" she asked.

"A quarter after midnight."

"What are you doing still awake?"

"Daeng says we're getting close to the turnoff for Washington. He wants to know what you want to do."

"You didn't answer my question."

"He needs me, Mom. I'm helping to navigate. So, should we go to Washington or not?"

He seemed to be enjoying himself, so she let his late night slide and thought about his question. Quinn had been very clear that he hadn't wanted them to get too close, but she knew if she hadn't been pregnant, he would have asked her to join him.

"Tell Daeng yes to Washington," she said. "He should head to Walla Walla."

"Walla Walla? You're making that up, aren't you?"

"It's a real place, honey."

"No, it's not," he said.

"Check the map."

"Garrett," Daeng called from up front. "The turnoff's coming up. What's the verdict?"

"Go on," Orlando instructed her son.

He turned to leave, but then stopped and said, "Your computer was dinging for a while so I turned down the volume." He headed to the cab.

Her laptop was still sitting on the table, her screen open but dark. Despite Mrs. Vo's insistence that Orlando rest right after she finished eating, she had spent a little time online, checking if using the name Dani instead of Danielle got her any closer to answers. It hadn't.

She woke the screen, typed in her password, and cringed in pain. Not indigestion this time, but another one of those stupid false contractions. She shot a glance toward the front of the RV to see if anyone had seen her, but the men were all up front watching the road and Mrs. Vo was asleep in her chair.

As the spasm receded, she braced herself for another. When it didn't come, she turned her attention to her computer.

The beeping Garrett had heard had been triggered by the facial recognition system. She brought the interface forward and saw it didn't just return a single result but three. She opened the first.

It was a potential match for one of Helen's attackers, the guy who'd been in the passenger seat of the car. She studied his face, comparing it with the image from the security cam. It looked pretty damn close to her.

The match's name was Harold Winston, nicknamed Tex.

Former military, dishonorable discharge, and three years in mercenary service with a well-known defense security operation before turning freelance.

Definitely sounded like a winner.

Match number two was for the driver. One look at the picture and she knew it was right.

Terry Kuhner. Driving specialist. Five years in prison for being the wheelman on a bank robbery. Scattered work history. Wanted for questioning in connection to several more robberies on the East Coast. His last known location was Chicago six months earlier.

If she could track down these two, she should be able to find out who'd hired them to take Helen. She might even be able to find out where Helen had been taken.

Orlando opened the last match.

The picture that stared back at her was of a woman, aged twenty-three. The recognition software put the match to the photo of Dani at only 53.2%. The name of the girl the software identified was listed as Marianne Trudeaux. The problem was that the picture was ten years old, which meant Marianne would be in her early thirties now, an age Dani had not reached yet. Orlando did have to admit, however, that there was more than a passing resemblance between the two women. Was it coincidental or was there a connection?

Before immersing herself in finding out more about Marianne, she pinged Quinn's phone to check his location, knowing he'd wanted to get back on the road by midnight.

A dot appeared on the map sixteen miles east of Walla Walla. She'd thought they'd be farther than that by now. She decided to call him.

"Shouldn't you be sleeping?" he asked.

"I was. Is everything all right?"

"Well, we *are* being chased. I mentioned that to you earlier, didn't I?"

"Ha. Ha."

"Oh, and someone spotted Nate in Walla Walla a little while ago."

She sat up. "What? Where is he?"

"Right next to me."

She waited for him to go on, and when he didn't, she said, "I swear to God, if you don't tell me what happened right now, I will find you before the sun rises and—"

"Calm down, honey."

In an instant, she went from worried to pissed off. "Don't you tell me to calm down!"

"I didn't mean it that—"

"Tell me what happened!"

"I will, okay? Just—"

"If you say relax, this is the last baby you will have the chance to create."

After a beat, he recounted the close call they'd had before leaving Walla Walla.

"They've got to be using traffic cams," she told him. "You need to get onto a road that's not covered."

"I know, but our options are pretty limited right now."

Orlando looked at the map. "I show you nine miles outside Waitsburg. Is that right?"

"Give or take."

"When you get there, take 124 west." It would take them in the opposite direction they wanted to go, but the likelihood of their being captured by any cameras would be near zero.

"We were already planning on doing that."

"Oh...well, then, good," she said.

"Get some rest, okay? It's late," he said. "You guys aren't still on the road, are you?"

Reflexively, she cupped her hand around the bottom of her phone to block the sound of the RV. "All tucked in for the night."

"Then sleep. I'll call if there's anything you can do."

"One thing."

"Yeah?"

"If you get a chance, ask Dani about a girl named Marianne Trudeaux."

"Who is she?"

"Facial recognition kicked her back as a possible match for Dani. She isn't, but they look enough alike that they could be related."

"All right, I'll ask. Now go to sleep."

EASTERN WASHINGTON

QUINN GLANCED AT Dani as he hung up the phone.

She was staring at the dark countryside, lost in thought, like she'd been doing since not long after Nate picked them up, so he decided to leave Orlando's question unasked for now.

At Waitsburg, they switched to the lesser used road and headed west. It wasn't the perfect solution. Once the others knew the three of them weren't on the highway anymore, they would quickly figure out what had happened. Route 124 was the only logical alternative in the area.

Darkness settled in tight around them as the lights of the town faded. For the first few minutes, theirs was the only car on the road. Then Nate's eyes paused on the rearview mirror. "Someone's back there."

Quinn and Dani looked out the rear window. There was a single pinpoint of light, maybe a mile back—a motorcycle or a car with one of its headlights out. Quinn watched it for several minutes. When he was sure the distance between them hadn't changed, he relaxed. Dani also looked less concerned, so he decided now was as good a time as any.

"My friend wanted me to ask you a question," he said.

She looked a little confused. "What?"

"Does the name Marianne Trudeaux mean anything to you?"

She sat up, her eyes wide. "Where did she hear that?"

"She didn't tell me. Is it your name?"

"No."

She seemed to be telling the truth. "Someone you know?"

More controlled than she'd been a few moments before, she said, "Sorry, I don't know her."

This time she was lying, but he knew if he pushed she'd completely shut down. He sent Orlando a text:

> She's not admitting it, but she knows the name.

BIANCA CAUGHT UP with the Lexus five miles before it reached Waitsburg and followed from a hundred yards back, tucked in behind a minivan. Tailing them through the small town had been trickier, the place all but dead at that time of night. But once she realized they were headed to the state road, she backed off.

According to the map, only a handful of roads led off the route. She could afford to give them plenty of space to get comfortable before she made her move.

She watched the Lexus's taillights. A few miles out of town, the car disappeared around a corner. When it was out of sight, she switched off her lights and increased her speed.

QUINN LOOKED OUT the back. The other vehicle had not reappeared after they took the bend in the road.

"Must have turned off," Nate said.

Quinn settled back in his seat. "Let's hope so."

"DONNIE, GIVE ME something, man. I should have caught up to them by now."

As soon as Orbits knew Quinn and his companions had

skipped town, he hightailed it down the highway, not worried about getting pulled over. A few minutes before, he had passed Waitsburg and continued east on US 12, but unless the others were driving as fast as he was, he should have seen them by now.

"Hold on, I'm scrolling through the footage."

"Faster!"

A pause, then, "Dammit."

"What?"

"I just caught up to the live feed and you just drove by but they haven't yet. You must have passed them."

Orbits braked to a halt in the middle of the road. "If I'd passed them, I would have known it. I've only seen four cars and none was a Lexus.

"The last image I have of them is from before Waitsburg. Maybe they stopped there."

Orbits executed a U-turn and headed back the other way. "Why would they stop? It doesn't make any sense." Waitsburg was only about thirty minutes from Walla Walla, where Quinn and the others had stayed for several hours. There was no reason to stop again so soon.

"How should I know?" Donnie said. "Maybe they had car problems, or maybe...oh."

"Oh what?"

"There's a road going west. Route 124. They must have gone that way."

"Goddammit, Donnie! I just lost ten minutes. You should have figured that out sooner!"

STEVENS KEPT THE helicopter on the ground until the techs had identified not only the targets' current vehicle but where they had gone. Once that information was received, he and his team lifted off, all running lights extinguished.

Instead of following US 12 to Waitsburg, they flew in a straight line northeast to the edge of the town. Stevens then ordered the pilot to parallel Route 124 a quarter mile to the south and fifteen hundred feet up.

One of his men spotted a car a mile outside of town, heading west. A check via night vision scope revealed the vehicle was not a Lexus.

Five empty miles of road later, a different spotter said, "Headlights."

About a half mile farther on, two lights cut a lonely path through the darkness.

When they confirmed it was a Lexus, Stevens consulted the map. "There's a small town coming up," he told the pilot. "After that, it's clear for a long stretch. Here." He tapped the map. "There's a curve in the road about twelve miles ahead. Take us there."

25

ROUTE 124, WASHINGTON

QUINN, NATE, AND Dani drove through the little village of Prescott and continued west. With each passing mile, the hills on the right closed in until they were right up against the road.

Three cars had passed the Lexus going the other way, but so far the only car on their side of the road had been the one Nate had spotted way back at the beginning.

In another twenty minutes, they should reach Kennewick. From there, they could take smaller roads to the Columbia River. They would have a decision to make at that point—stay in Washington or take a chance by crossing over via the interstate.

"I do know her," Dani whispered.

Quinn turned and found her staring out the side window.

"*Did* know her," Dani said.

"She's dead?"

A nod, her gaze still on the dark hills.

"Who was she?"

A long pause. "My sister."

"I'm sorry," Quinn said, meaning it.

"Thanks," she whispered.

He hesitated a moment before asking, "So your last name's Trudeaux?"

"That's…complicated. It was our mother's maiden name. Marianne and I used it sometimes. It was…easier."

"Easier why?"

Bright lights suddenly filled the cabin of the Lexus.

"Hold on!" Nate yelled as he slammed on the brakes.

With the tires screaming against the road, Quinn flew forward, his seat belt the only thing keeping him from smashing into the dash.

Plopped in the middle of the road directly in front of them was the large helicopter they'd seen in Ellensburg, a spotlight on the side of the aircraft aimed at them.

"Back!" Quinn yelled.

He yanked up the bag that contained his gun as Nate threw the car into reverse, but they had barely started to move when gunfire ripped into the front and rear of the Lexus, piercing the engine and hitting at least one of the tires.

"There are more behind us!" Dani yelled.

Nate hit the brakes at the same moment the engine gave out.

Quinn looked back. Sure enough, two men were on each side of the road, armed with automatic rifles.

"Out of the car, hands on your head." The voice came from a speaker on the helicopter.

"What are we going to do?" Dani asked.

In addition to the four men behind them, Quinn counted the silhouettes of four more by the helicopter.

"You can't let them take me," Dani said.

"Out of the car now!" the man at the helicopter ordered.

―――――――

BIANCA HAD THE advantage of not being surrounded by the metal and glass of a car as she followed a quarter mile behind the

Lexus. Even through her helmet, she was able to pick up the faint *whoop-whoop* of the helicopter.

She took glances at the sky to the south, until—

There, she thought as she spotted a dark blob moving fast against the background of stars.

She had been hoping Morse's men wouldn't make a reappearance, but so be it.

The helicopter raced ahead, disappearing in the night.

She increased her speed again, closing the distance between her and the Lexus to just over two hundred yards.

Things were about to get interesting.

ORBITS SPAT AN unending string of curses as he sped down the highway.

God only knew how far he had to go. He had seen absolutely no sign of Quinn's vehicle yet. If Donnie had led him astray again, the kid would soon be spending a lot of time in physical therapy.

Orbits leaned forward, his hands clutching the wheel like he'd never let go.

How far should he give it before going back? Five miles? Ten?

"Where are you, dammit?" he yelled at the windshield. "Where the hell are you?"

AHEAD, THE LEXUS took a curve around a hill, moving out of sight.

Bianca was about to close the distance a little more when suddenly a bright halo of light spilled onto the road from the other side of the hill. As she heard a screech of brakes, she brought her bike to a quick stop.

She was dismounting when automatic rifle fire erupted, the

bullets ripping into metal. She opened the seat and the kit that had been waiting with the gun.

"Out of the car, hands on your head," an amplified voice ordered, echoing around the curve.

She moved up the hill in a crouch and worked her way forward until the road beyond the curve came into view.

The helicopter was sitting right in the middle of the highway, the Lexus skewed on the road in front of it and lit up by a spotlight from the aircraft. She counted three heads inside the car, two men in front and the woman in back. They all appeared to be alive. Apparently the gunfire had simply been a warning.

She took stock of Morse's men. Four at the helicopter and four more behind the car—every single one of them focused on the Lexus.

"Out of the car now!"

It was an impossible situation for the targets. The attack squad may have been ordered to avoid injuring the woman, but it would have no qualms about hurting her companions. Morse's people undoubtedly had both men already locked in their sights. If the targets tried anything, it would be over in seconds.

She set her gun on the ground and opened the kit. Inside were three mini flash-bang grenades and an equal number of smoke bombs. She removed two of each, then, in quick succession, tossed one flash bang toward the men behind the car and the other toward the helicopter. By the time the canisters landed on the road, she'd already thrown the first smoke bomb and was readying the other. Right before it left her hand, the flash bangs exploded.

"WHAT ARE WE going to do?" Dani asked, desperate.

Quinn looked around again, hoping for another way out, knowing they had only one option.

"That's a lot of manpower," Nate said.

"Yeah," Quinn agreed.

"Government?"

"Let's hope so."

If the squad surrounding them was tied to US intelligence, Quinn and Nate might actually live through this. The fact that they hadn't already been shot supported the possibility.

"I don't see where we have a choice," Quinn said.

Dani's eyes widened. "Wait. No way. You can't let them get me. You can't!"

"Dani, if you have an idea about how we can get out of this, I am all—"

Even shielded by the car, the *bang* behind them was thunderous. As they ducked, a second went off in front of them.

"Flash bangs," Nate said.

Quinn raised his head and looked out the window. Through a stream of rising smoke, he could see that the men by the helicopter were on the ground, stunned. He looked out the back. Two of the four men there were in the same condition. The other two, however, were scanning the area, guns raised. More smoke was rising directly behind the Lexus.

Quinn's first thought was that Orlando and Daeng had arrived, but he knew that was impossible. They were too far away. For the moment, it didn't matter who it was.

"Everybody out," he said.

The car was angled so that Quinn's side was the one most shielded from the men behind them. He opened his door and motioned for Nate to follow him out. Dani had her door open a second later.

The smoke had built up enough so that they could no longer see the helicopter, but the rear cloud had not yet built to the same level. Quinn caught a glimpse of the two men who hadn't been dazed rushing toward the Lexus.

Thup-thup.

Both men dropped to the ground as muted gunshots cut across the road.

Quinn looked toward the hill, searching for the source, but his eyes had been affected by the spotlight and he could see little in the darkness beyond.

"Hold on to me and stay low," he said to Dani.

When she had a grip on his jacket, he signaled Nate to follow and led them around the front of the car.

Another *thup*, and a few seconds later, a fourth, both coming from behind the vehicle.

Quinn sneaked toward the edge of the road opposite the hill. His thought was if they could get into the field and work their way around the helicopter, they could lose themselves in the countryside beyond.

"There!" a man shouted.

Through a swirl of smoke, Quinn saw one of the men at the helicopter pointing at them, and then in an instant, the man disappeared again.

Quinn changed directions, heading back along the side of the car toward the men he'd seen shot. Behind them steps ran toward the spot where they'd been. For a moment, he thought they might be clear, but then a man rushed at them out of the smoke.

Nate shoved the barrel of the man's rifle toward the sky before the man could get a shot off. The attacker quickly flipped the stock end around and smacked it into Nate's shoulder, sending Quinn's partner staggering. But Nate was able to hold on to the rifle and rip it from the man's hands.

"I've got this," Nate said to Quinn as he threw a palm strike to the attacker's jaw.

"Come on," Quinn said to Dani, and pulled her fast along the car into the smoke.

As they crossed the asphalt, Quinn's foot hit the arm of one of the men he'd watched drop. He could see the guy's face now. A bullet hole dead center in his forehead.

Whoever had done this was a pro.

The smoke thinned as they started around the curve in the road.

"You can let go now," he whispered to Dani. "Just stay close."

Either she hadn't heard him or wasn't interested, because she kept clutching his jacket.

They were almost out of the smoke when they heard a voice behind them say, "I'll take over now."

Quinn turned.

Standing twenty feet behind them was a blonde woman wearing a leather jacket and dark pants. Her most important accessory was the pistol pointed at them.

He put himself between Dani and the woman.

"Deal number one," the woman said. "I get the girl, you live. Deal number two: I get the girl, you die. Your choice."

"No," Dani whispered.

The only hope they had was for Quinn to buy enough time for Nate to catch up to them. "She's no good to you," he said. "She doesn't even know where the location is."

The expression on the woman's face remained unchanged. "I don't know what that means. I'm here to recover the girl. So, if you please." She motioned with her free hand for Dani to come to her.

A footstep, faint and off to the side, behind the woman.

"Who do you work for?" he asked. "The Wolf, right?"

This time there was a tick of her head. Score one for Quinn.

"Why don't you give her a call? Tell her I'm willing to make a deal."

Dani's grip faltered, and he could sense her confusion.

The woman scowled. "I've already given you your choice of deals. Give me the girl."

Out of the smoke near the hill, a voice said, "Everyone freeze."

As much as Quinn had hoped it was Nate he'd heard approaching, it wasn't.

The blonde woman whipped around and pulled her trigger. At almost the same instant, a rifle yelped twice from the smoke. The woman jerked to the side, hit, and fired off four more shots as she sidestepped into the cover of the smoke cloud.

Quinn pushed Dani in front of him. "Run!"

She hesitated, looking at him.

"Just run. Find someplace to hide! Go!"

She took off.

Quinn ran back into the smoke in the direction the woman had disappeared, wanting to ensure she didn't come after Dani. As he reached the back of the Lexus, feet staggered toward him from the left. He twisted around, but it was Nate.

His partner had an arm around his ribs and blood on his face.

"You okay?" Quinn asked, not worried about what he could see, but what he couldn't.

"I'll be fine," Nate grunted. "Where's Dani?"

"She's okay. I sent her down the road."

They heard a *thup*, back closer to the helicopter.

The woman, Quinn thought. Though he would have loved to deal with her, with the smoke and the condition Nate was in, they needed to get away.

"Come on," he said, and headed after Dani.

BIANCA TOUCHED HER thigh again. The bullet had passed a half inch under her skin, hitting only meat before exiting the other side. It had been a while since she'd been shot, and it didn't make her happy.

The girl and her friends could wait. With their car wrecked, they weren't going to get very far.

Morse's men, however…well, she'd already taken out all four men behind the car. Now she wanted nothing more than to deal with the rest.

The first was easy. It was logical that one man would be tasked with staying at the helicopter.

Slinking through the smoke and ignoring the pain from her wound, she moved along the edge of the road until she reached the aircraft's tail section. There wasn't as much smoke here, but enough to limit visibility. She ducked under the tail and headed forward until she reached the main body. Peeking around the edge, she saw the shadow of the man standing right next to the floodlight.

She raised her gun, aimed for his exposed ear, and *thup*—one down.

She almost blew it with number two. As the first one dropped to the ground, she started to step out from under the helicopter. That's when a different shadow rushed at her.

He'd been standing next to his friend. Apparently two had been left behind.

She took him down when he was ten feet away, silencing him just as he started to yell for help. She expected to hear the third man running over to help, but the only steps were faint in the distance—the girl and her friends thinking they could get away.

She waited several more seconds to be sure, and then crawled the rest of the way out from under the aircraft.

The smoke was finally starting to lift. She could see the Lexus now, and the body lying beside it. She hadn't been responsible for that one. Whoever it was had lost the fight she'd heard.

She sneaked over and saw he was one of Morse's. She checked his pulse. He wasn't dead, but from the slack look on his face he wouldn't be waking very soon. She was deciding whether or not to waste a bullet on him when she heard a grunt coming from the other side of the car, near the hill.

Peeking over the hood, she spotted another person lying on the ground. She approached cautiously, her gun pointed at him. He held a rifle loosely at his side. When he noticed her, he tried to sit up and lift the gun but was unable to do either.

Blood covered his shirt from a bullet wound in his gut. More soaked his pants around his right knee.

This was the guy who'd shot her, she realized. Two of her blind shots had caught him. Nice.

She raised her gun to finish the job.

"No! Don't!" he begged.

Thup.

"WHAT THE HELL?" Orbits said as he neared the bend in the road.

A bright light was shining on the other side, smoke rising through its halo. As he rolled to a stop, he spotted the outline of someone running toward him.

"What the hell?" he repeated.

The runner turned out to be a woman, and not just *any* woman.

He toggled the window down as she neared. "Hey, something wrong?"

She slowed, looked back toward the light, and then at Orbits. "There's a-a robbery going on over there. Some men with guns. I barely got away.

"Guns?" He pushed the button unlocking the car. "Get in!"

One of his competitors had no doubt just blown it, and Orbits was in the right place to reap the benefits.

She hesitated.

"Come on," he said. "Hurry. I'm not going to hang around here and get shot."

She looked back toward the corner again. The smoke was still the only thing there.

"O-okay. Only for a little ways."

"Sure, sure. Just get in."

As soon as she was seated beside him, he executed a U-turn and headed east.

"You okay?" he asked.

She nodded.

"I'm Ricky," he said, extending his hand.

She looked at it for a moment and then shook it. "Dani."

26

NEW YORK CITY, NEW YORK

NO MATTER HOW late Morse stayed up the night before, he was out of bed by 5:15 every morning. This one was no exception.

He kissed his wife on the forehead and limped his long-ago damaged body into the bathroom. After closing the door, he turned on the wall-mounted TV, the channel preset to Prime Cable News. The volume was muted, not because he was afraid of waking his wife, but because he was interested in the images the network broadcasted, not the nonsense the on-air talent spewed.

Television news these days was not news. It was bouts of stupidity wrapped in ridiculous suppositions and opinions disguised as facts. Not that he minded. On more than a few occasions, he'd been able to make use of the medium for his—and his country's—benefit.

He had just lathered his face for a shave when the only surviving landline in the house trilled. It was his work line and had extensions in every room.

He wiped the foam from one side of his face and grabbed the receiver. "Yes?"

"Good morning, Director." Morse recognized the voice as that of Falcao, his assistant director of operations.

"Morning," Morse growled.

"There's been a complication."

"With?"

"Red team, sir."

"What kind of complication?"

"It's developing so we don't have all the details. Communications was lost with them approximately thirty minutes ago, and we just obtained satellite images from their last known position. Their helicopter's in the middle of a highway, and there are eight bodies on the road."

Morse had fully expected to wake this morning to news that the girl had been captured, not his team wiped out. "A crash?"

"No, sir."

"Do you have on-site confirmation of casualties?"

"Not yet, sir. A containment team is en route. There is, however, already local law enforcement on the way to the scene now."

"No way to divert them?"

"No, sir."

"Any sign of the girl?"

"None."

"I'll be there in forty-five minutes."

After Morse hung up, he wiped the rest of the foam from his face and picked up the phone again.

"Clark residence," the English butler answered.

"This is Morse. I need to speak with Mr. Clark."

"I'm afraid Mr. Clark is still asleep."

"And I'm afraid you're going to have to wake him up."

BERLIN, GERMANY

ASSISTANT TRADE ATTACHÉ Komarov had just risen from his desk to leave for lunch when his phone rang.

Annoyed, he hit the speaker button while pulling on his suit coat. "Komarov."

"Herr Komarov, it is Karl Schwartz."

He stopped, his arm half in the sleeve. "Herr Schwartz? What can I do for you?"

Why would Schwartz be calling again? Komarov's part in the operation was done. He'd already gone back to being what he really was—an agricultural trade expert.

"I have a request, if I may."

"Of course."

"It is concerning the hotel project. There is a problem with the original blueprint. I need to know if we should make an adjustment, but I have not been able to reach our partners in Moscow and was wondering if maybe you could do that for me."

Komarov closed his eyes. It was exactly as he'd feared. He was being pulled back into the middle.

Trying to keep dread out of his voice, he said, "I would be happy to help."

27

ROUTE 124, WASHINGTON

Q UINN HADN'T EXPECTED to see Dani when he came around the turn. He'd told her to hide and assumed she'd done exactly that. But he also hadn't expected to see the taillights of a car driving away. It was likely someone scared off by the lights and the smoke and the gunfire.

He cupped his hands around his mouth and said as loudly as he dared, "Dani?"

No response.

He tried again, knowing she couldn't have gone very far. "Dani? It's us."

Still nothing.

"She's probably too scared to come out," Nate said.

Quinn wasn't so sure about that. Though she'd been afraid as they made their escape, she hadn't come close to freezing up.

"Dani!" he tried again.

She didn't answer.

He looked behind them, knowing the woman with the gun would be coming soon. Dani would have to wait.

"Can you make it up the hill?" he asked Nate.

"I think so."

"Come on, then."

Up they went, Nate wincing with every step but keeping up with Quinn.

"This should be high enough," Quinn said.

They lowered to the ground. Nate propped himself up a few inches so that his ribs didn't touch anything.

When the female shooter came around the bend, she stopped, looked down the road, and started walking again, scanning side to side. She was still at it three minutes later when, in the distance, Quinn caught sight of a pair of headlights slowly heading their way. Since the woman didn't have the benefit of his higher vantage point, it was another thirty seconds before she saw them, too.

She turned and walked back toward the curve, but stopped about a hundred feet from it at the base of the hill. Quinn couldn't see what she was doing, but it became clear a moment later when he heard an engine kick on.

Her motorcycle must have been the one-eyed car they'd seen outside Waitsburg, he realized. More troubling was the fact she hadn't found Dani, either.

"Stay here," he told Nate.

He hurried down the hill and back to the Lexus. The trunk refused to open until he used one of the rifles to pry the lid loose. He grabbed their bags and carried them up the hill.

He was still several feet from Nate when the car he'd seen swung around the curve and skidded to a stop. He dropped down when he heard the door open, and watched the man who climbed out look around in surprise. A moment later, the guy jumped back in his car and reversed away.

Quinn double-timed it the rest of the way up and set the bags down next to Nate. The car's taillights were receding, but the driver, no matter how spooked he was, would soon be calling the authorities, if he hadn't already done so. As much as Quinn and Nate needed to get out of there, there was still the question of Dani's whereabouts.

Quinn opened the tracking app on his phone and input the

tracking ID number of the chip he'd hidden in Dani's shoe. A map filled the screen, and then the dot representing Dani appeared. She was still on Route 124 but was over halfway back to Waitsburg, moving steadily away from them.

"How did she get all the way over there?" Nate asked.

Quinn glanced down the road. The taillights he'd seen, not of the car that had just left, but of the one that had been there as he'd first run around the corner. She had gotten into it. That was the only explanation.

"It doesn't matter right now," he said. "We need to put some distance between ourselves and this place fast."

TRAFFIC ON 124 had picked up considerably since the discovery of the helicopter in the road and the bodies scattered around it. At first, the responders had been limited to police and fire department vehicles. In the last ten minutes, though, a convoy of a dozen military vehicles had passed Quinn and Nate's position.

They were approximately four and a half miles east of the crime scene, hiding in a copse of trees in the large front yard of a farmhouse along the road. A few more miles and they would have made it to Prescott, but Nate had been hurting too much, and carrying all the gear wasn't doing Quinn any good, either.

Another set of headlights appeared in the east at 4:12 a.m. As they neared the farm, the lights blinked twice. Quinn and Nate stepped out of their hiding place and Mr. Vo's RV slowed to a stop.

The side door popped open and Daeng leaned out. "Are you the ones who requested a ride?"

Quinn handed him the duffels, then let Nate board first before climbing in himself.

"Good to see you," Daeng said.

As they shook, Quinn said, "You, too."

"So, where do you want to go?"

"East."

"Consider it done."

Daeng moved back into the driver's seat and pulled them onto the road.

"You hurt, too?" Mrs. Vo asked Quinn. She and her husband had helped Nate into the chaise longue.

She scanned his face, looking for injuries.

"No, I'm all right."

Her eyes narrowed. "What you do to Nate?"

"I didn't do anything to him. He, um, fell down."

Mr. Vo, in the process of cleaning the dry blood off Nate's face, said, "Then he fall on pile of rocks, I think."

"You need to eat?" The way Mrs. Vo asked Quinn the question, it sounded almost like an accusation.

"Only if there's something handy," he said.

"Everything handy. Is mobile home. I get you pork chop." She looked him over. "Two, maybe."

"Thank you, Mrs. Vo."

She grunted and moved over to the kitchen.

Quinn made his way past her to the back where Orlando was sitting at the table. "Hey," he said softly. He leaned down and kissed her.

"Sorry I didn't get up," she said.

"I didn't expect you to."

She sniffed the air around him. "You need a shower."

"I missed you, too." He put a hand on her belly. "How's the little one?"

"Active," she said. "Where's Dani?"

He pulled out his phone and showed her.

"How long has she been stopped?" she asked.

"About twenty minutes."

In the three-plus hours since he'd last seen Dani, her tracking chip had traveled the hundred and fifty miles to Spokane and then stopped—not just paused, but stopped dead.

"Maybe she's asleep," Orlando said.

"That's what I was thinking. What I don't understand is why she got someone to drive her that far. From what I could tell, her tracking chip made only one quick stop the whole time."

"I'll double-check the data." Orlando opened the laptop version of the software. "Chip number?"

He gave it to her and sat down across the table. "Where's Garrett?"

Orlando nodded toward the bed above the cab. "He knocked out a few hours ago. I don't expect him to stir again until lunchtime."

He scanned the rest of the interior. He'd never been in the RV before. "This place is...cozy."

"I was thinking we could start taking it on jobs and using it as a mobile office."

"You were?"

She looked at him over the top of her computer. "Don't be stupid."

She concentrated on her screen again. A minute later, she said, "You're right. Whoever picked her up took her all the way to Spokane, with just one stop of two minutes and seventeen seconds."

"I don't like it."

"Neither do I." She paused. "What now?"

"Go to Spokane," he said without hesitation.

"So we're playing the white knight again."

"Is that a problem?"

She squeezed his fingers. "When has that ever been the case?"

She started to lean forward to kiss him, but her belly kept her from getting very far, so she yanked on his arm and pulled him across to her.

28

EASTERN WASHINGTON

DANI HADN'T REALIZED something was wrong until they reached Waitsburg.

"You can leave me here," she said. "Anywhere's fine."

"Here? Nah. You don't want to get out here," Ricky said.

He then raced straight through town, ignoring all traffic signs.

When she had tried to open the door and jump out, he grabbed her arm, pulled her back, and punched her in the jaw. That had knocked her out. How long, she wasn't sure, but when she woke, they were rambling down a highway, the sky still dark.

"I suggest you not try that again or I'll really hit you next time," Ricky said.

Dani scooted as far away from him as she could, biding her time until an opportunity to escape presented itself.

One never came.

As they neared Spokane, he grabbed her again and pulled to the side of the road. This time, instead of punching her, he manhandled her into the back.

He flashed her a look at the gun in a holster under his arm. "Don't try anything."

He climbed out of the car and retrieved something from the

trunk. After opening the passenger-side rear door, he slid in next to her and held out a bottle of water.

"Drink it."

"I'm not thirsty," she said.

He pulled out his gun and pointed it at her ribs. "Drink it."

"You won't kill me."

He chuckled. "You know, you're right." He switched his aim to her thigh. "But I have no problem hurting you a little bit. Now drink."

She reluctantly took the bottle from him. As she unscrewed the top, she realized the seal had already been broken.

"Go on," he said.

She pretended to take a sip.

"That was very pretty. Now take a nice, big gulp, or in a few seconds I'll put a new hole in your jeans."

She did as he ordered.

"Now finish it," he told her.

She downed the bottle.

The first wave of dizziness hit before she had even removed the bottle from her lips. Within moments, she was leaning back, barely able to keep her eyes open.

Ricky took the bottle from her and laid her down across the seat. "Don't worry. You'll only have a little bit of a headache when you wake up."

The last thing she remembered was hearing him get out of the car and shut the door.

———

ORBITS HAD BEEN doing a lot of thinking on the drive to Spokane.

It was possible the Californians were responsible for the road-block, but he hadn't seen any sign of them since Yakima so he wasn't going to jump to that conclusion. Whoever it was had access to some pretty extensive resources. Considering that and what he had seen of the Californians' operation, he couldn't ignore the fact that a hell of a lot of money was being poured into capturing the girl. Which led him to one very annoying conclusion: Even with his fee doubled, he was being woefully underpaid.

He began to wonder how many others were looking for the girl.

There was his client, plus the Russians who'd tried to hire him, and the Californians at the very least. He was willing to bet there were more.

His dour mood brightened as the outline of a new business opportunity formed.

After drugging the girl, he found a quiet motel on the edge of Spokane. The room was ratty and nowhere near the standards he preferred, but it would do. Setting his alarm for three hours, he lay down and contemplated the windfall he was about to receive until he fell asleep.

ORBITS ROSE AGAIN at 7:30, even more convinced he could pull off his idea.

He checked the girl and called Donnie.

"I need three things right away," he said.

"Hold on." Movement on the other end, the rustling of sheets and then paper. "I'm ready. Go ahead."

"One, a secure location in or near Chicago. Clean, you understand? Nothing to tie it to any previous operation. Two, a four-man support team with their own gear. They can't be afraid to get dirty if needed. And three, a private jet from Spokane to Chicago that can leave within the hour."

"All that's going to be expensive."

Orbits knew the costs would be a drop in the bucket if everything went as planned. "I don't care. Just do it. The plane first. You can work on the rest while I'm in the air."

Donnie called back ten minutes later with flight information, and a half hour after that, Orbits and the girl arrived at the specified airport entrance.

As he'd hoped, no one questioned his story of a sick sister he was taking home to their parents' house. It was all in how you sold your story, and boy, could he sell. He even doted on her during the flight, just because it amused him.

When they arrived in Chicago, Donnie had an ambulance waiting, driven by one of Orbits's temporary team members.

They headed south from O'Hare airport, along the western edge of the city to an empty industrial building in Broadview. They passed through a gate in the fence that surrounded the property and drove straight into the building, courtesy of a large metal door rolled up.

The three other members of Orbits's team were waiting inside. After instructing them to take the girl into the most secure room, Orbits found an empty office where he could have some privacy. He pulled out the piece of paper he'd used to work out the details of his plan and called Donnie again.

"I think you're going to enjoy this," he said before laying out his plan.

"Whoa," Donnie whispered when Orbits finished.

"Whoa as in you can't do it?" Orbits asked.

"No, as in that's pretty crazy. I mean, good crazy, you know?"

"Then you *can* make it happen."

"I'll need an hour or two to work out the details, but I don't foresee any problems. What's the timeline?"

Orbits thought for a moment. He needed this to happen fast so that no one could waste time looking for him. He glanced at his watch. It was already 2:30 in the afternoon, Central time. Assuming Donnie would need all of the two hours...

"Start it at four thirty my time, with a two-hour time limit. But use Pacific time since that's where everyone will think she is."

"DAMMIT," ORLANDO EXCLAIMED.

Quinn twisted around in the front passenger seat, where he'd been keeping Daeng company. "What is it?"

"Come back here."

"Garrett, you've got copilot duty," Quinn said.

Smiling, Orlando's son moved to the side to let Quinn out, and then took the passenger seat.

"Did she stop again?" Quinn asked. Twenty minutes earlier, Dani's tracking chip had started to move once more.

From the look Orlando gave him, he knew it wouldn't be good news. "She's flying."

"Flying? Are you sure?"

She turned the screen toward him. The blip representing Dani was now moving eastward, heedless of any roads and at a clip no car could match.

"Where is she going?" Quinn said under his breath.

Though he hadn't expected an answer, Orlando said, "Their current course will take them anywhere from Minneapolis in the north to St. Louis in the south, and as far east as New York or possibly Boston."

"She can't be doing this on her own. Someone must have her."

Orlando nodded. "There can't be that many places in Spokane to rent a jet. I'll make some calls."

"While you're at it, see if you can arrange one for me," he said.

She frowned at him, and then opened the browser on her computer.

OUT OF THE corner of her eye, Orlando watched Quinn return to the front of the RV. She was angrier than she had a right to be, but she couldn't help it.

He had asked her to arrange a plane for *him*, not them. He'd probably take Nate and Daeng but clearly intended to leave her behind. Was it the right call? Maybe, but she didn't care about the right call. She needed to be where she was useful, and that was wherever he was.

The baby pushed against her stomach. "Quiet, you," she whispered, taking the baby's movement as traitorous support of its father's viewpoint.

She'd been right about jet rental places. There was only a handful in the city. She worked her way through the list and found the winner at number four. Someone there told her a man had chartered a flight that morning to take his ill sister home. But when Orlando pressed for more details, the person had clammed up and not divulged the jet's destination.

That wasn't a big problem, though. She had the name of the company now, so it was easy to find a listing of tail numbers of all the company's aircraft. Since flight plans were public record, all she had to do was plug in the different numbers until she found the right one.

Chicago.

She almost hollered out the info, but remembered she was annoyed with Quinn. She decided it could wait. She arranged for a jet from a rival company that could hold up to ten passengers, and then switched back to the tracking map. Though she feared the flight plan was false, Dani's plane was still on course for the Windy City.

A *ding* signaled the arrival of an e-mail. It was from Gordon Evert, a fixer in San Diego she had known before either of them had entered the business.

Hey O,

You're mixing with some nasty stuff if you're interested in Tex Winston. Might have something for you.

G

"How did I know you'd try me right away?" Evert said when she called.

"How's it going, Gordon?"

"You know, all sunshine and pretty ladies. When you coming home for a visit?"

Orlando had spent much of her youth in San Diego. It's where her mentor, Abraham Delger, had recruited her. "Soon. Tell me about Tex Winston."

"What do you want to know?"

"Ideally, where I can find him right now."

"I believe I can help you with that."

When she finished talking to Gordon, she called the jet company back and reserved a second plane.

"ABSOLUTELY NOT," QUINN said.

They were in the RV, parked in the airport lot next to the private jet terminal. Mr. and Mrs. Vo had taken Garrett out to look at the planes.

"Who else are you going to send?" Orlando argued.

"Daeng can do it."

Orlando glanced at Daeng. "No offense…"

"Why do I think I'm about to be offended?" Daeng said.

Orlando turned back to Quinn. "Daeng isn't the best interrogator. He's too nice."

"It's true," Daeng agreed.

"Besides, we can't send him in alone," she added.

"I wasn't planning on sending him in alone," Quinn said. "I was planning on getting him some help."

"Just not me."

He hesitated before saying, "I was thinking Ananke."

Orlando threw her arms up. "Oh, that's just great. You think Ananke is a better interrogator than Daeng? She *kills* people for a living. She doesn't talk to them."

"She can handle the job."

"*I* know what to ask him. *I* know what we need to know. *I* need to be the one who goes."

"You and Daeng can't do it on your own."

"Fine! Then...call Ananke, if you want. She and Daeng can do their thing but I'll talk to him."

"Orlando, look at yourself. You're going to have a baby at any minute."

"My due date isn't for two weeks."

"Nine days."

"Okay, nine days. That's still not today."

Quinn knew she would not let go of the idea. Though he was sure he'd regret it, he said, "All right, all right. Go. But anything dangerous you leave to the others." He turned and pointed at Daeng. "And you are responsible for anything that happens to her."

"Me?" Daeng said. "This wasn't my idea."

29

PALM SPRINGS, CALIFORNIA

T HE JET CARRYING Orlando and Daeng touched down at
Palm Springs International Airport a few minutes before
noon local time. Outside the terminal they found Ananke waiting
for them.

The assassin smiled at Daeng, looking him up and down as
she offered him her hand. "You must be Daeng. I've heard so little
about you, which is clearly unfortunate."

"Nice to meet you," Daeng said, shaking her hand and looking
only a bit flustered.

"And Orlando, you look so…big."

She opened her arms, offering a hug, but Orlando took a step
back.

"No, thanks," she said. "Did you get the car?"

Ananke shook her head. "I only arrived five minutes before
you."

Orlando checked her e-mail and found out where the car she'd
arranged for was parked.

"Why doesn't Quinn trot you out more?" Ananke said to
Daeng.

Before Daeng could respond, Orlando said, "Follow me," and
led them to the waiting BMW 535i.

With Daeng as driver, Orlando in the front beside him, and Ananke relegated to the back, they headed west into town.

"So when are you due?" Ananke asked after they'd been on the road for several minutes.

Orlando ignored the question as she tracked their progress on her phone.

"You're not having twins, are you?"

Orlando looked out the window. "Three more streets and take a left."

"Got it," Daeng said.

"Does the father know?" Ananke asked.

Orlando whirled around. "*That* is over the line. Not another word out of you."

Ananke had veered into the topic that had caused the rift between them—Orlando's former lover and Garrett's father, Durrie. Back when Orlando lived with him, Durrie had confessed that Ananke had tried to get him into bed. Orlando never knew if she'd been successful or not, but that the girl tried was enough.

"You're right," Ananke said, the playful quality in her voice gone. "I'm sorry."

Orlando settled back in her seat.

Evert had told her that Tex Winston owned a townhouse near the city center.

"I know for a fact that he was there last night," Gordon said after giving her the address. "He called me looking for work."

"Do you think he's picked up something by now?" she asked.

"I doubt it. People don't like working with him. He has a short fuse and no sense of humor. Not a great combo."

They found the townhouse complex on a wide, quiet street three blocks east of Palm Canyon Drive. They parked out front and entered through the guest gate, the electronic lock no match for even the greenest operative.

Winston's place was number nineteen and in the back row. A

vehicle was in its assigned spot out front, and when Orlando listened at the townhouse's door, she heard a TV inside.

They had a quick discussion on what tactic to use, then Daeng and Ananke moved to either side of the door. Once they were set, Orlando pushed the doorbell. After a few moments, she heard feet shuffling on the other side. The peephole darkened and a voice called through the door, "What do you want?"

"It's Deedee," Orlando said.

"That supposed to mean something to me?"

"It's *Deedee*. I'm here to—"

Instead of finishing her sentence, she grabbed her stomach, let out a little cry, and bent forward.

Winston let her stay like that for a beat before asking, "What's wrong with you?"

"Please," she said. "I need...I need to sit down."

The door remained closed.

She looked at the peephole, her face straining from the imaginary pain. "Please."

Nothing for a few seconds, and then the door cracked open. "Are you sick?"

"I'm pregnant. I just need to rest for a minute."

When he started opening the door wider, Daeng and Ananke shot around the jamb in unison and knocked him back into his house. Not giving him a chance to recover, they grabbed his arm and pushed him against the kitchen counter.

Orlando followed her colleagues in and closed the door.

"Let go of me!" Winston roared. He twisted back and forth, trying to break free.

"I'd stop that if I were you," Orlando said.

His gaze turned to her, then switched quickly to the gun she was pointing at his chest. His mouth contorted into a snarl. "You wouldn't shoot me."

"I wouldn't challenge her, buddy boy," Ananke said. "Her hormones aren't exactly balanced at the moment."

Winston relaxed and donned a you-got-me look, then suddenly pushed up with his feet and threw his legs into the air, as if to flip onto the counter. It was all very Bruce Lee. The only flaw in his plan was that once he was airborne, Daeng and Ananke let go.

Down he went, the back of his head cracking on the edge of the counter as he fell to the floor.

Daeng toed Winston's unmoving body.

"Oh, great," Orlando said. "Please tell me he's still breathing."

CHICAGO, ILLINOIS

QUINN AND NATE landed at O'Hare International Airport forty-five minutes after their colleagues reached Palm Springs. Following the signal from Dani's tracking chip, they headed south until they reached an area of warehouses and small manufacturing facilities in Broadview.

The building Dani's signal was coming from was set back from the road, behind a ten-foot-high chain-link fence. The building was a long, rectangular structure, two stories tall and made of brick. Attached to the front section of the fence was a sign that read FOR LEASE.

"I count three entrances," Quinn told Nate as they drove by. One in front, and two on the left side—a set of double doors and a large roll-up. "No sign of anyone."

They continued down the block and pulled into the parking area of a wholesale plumbing-supply business.

"How do you want to handle things?" Nate asked as he killed the engine.

To get to the building, they'd have to go through the fence, but the only gate Quinn had seen would likely be watched. He pulled up a satellite image of the area.

"The lot backs up to a distribution center." He showed the

image to Nate. "If these are still there"—he pointed at several shipping containers near the back of the other business—"we can get in behind them and cut a hole in the fence."

"Works for me," Nate said.

Before leaving Spokane, they had equipped themselves from Orlando's stash in the RV, but had failed to bring along a pair of heavy-duty wire cutters. After a stop at a nearby hardware store, they made their way to the distribution center.

The good news was that the containers were still at the back of the lot. The bad was that the entrance to the facility was guarded so they couldn't drive on. The property next door, however, did not have the same issue.

The sign on that building read EPSTEIN SYSTEMS. Quinn had no idea what they did but apparently it involved only a few people, as there were just four cars parked out front.

Nate drove along the side of the building and turned around the back. As Quinn had hoped, there were no other cars, and no way for anyone inside to know Quinn and Nate were there. At the corner shared with the distribution center, they cut enough of the fence away from the pole to bend it back and slip through.

They walked fast across the thirty feet of open space between the fence and the containers, without anyone back at the main building noticing them. When they were in position, they studied the back of the building Dani was in. No doors, just a strip of long, narrow windows running across the building a few feet below the roofline.

Quinn pointed at an old Dumpster sitting to the side. "If we move that over to those pipes, we can scale up."

The pipes were a set of four electrical conduit tubes running up to the roof, each no more than an inch in diameter. They weren't optimum but Quinn and Nate had climbed walls using less.

Nate cut a flap in the fence, held it out of the way so Quinn could pass through, and then he followed. Moving the Dumpster was tricky. It had a bad wheel that wanted to squeak with every turn. Quinn had to lift the corner off the ground while Nate pushed.

"Why don't you stay down here," Quinn suggested when he noticed Nate rubbing his bruised ribs. "I'll go up and scout around."

"No way," Nate said.

He pulled himself onto the Dumpster and started up the skinny pipes to the roof. Quinn waited until Nate was finished before making his own way to the top.

The roof was massive. Scattered across it were several old air-con units, dozens of pipe vents, and several other items that made up the building's systems. Quinn had hoped to find a stairwell entrance but didn't see any.

"Are those hatches?" Nate asked a few moments later, nodding toward the far end.

It was hard to tell from where they were. To get a better look, they stuck to the edges, where their steps had less chance of being heard, and headed over. One of the metal plates was indeed a hatch, while the other was some kind of vent.

They knelt beside the former. Quinn ran his fingers underneath the lip until he found a release lever. He had to push hard to get it to move, and when it finally slid to the open position, it did so with a much louder *click* than he would have liked. He and Nate froze. When no one came to check out the noise, Quinn grabbed the lip again and lifted.

The hatch moved up four inches before it was stopped by something inside. Leaning down, he discovered a rod, one end attached to the hatch and the other running down below the frame, out of sight. He moved his hand through the opening and felt around. The problem was a hook on the bottom, and the only way to dislodge it was to lower the hatch.

"I need something thin but strong," he whispered to Nate. "At least a foot long."

With a nod, Nate crept back to the edge of the roof and soon returned with several twigs, none more than an eighth of an inch in diameter.

Quinn chose one, notched a V into the end, and slipped it through the opening, placing it so that the cut cradled the rod. He then lowered the hatch until there was just enough space for the twig. With a push of the stick, the hook swung out of its mooring point, allowing him to open the hatch all the way.

He leaned through the hole. An empty hallway, the only illumination coming from the sunlight streaming past Quinn.

He lowered Nate in first, and then slipped into the opening. Nate grabbed on to him as Quinn hung from the frame and helped him down without making any noise.

Nate winced as he straightened up, but Quinn acted like he hadn't noticed.

There were several more doors along the corridor, but the one at the very end interested Quinn the most. He was sure it would lead them farther into the building.

It opened with a slight squeak. Again, they paused.

Though they heard no one heading their way, they did hear a voice.

PALM SPRINGS, CALIFORNIA

WINSTON'S TOWNHOUSE WAS an end unit, designed so that the master suite didn't share a wall with anyone else. Perfect for their needs.

Daeng and Ananke brought two dining room chairs up to the master bathroom. One they placed in the large Jacuzzi tub, then dumped Winston onto it and tied him up. The other was placed just outside the tub for Orlando.

"Daeng, if you will," Orlando said, when everything was ready.

Daeng picked up a bucket of ice water they'd prepared downstairs and began pouring it over Winston's head. The man woke with a jolt, gasping for breath.

Orlando let Daeng douse him for a few more seconds before saying, "Enough, I think."

Daeng tipped the bucket back.

"What the hell, man?" Winston said between pants. "Who are you?"

"We have a few questions for you, Mr. Winston, and would appreciate your cooperation," Orlando said.

"Fuck you!"

Orlando glanced at Daeng and tilted her head ever so slightly. He stepped forward again and dumped the remaining water over the man's head.

Winston sputtered and started panting again. With a shiver in his voice, he said, "You think that's going to make me talk?"

"Of course not," Orlando said.

This time her nod was to Ananke.

The smiling assassin approached Winston slowly and leaned forward until her mouth was only a few inches from his ear. "She doesn't like it when you don't cooperate," Ananke whispered. As the last word left her lips, she stabbed a syringe into his arm and shoved down the plunger.

Winston yelled out and tried to pull away, but there was nowhere to go.

As Ananke stepped back, Orlando said, "In about an hour you'll start to feel the sweats. Nothing too drastic. Under normal conditions you might not even notice. Another hour after that, your gut will begin to clench, and soon you'll be vomiting up everything that's in your stomach. But the spasms won't stop. As you continue to dry heave, your temperature will spike. It'll probably be a good five or six hours before you start bleeding from your nose and your eyes, but it will come. And the pain—" She sucked in a breath and shook her head. "I'm not going to lie to you. It's going to be bad. Every nerve ending is going to feel like it's being smashed under a hammer. You're going to die, Mr. Winston, but not until morning. Unless, of course, you take your own life. Most in your position do."

Throughout her speech, he stared at her, his eyes growing wider and wider.

She reached over to the sink counter and picked up a hand towel. Unfolding it, she revealed another syringe. She held it in the air and admired it.

"This," she said, "will stop all that from happening."

It was a lie, of course. Her syringe contained the same harmless saline solution that had just been injected into him. This part of the plan had been Ananke's idea, a riff, she told them, on the method she'd used on Edmondson.

"Give it to me," he said. "Please. I'll tell you whatever you want."

Orlando frowned. "You'll answer our questions first, and *then* you get it."

"No way, man. You give it to me first. If I die, whatever it is you want to know goes with me."

"That's where you're wrong. I'll admit it would be easier to get the information from you, but there are other ways to obtain it. So, if you're refusing to cooperate, I guess we're done here." She stood up. "Have a good life, Mr. Winston. What little of it that's left."

She started for the door. Daeng and Ananke turned to leave with her.

"No!" Winston yelled. "All right, all right. I'll talk first. I'll talk!"

CHICAGO, ILLINOIS

BEYOND THE DOOR, Quinn and Nate found stairs leading down to the first floor. Walls lined both sides, the one on the right stopping near the bottom, while the one on the left continued on for another dozen feet until it met the front corner of the building.

Quinn went first, stopping four steps from the bottom.

The voice was a bit louder, but still too distant to make out the words. He *could* tell the speaker was a man.

He peeked around the end of the wall. A huge room extended all the way to the far side of the building and back nearly to the center point. To his left, at the front of the structure, was a walled-off room, probably a lobby.

If he had to guess, machinery had once filled the space. Now, the only machine in the room was an ambulance parked near the closed roll-up door. The room appeared otherwise deserted.

He heard the voice again, and realized it was coming from an open doorway along the back. After letting Nate take a look, he pointed at the walled-off room up front. It would provide a considerably better vantage point than the stairs. Staying low, they crept over to it and worked their way down the wall until they came to a door. All was quiet on the other side, so Quinn inched it open. Taking the darkness within as a good sign, they slipped inside.

Quinn did a quick scan with his penlight to make sure they were alone, and then said, "Head for the ambulance. While you disable it, I'll check out that back door to see if I can figure out what's going on."

"Got it."

Quinn eased the door open, and immediately stopped.

Someone was walking across the big room. Make that two people. When they stopped, Quinn heard one of the ambulance doors open. A third set of steps, farther away.

Quinn mimed for Nate to switch places with him and hold the door. He then slipped his phone through the narrow opening until the camera lens cleared the jamb.

On the screen was a view of the other room. He changed the angle until the ambulance was the focus, and zoomed in. The rear door was open wide. One man was standing in front of the opening, pulling out a gurney. Another was walking toward the man from the back of the room.

As the back end of the gurney came out of the vehicle, the rear legs and wheels automatically deployed. The third man climbed out of the ambulance a moment later, set something on top of the rolling bed, and grabbed the end.

The two with the gurney rolled it toward the back door, while the other man continued to the ambulance and circled to the driver's side.

"Are they going somewhere?" Nate asked.

Quinn had been wondering the same thing, but remained silent as he tried to figure out what to do.

Their choices were few, and none of them good.

PALM SPRINGS, CALIFORNIA

ORLANDO, DAENG, AND Ananke left Winston a huddling mess under a steady stream of cold water in his shower. That had been Ananke's doing, a little ad-libbed addition to what Orlando had told the guy.

"You may feel clammy for the next twenty-four hours," Orlando had said as she administered the "antidote." "There's a chance you'll have a headache, too."

His fear ticked up another notch. "I-I already have one."

She nodded. "If you're lucky it won't get too bad. Sometimes…" She shrugged. "Let's just say, to lessen the side effects of the antidote, you'll want to do nothing for at least the next twenty-four hours. Forty-eight would be even better. Can you do that?"

Lips shaking, he said, "Yes."

"I would stay in bed and sleep. Wouldn't even turn on the TV. But that's just me."

Though he said nothing, Orlando knew he would do exactly that.

When she signaled Daeng, he cut Winston loose from his chair. The man immediately threw the ropes off.

"Slowly," Orlando warned. "If you increase your heart rate, you'll speed up the spread of the poison, making it all that much harder to rid it from your system."

The man's movements switched from high speed to slow motion in an instant.

"We'll be off now, Mr. Winston. We thank you for your cooperation."

"There is one other thing he can do," Ananke said as Orlando and Daeng were turning for the door. "I heard one's chances are greatly improved by soaking in cold water for thirty minutes every three hours." She looked directly at Winston. "I don't know if it's true, but you might want to give it a try."

He pushed the last of the rope away, stumbled out of the tub into the shower.

As he turned on the water, Ananke said, "Cold, remember. Only cold."

"Cold. Right." He moved the dial all the way to C and slipped down the wall to the tiled floor.

When they were outside, Daeng said, "The water was a nice touch."

Ananke smiled. "Thank you very much, Daeng. It was one of those spur-of-the-moment things."

Orlando had to admit it had been a good addition, but she kept the thought to herself.

Once they were in the car, Daeng said, "Where to now?"

"You heard him," Orlando replied. "L.A."

"We're not done, then?" Ananke asked.

"No."

"Oh, goody." She sounded genuinely excited.

Daeng looked less enthusiastic. "Maybe we should pass the information on to Helen's organization. They'd probably want to deal with it."

"You have more confidence in them than I do," Orlando said.

"Okay," he said, "but shouldn't we at least let Quinn know what we're doing?"

Quinn would shut her plan down before they even pulled away from the curb.

"Just drive," she said.

30

BROADVIEW, ILLINOIS

"HIGHER," ORBITS SAID, his voice echoing through the otherwise empty room.

Branson, one of his new team members, tilted the girl's head back.

"That's good," Orbits told him.

He snapped off three more photos.

"All right, give me a moment."

Branson let the captive's chin fall back to her chest.

Orbits scrolled through the shots he'd taken. Of the last three, two were fine, but in the third he'd captured part of an eye, showing it was closed. He couldn't have that. Someone might get the idea she was dead. He trashed it, and then looked through all the others to see what else he might need. The problem was, he didn't know exactly what would identify the girl to someone, and if his plan were to work, others had to know for sure he had her.

He'd already shot pics of the pads of her fingers, and the small butterfly tattoo on her waist. There were other torso photos, lower-face photos, back photos. He'd even shot a full range of her nearly bald head. What else could there be?

He was about to tell Branson they were done when the picture of her face gave him one last idea.

"Pull her lips back," he said. "I want to take a few of her teeth."

"You got it," Branson said. He tilted her head up and peeled back her lips.

Orbits took a shot. "Now open her mouth."

When Branson pried the woman's jaw apart, she stirred slightly, moaning. Apparently it was almost time for Orbits to force some more of the sedative down her throat.

He moved in really close, took several shots of her upper teeth, and then switched his angle to do the same with her lower. Her tongue had lolled to the side, though, and partially blocked the shot. He grabbed it to move it out of the way, but as his thumb touched the underside, she flinched.

It couldn't have been from pain. He had barely touched her. Curious, he bent her tongue back and spotted several black marks. They were small and the angle made them hard to see clearly. He took a picture and brought the photo up on the display.

Not random marks—a tattoo of numbers.

"Is that it, or do you want to take some more?" Branson asked, still holding the girl's mouth open.

Orbits looked up in surprise, having momentarily forgotten anyone else was there. "Yeah, yeah. I got what I need."

He walked away, staring at his phone. Could this be the reason everyone wanted the girl?

He zoomed in on the tattoo a bit more. Two sets of eight digits, with a period after the first two numbers in each set, and, in front of the second set—the one beginning with 95—a minus sign.

Whoa. Whoa. Whoa.

He knew what this was. GPS coordinates.

When he entered them in his phone, up popped a map of northeastern Kansas, an arrow dropping into the countryside not too far from a town called Meriden. He clicked on the satellite view but it didn't make things any clearer. The surrounding area was mostly farmland, while the exact spot was a small, grass-covered clearing encircled by a thick grove of trees. After zooming in as far as he could, he saw a few spots of white within the grass —rocks, probably—but nothing else.

This had to be what was so important about the girl.

He thought for a moment.

Though this put a whole new spin on things, there was no reason to scrap his original plan. He could still reap its benefits *and* snag an even bigger score. It would not be without risks, but hell, he was Ricky Orbits. If anyone could pull it off, he could.

He e-mailed the girl's pictures to Donnie, with a note telling him to move up the start time to immediately, and then turned back to Branson.

"Pack everything up," he ordered. "We're moving out."

AFTER THE AMBULANCE'S engine rumbled to life, the driver headed back into the rear of the building, leaving the vehicle unattended.

"Do you have a tracking chip?" Quinn asked Nate.

"No."

Quinn didn't have one, either. They'd brought several on the flight east, but they were in a bag in the back of their car.

"Your phone," Quinn said, holding out his hand.

"What?"

"Your phone. Quick."

Nate pulled out his cell.

"Call me," Quinn said.

When Quinn's phone vibrated, he answered, and then switched devices with Nate.

"What are you doing?" Nate asked.

"Just stay here," Quinn said.

He moved into the large room and hurried over to the ambulance. He would have liked to put Nate's phone in the back portion of the vehicle, but if the others returned while he was doing it, he'd be seen right away. He settled for the front cab. Making sure the cell was on silent mode, he jammed it under the driver's seat, the microphone end as close to the edge of the cushion as possible without revealing itself.

Before he could make his retreat, he heard footsteps enter the room. Sneaking around the front of the ambulance, he crouched beside the grill and peeked under the vehicle. He could see the legs of two men approaching the back. When they arrived, they stopped and seemed content to just hang out.

Quinn heard the clatter of wheels coming from the back of the building. Knowing there was only one way he would be able to remain unobserved, he snaked under the ambulance until he was completely beneath the rear section. Across the room, the gurney appeared in the doorway, escorted by two more men. No, three, he realized, the last mostly hidden from view by his companions. Though his was a low angle, Quinn could see Dani on the bed, unconscious. As the group moved across the room, one of the guys waiting at the back of the ambulance climbed inside.

Quinn calculated the odds, but he couldn't take out all five men on his own without Dani getting hurt. He shot a look toward the front room. The door was closed, Nate remaining hidden as ordered.

The men loaded the gurney into the vehicle, and then two of them climbed in with Dani and the man who was already inside. One of the remaining two took the driver's seat while his companion walked over to the wall and started pulling the chain to open the rolling door.

The ambulance began moving forward.

Wonderful, Quinn thought sarcastically.

The second he was clear of the rear bumper, he hopped into a crouch and moved with the vehicle, staying tight to the back and below the rear windows. Though this kept him out of sight while the vehicle headed for the exit, his makeshift plan had one glaring problem—when the ambulance passed the rolling door, the man holding the chain would see him.

Quinn moved as close as he could to the passenger side, and the moment the man came into view, he flew at him.

The chain ripped from the guy's hands as he sailed backward. Grazing the outer wall, he twisted around, hit the floor shoulder first, and tumbled onto his chest, his forehead bouncing off the concrete. Quinn jammed a knee into his back and raised his palm, intending to hit the man in the head, but realized the guy had been knocked out.

Quinn pulled out his gun and jumped to his feet, knowing what would come next.

A LOUD METALLIC rattle filled the air as the ambulance pulled outside.

Orbits turned toward the back window just in time to see the rolling door sail downward, barely missing the ambulance.

The driver, Stafford, hit the brakes and looked back at Orbits. "That asshole nearly took us out. What was he thinking?"

"Must have lost his grip," Parnell, another member of the team, said.

Orbits was tempted to tell Stafford to drive on and leave Conway here, but given what was about to go down, he might need all the help he could get.

They watched the pedestrian door. When Conway didn't come out, Branson said, "Maybe he's hurt."

"Shit," Orbits said under his breath. "Someone go get him."

"On it," Branson said.

QUINN MOVED BEHIND the pedestrian door and waited. It wasn't long before he heard steps heading his way.

When the door opened, the new arrival's focus was in the

other direction, toward the rolling door. As soon as the man saw his colleague on the floor, he hurried over.

Quinn followed, and placed his suppressor against the man's neck as the guy knelt down next to his friend.

A moment of frozen time—the man motionless as he assessed his options, Quinn steady as he watched for the first sign of resistance.

There.

The man twisted around to grab Quinn's weapon, only the gun wasn't there anymore.

Thup.

The bullet ripped through the guy's calf. As he yelled out in pain, Quinn whacked the hot barrel against the base of the man's skull. He was dazed, but not out. Quinn hit him again and sent him to the ground with his buddy.

He rushed back to the door to await the next one.

ORBITS STARTED GETTING antsy after twenty seconds. When forty had passed, he became downright anxious.

"Should I go see if they need help?" Parnell asked

Orbits stared at the building. Something was wrong.

"If he needed help, he would have come back and asked for it by now," he said. He turned toward Stafford. "Go. Get us out of here."

Stafford didn't need to be told twice.

As they raced away, the door to the building opened.

For half a second, Orbits thought it was Branson, but whoever it was never stepped outside.

The hunter fumed. Somehow their location had been discovered.

QUINN WATCHED THE ambulance race away. It had been too much to hope they'd keep coming in one by one. But he had taken out two of them, reducing their manpower by forty percent.

He yelled for Nate to join him. When his partner appeared, he was holding Quinn's phone up to his ear.

"Is it working?"

"Yeah, but they're not talking much."

"Have they at least said where they're going?"

"Not yet."

Quinn looked over at the two unconscious men on the floor. One or both of them might know where the ambulance was headed. But with Dani's chip and now Nate's phone, he and Nate didn't need to waste time questioning them.

They left the men where they lay and headed back to their car.

31

A T 4:23 P.M., Central time, an auction appeared on the darknet. The item being offered was a Caucasian female in her mid-twenties. A list of her physical traits was included, as were several photographs and the name she was currently using: Danielle Chad.

The reserve opening bid price was $1.5 million.

Because the identities of most interested parties were unknown, e-mail alerts were sent to several people and organizations who might or might not care, in hopes that word would get to those who did.

WASHINGTON, DC

AN E-MAIL ARRIVED in Scott Bennett's inbox, marked urgent.

This wasn't unusual. Almost everyone who e-mailed Bennett marked their messages urgent. What made this one stand out, though, was that it had come from one of his superiors in the ultra-secret, America-first organization known as Valor. The first line read:

Handle this.

The second line was a link. And the third a random-looking string of letters, numbers, and symbols.

Bennett copied the last line and clicked on the link. His screen went black for four seconds before an empty text box appeared. After inputting the copied string of characters, he hit RETURN.

The new page was some kind of auction that was already twelve minutes into a two-hour time limit.

His confusion as to why Valor would be interested vanished when he saw the item on the block.

His first move was to send Ricky Orbits a text telling him his services were no longer needed. His second was to put in a bid.

BERLIN

FOR A TEN-minute period, Assistant Trade Attaché Komarov felt like he was nothing more than a glorified switchboard operator. First Schwartz with a message for Moscow, then Moscow with an immediate reply, then Schwartz again, and Moscow, and Schwartz, and finally Moscow.

Whatever was going on was big enough to ignore normal protocols. Komarov had no idea what it could be and was glad for that.

When he passed the last message on, Schwartz told him to stay close for the next hour and a half in case he was needed again.

Komarov didn't like the sound of that.

NEW YORK CITY

MORSE STARED AT the monitor. On it was an auction page, the item for sale one Danielle Chad.

"Can we figure out who sent this?" he asked the tech.

"We're attempting to trace, but unlikely."

"What about a location off the photographs?"

"They don't have any geo-tags and the background's just a wall, sir. It could be anywhere."

"There's nothing that can help us?"

"Nothing yet. We should be able to trace the money once the winning bid is paid. That would give us—"

"That'll be too late."

There was one thing they could do, Morse knew, but authorization for that would have to come from above.

"Keep working at it," he told the tech, and then returned to his office and called Clark.

After Morse laid everything out, the older man said, "It seems we've been handed a second chance."

After red team had been all but wiped out early that morning, the agency had had no choice but to remove itself from the physical chase for the Hayes girl until another team could be freed up.

"It could be a trick," Morse said. "They might not have her at all."

"Have you been able to verify her identity in the pictures?"

"Preliminarily, yes. But—"

"Then I say we have no choice."

"So that's a green light?"

"Yes."

"How high can I go?"

"As high as needed."

LOCATION UNKNOWN

THE WOLF PUSHED the button again, and immediately Director Cho arched on the table from the electricity coursing through her body. At the preset time, the shock cut off and Helen dropped back down.

"Another, I think," The Wolf said, and tapped the button once more.

Cho had just started to arch again when the door opened.

Braun stuck his head into the room and motioned to his boss. She acknowledged him with a nod, and then watched Helen finish the latest round.

When the cycle was done, she said, "Don't go anywhere. I'll be right back."

She found Braun in the hallway, holding a laptop.

"What is it?" she asked.

"Someone found the girl."

She tensed. "Who?"

"It's not that easy. Look."

He opened the computer and showed her the screen for the Danielle Chad auction.

After reading through it and studying the pictures, she said, "It looks like her, but are we sure?"

"It's her," he said. "The fingerprints are a match."

The Wolf finally allowed herself to smile. So her dead partner's daughter had finally been found. Now all she had to do was find out who was behind the auctioning, because there was no way she would let anyone else have the girl. She'd been waiting so long for Danielle Hayes to reappear, and had already borrowed heavily to fund the hunt for her. The secret the girl held rightfully belonged to The Wolf. Not only would it pay off her debts, it would allow her to finally regain the life she'd once had.

She glanced back at the door to the playroom. "I fear Ms. Cho has just become obsolete. Hold her until you hear from me in case this is some kind of scam. If they really do have the girl, eliminate her and thank our host for his hospitality."

32

LOS ANGELES, CALIFORNIA

ONCE WINSTON started talking, he hadn't held back. He'd told Orlando and the others that he and Terry Kuhner had taken Helen Cho to a private airfield in Marin County, where they caught a waiting Gulfstream jet south to the Van Nuys Airport in Los Angeles. From there, they transported her to a construction site in Koreatown.

"The night guard waved us right through," he'd said. "There was a Suburban waiting for us in the underground garage. You know, a black one with tinted windows. Like you see in all the spy movies. Two guys get out and take the woman from us. While they're putting her in the back of their car, another guy gets out. I was surprised because it was Mr. Rachett."

"*Thomas* Rachett?" Orlando said, an eyebrow raised.

Winston nodded. "His people have hired me a few times, but I had never seen him in person before. He quizzed us on how things went down, and then told us our money would be in our accounts within the hour. After that we went our way and they went theirs."

"So he'll know where she is."

"Uh-huh. Yeah, he should know. Can I have the antidote now?"

"Does he still work out of that old theater?"

"I, uh, think so. Last I heard, he did."

The Imperial Theater was one of the old downtown Los Angeles movie palaces. For decades most of them had sat unused and decaying, sad reminders of the area's sparkling past. In recent years, many had been restored to their previous splendor and reopened to the public. Rumors were that the Imperial, too, had been redone, though no one but the invited was allowed inside.

Rachett's public face was that of a successful businessman who had his hands in a lot of different things—construction, restaurants, real estate, and parking lots. His other face, the one the public doesn't see, was that of a big-time fixer who meddled in politics, torpedoed rivals, and used whatever means necessary to exert influence on whomever he chose.

Orlando, Daeng, and Ananke were still thirty minutes from downtown when Orlando's phone rang. On the screen was a single letter: M—Orlando's shorthand for the Mole.

She hit ACCEPT. "To what do I owe this honor?"

"Have you…seen the auction?" he said.

"Auction? What are you talking about?"

"Open…your e-mail."

She logged on to her laptop and opened the e-mail that had just come in from the Mole. It contained only a link.

After clicking it and reading the page that appeared, she said, "Holy crap."

ILLINOIS

ORBITS COULDN'T STOP thinking about the fact that someone had known where he'd taken the girl.

He went over it and over it as they headed south. If someone had found out about his flight from Spokane, the person might have been able to have people in position to follow him when he landed. But he couldn't see how that was possible. No one had seen him pick up the woman, so how could they have known he'd even gone to Spokane? Maybe they would have eventually figured it out, but he'd have landed and been long gone by then.

After several minutes of mulling it over, his gaze turned to Danielle. There was only one possibility.

Leaning over her, he checked pockets and hems, and patted down her legs and arms. Nothing. He rolled her onto her side and had Parnell hold her there while he searched her back. Still no bug.

He almost gave up, thinking he must have been wrong, when he glanced at her feet. He yanked her shoes off. The tracking chip was underneath the insole of her right shoe. A square hole had been cut into the rubber so it would fit nice and snug.

"Got you," he said.

He moved up front to the empty passenger seat, rolled down the window, and tossed the chip and both shoes onto the side of the road.

With a laugh, he said, "Whoever you are, you're out of luck now."

WITH DANI'S TRACKING chip as their guide, Quinn and Nate were able to stay half a mile back as they followed the ambulance.

Quinn had plugged a set of earbuds into his phone to better hear the open line coming from the other vehicle. Unfortunately, what little conversation there had been came from the back of the ambulance, and he could barely make out every third or fourth word.

He leaned forward, concentrating, as a new noise came over the line. It sounded like someone moving around. He closed his eyes and tried to picture what was happening.

Definite movement. Perhaps—

A loud beep in his ear signaled an incoming call.

It was Orlando, so he put the connection with the ambulance

on hold, clicked over, and turned off MUTE. "Did you find Winston?"

"We did," she said. "Did you find Dani?"

"Kind of. They had her in this building but left a little while ago. We're following."

"Did you know her new friends just put her on auction?"

Quinn disconnected the earbuds from his phone and switched to speaker so Nate could hear. "Say that again."

"An auction to buy Dani went live about ten minutes ago." She filled in what details she knew.

"Any bids yet?" Quinn asked.

"Two were just posted. One for two-point-five million, and the next for four."

"Does it say anything about how the winner will receive her?"

"No," she said. "Whoa. First bidder just re-bid. Five million."

"The ambulance stopped," Nate said.

"Stopped?" Quinn asked, surprised.

He had pulled a dedicated tracking device out of their kit and propped it in the cup holder. He looked at it. Sure enough, the chip was now stationary. But that didn't make any sense. They were on the interstate and Quinn and Nate had encountered no sign of slowing traffic.

"I've got to go," he told Orlando, and hung up.

A few seconds later, Nate said, "It's coming up. Right...about..."

Before he could say "now," Quinn saw them.

"They found the chip."

Dani's shoes were lying on the side of the road, right where the tracking dot had stopped on the display. Though the chip's loss was unfortunate, it wasn't the end of the world.

Nate's phone was still in the ambulance; they could track its location. But because the dedicated tracking device was able to only recognize the signal from homing chips and not from phones, they couldn't listen in and track the phone at the same time. Still, as long as the others continued to use the ambulance, it would be okay.

Quinn was tempted to have Nate move within visual range, but held off. It turned out to be a smart move when a minute later, the ambulance exited the interstate and randomly worked its way through the local neighborhood before rejoining the main road. Clearly the men had assumed that after ridding themselves of the chip, their pursuers would close in and therefore had attempted to lose them.

Once they were back on the interstate, Quinn had Nate close the gap.

LOS ANGELES

THE IMPERIAL THEATER was on South Spring, in an area of parking garages, recently converted lofts, and trendy restaurants. It hadn't always been that way. For decades, most of downtown had played host to only office workers during the day while serving the homeless around the clock. The turn of the century saw the start of a gentrification movement that spit and sputtered for several years before finally beginning to take hold.

The marquee of the Imperial stuck out over the sidewalk like a giant spike. It had been refurbished not long ago but carried no message. The front entrance of the theater was hidden from the street by a wooden wall painted black. Elsewhere such a wall would be covered with posters and graffiti, but this one was not. Orlando knew this had everything to do with who owned the place. No one—not even a wannabe gang member with a spray can—wanted to mess with Thomas Rachett.

"How does one get in?" Ananke asked as they drove by.

"There's got to be a door off the alley," Orlando said. With the front walled off and buildings to either side, it was the only option.

"Do we just walk up and knock?"

"No, we don't just walk up and knock," Orlando replied, trying to contain her temper. She knew Ananke was only being funny, but Orlando's sense of humor had a blind spot when it came to the assassin.

She had Daeng pull to the curb a few blocks away, then searched the Internet for info on the building. She turned up old plans from before Rachett had purchased the place. As she studied them, she realized what their choices were.

When she explained what they would have to do, Ananke raised an eyebrow. "So we *are* going to knock on the door."

Orlando wanted to punch her in the face.

TWO MEN STOOD outside the Imperial backstage door—bouncer types, one bald, the other ponytailed, both with more muscles than they would ever need.

They were chatting with each other when Orlando entered the alley, but stopped as they realized she was heading all the way down to them.

When she neared, the ponytailed guy said, "Afternoon, ma'am. Are you lost?"

She stopped and put a hand to her belly. "Whoa. I didn't expect it to be so hot today."

"Is there something we can help you with?" Baldy asked.

She took a few steps closer and suddenly leaned forward, panting.

The men moved toward her.

"Are you all right?" Baldy asked, concerned.

"Give me…a second," she said between breaths.

She stepped past them a few feet and then turned slowly around. The men naturally swiveled to face her, turning their backs to the street entrance, allowing Daeng and Ananke to slip unnoticed into the alley.

"That…was a strong…one," she said.

"You're not about to have a baby, are you?" Baldy asked.

"Not supposed to…but…maybe."

"Maybe I should call nine-one-one," Ponytail said.

Orlando held up a hand, like she was having another contraction and needed a moment. Finally, she said, "No need to call. It's not labor."

Daeng and Ananke each threw an arm around their respective target's neck and squeezed. Caught off guard, it took the men a moment to react. They twisted side to side, lifting Daeng and Ananke into the air as they attempted to pull the arms from their necks. They would have been more successful if they'd tried to help each other instead, but their instinct for self-preservation was too strong and soon both dropped to the ground, unconscious.

"Wow!" Ananke exclaimed. "That was a ride, wasn't it? How about it, Daeng? We should wait around until they wake up and do it again."

"I think I'll pass," he said.

Orlando would have liked to extend the bodyguards' sleep with a little knockout juice, but after dumping the sedative out of two syringes so they could be used on Winston, only one was left and she'd rather keep that one intact, just in case. They settled for dragging the men to the far end of the alley and zip-tying their wrists and ankles.

"That pregnancy act is really working for you," Ananke told Orlando as they finished up.

"It's not an act," Orlando said.

"That's what so cool about it. Imagine if you get yourself a false belly in the future. It's the ultimate distraction."

Orlando ignored her.

The bald guy had a set of keys on him that unlocked the theater door. A series of short hallways brought them to a T-bone intersection. On the wall was a sign that read HOUSE with an arrow pointing to the right, and STAGE with an arrow to the left. Below this was another, subtler sign.

RACHETT ENTERPRISES
Thru House

Orlando motioned toward the stage, hoping there was a back way to Rachett's office. They quietly made their way into the wings. A single bulb glowed from a stand on the stage, but it was bright enough for them to get a sense that the whole stage area had been refurbished—vibrant gold curtains, freshly stained floor, and a brand new movie screen waiting to be used.

Orlando peeked around the curtain and furrowed her brow. In place of rows of seats that should have filled the space was an intricate jigsaw puzzle of custom couches and lounges and mattresses, all very high end. At the very back of the room were two sets of emerald green double doors.

Thinking they could cut across, she motioned for Daeng and Ananke to follow her.

"What in God's name is this?" Ananke whispered as she came around the curtain.

"Quiet," Orlando said.

Daeng helped Orlando off the stage and into the audience area. She led them around the furniture toward the back doors.

"Does anyone else feel…dirty?" Ananke asked.

Orlando shot a look back at her.

"Sorry," the assassin said. "I'll shut up."

Upon reaching the doors, they heard voices on the other side, at least three people, moving to the left. When the voices faded, Orlando cracked open one of the double doors.

A grand lobby with gold carpet that matched the stage curtains, and at the far left, at the edge of her view, the beginnings of a wide stairway. She closed the door and opened the other half so she could look in the opposite direction. A guard stood ten feet away, his back to her. She eased the door closed, motioned for Daeng and Ananke to stay where they were, and then sneaked over to the other set of double doors. She went through the same routine as with the first set. This time she was able to see that the stairs went up to a second level, where a sign on the wall read:

RACHETT ENTERPRISES

There were no more guards, however.

Daeng took care of the one guard who was present, manhandling him back into the theater where Orlando injected him with a quarter of the remaining sedative. They then entered the lobby and moved over to the stairs. The second floor curved around the theater so they couldn't see anything beyond the upper landing. But they could hear voices again.

"So?" Ananke whispered.

Orlando glanced around until she spotted an elevator. "You guys take the stairs. I'll meet you at the top."

When Ananke saw what Orlando was looking at, she said, "Unfair. I want to be lazy, too."

Really, just one punch. Is that too much to ask? Orlando thought as she hurried over to the elevator and climbed into the waiting car.

There was a soft *ding* before the door opened on the second level. She waited by the elevator until the others joined her, and then they headed around the corner like they were there on business.

The corridor opened up into a larger room that reflected the Hollywood grandeur of the theater's past. Reds and golds and browns danced through metal and wood and fabric, turning the space into a showpiece that had surely impressed more than a few potential clients.

The reception desk in front was a combination of wood and glass that must have cost tens of thousands of dollars. No receptionist, though. In fact, no one was at any of the desks scattered throughout the room.

"Something's up," Orlando whispered. She pulled out her gun.

Seeing Orlando's weapon, Ananke said, "Finally," and retrieved her own.

Daeng followed suit.

Several offices were on either side of the open bullpen area. The voices seemed to be coming from an open door along the right and toward the back. Orlando and her team snuck along the wall and stopped a few feet from the open door.

"…back from her?" The voice was male, maybe fifties or sixties.

"I'm sure it won't be long. A few hours." Another man, younger.

"Good. I suppose you want me to take care of the disposal arrangements?"

"If it wouldn't be a problem."

"It won't be as long as it gets done today. I can't have this going any longer. I have a big event tomorrow night so I can't keep my staff off site for another day."

Orlando cocked her head. *My* staff? Was the speaker Rachett?

"We understand. The Wolf wanted me to express her appreciation for your help, and told me to let you know she will never forget your hospitality."

The Wolf. It seemed they were in the right place.

Orlando motioned for Daeng to watch their backs, then raised her gun and led Ananke inside.

The office was huge, with not one but two sitting areas, floor-to-ceiling bookcases, and a cruise ship of a desk in the middle. Behind the desk was the unmistakable figure of Thomas Rachett. A second man stood beside him while three others were in front of the desk.

The guy next to Rachett saw them first and started to pull out a gun.

Thup.

The sound had come from Ananke's weapon, the bullet dropping the man where he stood.

One of the men in front grabbed for his weapon, but it hadn't even cleared his jacket before Ananke dropped him with a second shot.

She smiled. "Anyone else?" When no one took her up on her offer, she said, "Well, that's disappointing."

Orlando looked at the duo in front of the desk. "I'm familiar with Mr. Rachett, but who might you two be?"

"People you would do better to leave alone," one of them said.

"Oooh. Scary," Ananke said.

The guy's buddy, the smaller of the two, piped up. "If you have business with Mr. Rachett, there is no reason for us to stay."

"I believe our business is with all of you," Orlando said. "If I'm not mistaken, you represent The Wolf, correct?"

"Who are you?"

"I'll tell you who we aren't. We aren't the ones who kidnapped the director of a United States intelligence organization and have been holding her against her will."

"Are you with the Agency?" Rachett asked. "Look, we can work this out. I know people who can—"

"You want to work this out? Tell us where Helen Cho is."

The smaller man narrowed his eyes. "You're not Agency, are you? I bet you're just a couple of hired…freelancers out for a quick buck. If it's cash you want, we can accommodate."

"Can I kill him?" Ananke asked.

"Not yet," Orlando said.

"Can I at least hurt him?"

"Be my guest."

The smaller man smirked. "You wouldn't shoot an unarmed —" He screamed as a bullet from Ananke's gun tore through his knee.

"Jesus!" Rachett said.

Orlando locked eyes with him. "Where is she?"

"She's downstairs!"

"She's here?" Orlando asked, surprised.

"Yeah. In the playroom."

"Playroom?"

"It's-it's in the basement."

"Show us."

WHILE DAENG TIED a tourniquet around the shorter man's leg, Orlando used a portion of the sedative on the man they hadn't shot. There was no need to waste any on the injured man, as he'd already passed out.

Rachett led Orlando, Daeng, and Ananke to a service elevator behind the stage.

As they traveled down, Orlando said, "How many more men?"

"I don't know," he said.

She tapped her gun against his back. "Try again."

"I'm not sure. At least two, and maybe as many as four."

When the elevator stopped, the doors opened onto a fairly large room that contained a few pallets of building materials but was otherwise empty.

"Which way?" Orlando asked.

"To the left. There's a hall. She's in the last room."

"The playroom."

He hesitated and then nodded.

"Are the men with her?"

"How should I know?"

Putting him in front, Orlando held on to his belt loop, her gun still pressed against his back.

As they neared the end of the hallway, a man stepped out of the second-to-last room. "Hey, I was—"

The moment he realized they weren't his colleagues, he dived back inside.

"Mine," Ananke said, passing Orlando.

She went low into the room, firing, and returned less than fifteen seconds later.

"Three," she said. "They won't bother us."

The last door had a pictogram on it, depicting a pair of feminine eyes and a seductive smile.

"This is it?" Orlando asked.

"Yes," Rachett replied.

"Open it."

The man did as ordered.

Using him as a shield, Orlando scanned the space as they moved in. The playroom was a sexual dungeon, with all manner of contraptions scattered throughout the room, and designed to have multiple guests at the same time. She suddenly realized what kind of movies were shown in the theater upstairs and almost shivered at the thought. Rachett's private sex club, where he no doubt played the welcoming host while using his guests' sexual predilections to further his business interests.

Helen was tied to a chair with a bag over her head. No one else was present.

Orlando's client was only semiconscious when Orlando pulled the bag off her head.

"Hey, wake up." Orlando gently tapped Helen's cheeks.

A blink.

"Helen, it's Orlando."

Helen slowly turned to her. "Orlando? What…what are you doing…here?"

"Getting you out." Orlando cut the bindings loose. "Do you think you can stand?"

"Um, I think so."

Orlando helped her to her feet and held on to her as Helen took a few tentative steps, gaining more confidence with each one.

"Where are we?" Helen asked.

"Los Angeles."

"How long?"

"You were taken two nights ago."

As they passed Rachett and Ananke, the man glared at Orlando. "I won't forget any of this, especially you. I'd watch your back from now on."

"Daeng," Orlando called.

Her friend stuck his head into the room.

"Can you take Helen for a moment?" she asked.

Once Daeng had collected the director and escorted her out of the playroom, Orlando stepped over to Rachett.

"I'm afraid you misunderstand your situation. Your life is over. That woman is not some low-level bureaucrat you can crush. She has resources available to her that you can only dream about. You might be thinking that you have friends in some pretty high places that can keep her down, but you'd be wrong. She will pay you back for your part in this. And when she does, you're going to wish my friend here had killed you already, because at least then you might have had a nice funeral."

With Ananke's help, Orlando used the last of the sedative on Rachett, tied him to the chair Helen had been in, pulled the bag over his head, and left.

ILLINOIS

HAVING NEARLY BEEN thwarted in Chicago and then finding the homing beacon on the girl had put Orbits on edge. Before leaving the building in Chicago, his intention had been to hire a plane to take them to Topeka, Kansas—the closest airport to the girl's GPS coordinates. But as he was reminded after his flight from Spokane, planes could easily be tracked. Now that they'd lost their tail, staying on the road felt like the better option. Besides, Topeka was only eight hours away by car, which meant they could get there not long after midnight.

After tossing the girl's shoes out the window, he'd stayed in the front passenger seat, staring at the road. It took a while, but around an hour southwest of Chicago, he finally started to relax, his mood helped by the auction heating up. For a while, Donnie called him with updates every five minutes or so, but as the bids began coming in faster and faster, Orbits decided to keep him on the line.

At one point there had been seven participants, but when the price continued to soar, two had fallen by the wayside. Those who remained were playing a feverish game of who would be last on top.

"New bid," Donnie said, his voice coming through Orbits's headset. "Fifteen million seven hundred and fifty thousand. That's a three-million-dollar jump."

"Who made it?"

"C."

To participate in the auction, bidders had had to deposit five million in special accounts Donnie had set up. Once this occurred, they were assigned a letter to "maintain anonymity." In reality, Donnie had collected the information on where each deposit had been transferred from, and already had automated bots working to uncover identities.

Bidder C had entered the auction when the price was sitting at five million. C had made a few incremental bids since then, but this was by far his or her largest jump.

If all stayed to pattern, bidder E would up the ante next, and then the remaining three—A, F, and G—would fight it out over who followed.

The delay seemed unusually long, and Orbits began to think that 15.75 million was going to be the final price. Not that he would complain.

"New bid," Donnie said. "Sixteen even. Bidder A."

A? Had they just lost another bidder?

"New bid. Sixteen one. G." Donnie barely had time to take a breath before saying, "New bid. Seventeen. E."

Apparently E was still in.

"Damn, Donnie," Orbits said. "We're going to hit twenty yet!"

QUINN AND NATE could hear only half of the conversation, but it was enough to confirm that those in the ambulance were indeed the ones conducting the auction. Not only that, it sounded like the person in charge was in the vehicle.

Quinn looked at his watch. They'd been on the road for an hour and a half. Not for the first time he wondered where the ambulance was going. They weren't randomly heading south-west, he was sure of that. If they'd just been trying to get lost, they would have stuck to the city.

No, they had a destination in mind. He wished one of them would say where it was.

TWENTY THOUSAND FEET OVER THE MOJAVE DESERT, CALIFORNIA

"ADDRESS CONFIRMED. TEXTING it to you now."

"Thank you," The Wolf said, and hung up.

33

LAS VEGAS, NEVADA

LIKE A NUMBER of freelance operatives, Donnie Lupo lived in Sin City. Unlike most of them, he did all his work from his basement office, often not seeing the outside for days or even weeks on end.

He had five regular clients, and a couple dozen others who would come to him now and then with work. Ricky Orbits was one of the five biggies, and the one currently occupying most of his time.

Donnie had been asked to do a lot of things over the years, but auctioning off a woman was a first. Perhaps he should have been repulsed by the idea, but he'd shed his morals long ago in favor of making a good living.

When he set up the auction, he'd worried that Ricky's reserve bid price was too high, but boy, had he been wrong. There was still time left and the bids were already inching toward nineteen million. With the ten-percent cut Ricky had promised him, Donnie was looking at nearly two million dollars. A tax-free payday like that would be all the motivation he needed to walk away from his job and become a thirty-three-year-old retiree.

The digital clock on his screen was counting down the time remaining. Fourteen minutes and thirty-seven seconds.

Donnie could barely contain his excitement.

———

THE GATED COMMUNITY was located in the Summerlin section of Las Vegas. A phone call placed fifteen minutes earlier ensured the two SUVs had no problem entering.

The house in question was located on a cul-de-sac that provided its residents with gorgeous views of the western mountains. The homes were large four- and five-bedroom places, all with identical red tile roofs, tan walls, and beautifully landscaped, drought-tolerant yards. A postcard for desert suburban life.

Visual evidence suggested that only two of the five houses were occupied at that moment, but those in the SUVs knew that the owner of a third—the house at the very top of the cul-de-sac—was also home.

They parked their vehicles on the road just outside the cul-de-sac but did not get out.

When the dash clock clicked down to two minutes left in the auction, The Wolf said, "Take us in."

———

BIDDING STALLED AT nineteen-point-five million dollars for a full five minutes.

But when the clock clicked down to two and a half minutes remaining, things began to move again. The first few bids came in at fifty-thousand-dollar increments, but as the time continued to run out, both the amounts and the speed picked up.

"Nineteen seven-seventy-five," Donnie said into his headset. "Nineteen eight…nineteen nine twenty-five…twenty million."

"Woo-hoo!" Orbits shouted through the phone. "Told you, man!"

"Twenty-one million," Donnie said. "Twenty-one five. Twenty-three." He paused, staring at the screen. "Whoa! Thirty million!"

"Are you shitting me?"

The bid seemed to stop everyone. "It's from bidder C," Donnie said. "Wait. Thirty-one million five. From B."

"B? I thought B was out of it."

B hadn't made a bid in well over ninety minutes. "Must have just been waiting."

Something creaked in the house above him, but Donnie was so wrapped up in the excitement that his mind didn't register it as significant.

The bids started coming in fast again. "Thirty-four. Thirty-four five. Thirty-five. Thirty-six." He glanced at the countdown clock. Fifteen seconds left. "Thirty-six five."

THE WOLF'S TEAM had the security system disabled and the door opened within twenty seconds.

They then split in two, half searching the ground floor and half doing the same upstairs. Though the target was not on either floor, a basement door had been discovered. As soon as the door was opened, a voice drifted up.

"...thirty-eight...thirty-eight seven hundred...dear God, forty million!"

The Wolf glanced at her watch. The auction was almost over.

She motioned her team down the stairs.

DONNIE'S GAZE FLICKED back and forth between the incoming bids and the countdown clock.

Five seconds.

"Forty-one."

Four seconds.

"Forty-one five."

Three seconds.

"Forty-two."

Two seconds.

"Forty-three."

One second.

"Forty-three five."

Four bids came in right as the auction ended. One was for forty-four, and three at the same higher amount. Donnie had to adjust the data so he could see the entry times to the hundredth of a second.

"Well?" Orbits asked.

"Forty-seven million," Donnie told him, hardly believing it.

"Son of a *bitch*! Seriously? Forty-seven?"

"Yes, indeed. Forty-seven."

Orbits laughed. "Who's our winner?"

"B."

"B? Well, how about that? Please inform our winner that we await the transfer of his funds. Once that's confirmed, we'll pass on instructions for—"

Donnie didn't hear the rest as the headset was ripped from his ear and a hand slapped tight against his mouth.

He started to struggle, but stopped just as fast when cold steel pressed against his cheek.

"There's a good boy," a female voice behind him said.

Someone twirled his chair around so that he was facing the rest of the room. There were five of them, four men and one woman. In the woman's hand was Donnie's headset, her palm covering the mic.

"What's your boss's name?" she asked.

Donnie said nothing.

She looked at the man holding the gun against Donnie's head. "Kill him."

"Orbits!" Donnie blurted out. "Ricky Orbits."

ILLINOIS

"ONCE THAT'S CONFIRMED, we'll pass on instructions for picking up the merchandise." Orbits paused, expecting a response. "Donnie, did you hear me?"

There was some noise over the line but no Donnie.

"Hey! You still there?"

Was that a voice?

"I think there's something wrong with the line. Let me call you—"

"Mr. Orbits?" Not Donnie's voice. A woman's. "There's been a slight change in the winning bid. The good news is that it's in your favor. Fifty million dollars, and you give the girl to me."

The initial moment of panic he'd felt when she came on the line all but disappeared when she mentioned the amount. Cautiously he said, "I appreciate your initiative, but I don't know who you are. You could be screwing with me."

"Have you ever heard of The Wolf?"

The name tickled something in the back of his mind, but it could have just been a memory of some Animal Planet show he accidentally saw.

"Sorry, I don't know anyone called The Wolf. And I'm certainly not doing any business with you until I see the cash."

"Of course not. That's why I've created two escrow accounts, each holding twenty-five million dollars. With the help of your colleague here, I'll send you information on the first account."

"The terms are full price, up front," he said.

"Half now, and half when I see the girl. That's *my* terms, Mr. Orbits. They are more than fair."

Orbits wanted to tell her where she could stuff her terms, but if she'd been able to get to Donnie, then she might be able to get to him, too. He'd much rather keep things civil.

"I let you see her, but I get the money before you take possession," he said.

"Agreed," she said. "When and where?"

"Nine a.m. tomorrow morning," Orbits said. "As for the where, give me your phone number."

"I'm not sure I like where this is going," she said.

"You don't have to like it. Just give me the number."

He wrote down the number as she recited it, and then said, "Be in Minneapolis by seven a.m. local time, ready to fly. I'll call you then with further instructions."

Before she had a chance to reply, he disconnected and turned his phone off.

NATE GLANCED OVER at Quinn. "Sounds like the party just got hijacked."

"It certainly does," Quinn said.

"By The Wolf."

"Apparently."

They were silent for a few moments.

"So if he wants her in Minneapolis by seven," Nate said, "and the meeting's at nine, then, assuming they have to do some ground traveling when they arrive, wherever we're headed can't be much more than an hour and a half's flight away from Minnesota."

Quinn nodded. The direction they were headed narrowed the choices down to somewhere in an area consisting of western Illinois, most of Missouri, eastern Kansas, and the northeast corner of Oklahoma.

He figured that St. Louis, the biggest city in the target area, was probably their destination, but less than fifteen minutes later, the ambulance transitioned onto the I-72 westbound, knocking St. Louis out of the running.

Conversation in the other car had dropped to almost zero.

"How much battery life did your phone have left when you gave it to me?" Quinn asked.

"Not sure. Maybe eighty percent."

Both phones had already been on and active for a few hours, and while Quinn's had been plugged in as they drove, Nate's had not. If the battery ran out of juice, they'd lose the ability to even passively track it.

Quinn hesitated a moment longer, and then disconnected the call.

34

LOS ANGELES, CALIFORNIA

ORLANDO HAD DAENG take them to Nate's house in the Hollywood Hills. Technically, it was Quinn's, but he'd moved in with her in San Francisco and had allowed Nate to use the property rent free. Nate had, in turn, let Daeng use one of the guest rooms.

"So this is the famous L.A. bachelor lair," Ananke said as they walked inside. "I've heard so much about it." She looked at Orlando, an eyebrow raised. "Tell me, is this where Quinn made his move on you?"

And I was just beginning to tolerate her, Orlando thought.

Stifling the string of obscenities that wanted to leap from her lips, she asked Daeng, "First-aid kit still in the same place?"

"Yeah," he said.

While Orlando was grabbing the kit out of the closet by the bathroom, the muscles in her lower abdomen contracted. She latched on to the shelf to keep from staggering, and took a few deep, quiet breaths. When the pain subsided enough for her to walk again, she returned to the living room.

Orlando sat next to Helen on the couch. The woman was clearly exhausted, but the dazed look she'd had in her eyes when they first found her was gone. Now there was only anger.

Using a damp towel Ananke had brought in from the kitchen, Orlando started to clean the dried blood from the director's face.

"You don't have to do that," Helen said.

"I know," Orlando replied.

"Did you get her?" Helen asked.

"Who?"

"Nanou Deschamps."

"I don't know who that is."

"The Wolf. Did you get her?"

Orlando shook her head. "She wasn't there."

Helen stared off in the distance for a moment before turning back to Orlando. "Tell me what's happening."

Two hours later, weakened from her ordeal but out for blood, Helen flew north to San Francisco.

WHEN THE AMBULANCE stopped to refuel in Hannibal, Missouri, Quinn and Nate did the same at a station a block away. While Nate filled the tank, Quinn walked down the street and found a place where he could watch the others without being noticed.

The driver was out of the vehicle, pumping gas. After a few moments, the ambulance's back door opened and another guy got out. He shared a few words with the driver before heading toward the snack shop.

When the driver returned the nozzle to the pump, the third man got out and stretched. He was the one who'd been shielded from view back at the building in Broadview, so this was the first time Quinn was able to get a good look at him.

Suddenly, Dani's disappearance at the roadblock in Washington made more sense. Quinn knew this guy. Orlando had forwarded him the man's picture the night before.

Ananke's hunter friend.

Ricky Orbits.

THANK GOD THE ambulance had a good air conditioner, because even with the sun down, it was still blazing hot and sticky outside. Orbits let the thing run at full blast for a while after they left Hannibal before finally turning it down again.

He should be happy, he thought. He was on the cusp of receiving a fifty-million-dollar payday. He already had the account number for where half was waiting. He'd checked, and it was all there. The only problem was that it was time locked to prevent him from transferring it into one of his own accounts until 9:01 a.m. the following morning, and only after The Wolf gave a final authorization.

She could be tricky in her way, and he could be tricky in his. He was going to get a kick out of handing the girl to her within miles of her ultimate destination. No doubt, the woman would fly the girl somewhere else to question her. By the time The Wolf discovered the truth, Orbits would have already taken whatever was of value at the location and gotten the hell out of there. The only thing he would have to worry about for the rest of his life was whether or not he was getting too much sun as he lay on the beach of some tropical paradise. He just needed to get the combo out of the girl.

"Boss," Parnell called from the back. "She's waking up."

Orbits unlatched his seat belt and worked his way to the rear of the ambulance.

Moaning, she moved her head side to side in a slow roll. Her whole body began to tense in a stretch, but when she knocked against the straps holding her down, she stopped and opened her eyes.

"Evening, princess," Orbits said. "I trust you had a nice, comfortable sleep."

Even though she was tied down, she lunged at him, rocking the gurney.

"Careful, sweetheart. You're going to hurt yourself."

She settled back, seething.

"Let me tell you what's going to happen," he said, smiling. "A nice lady with lots of money has shown a real interest in you. In the morning, she's going to give me some of that cash and I'm going to give her you. She calls herself The Wolf. That familiar to you?"

He could see that it was.

"You know how much she's paying? Fifty million. That's dollars. Not bad, huh? I bet it's even some kind of record." He paused. "I wonder if Guinness keeps track of that."

Again, she lunged. This time the gurney popped from one of its holds and moved a few inches toward Orbits. He jerked back, ramming his head into an equipment cabinet.

"You *bitch*! You think you're so damn smart." He wrapped his hand around her neck and squeezed. "But guess what? I know your secret. I know about the numbers under your tongue. Who's the clever one now, huh?"

He shoved her down and let go, then returned to his seat up front to the sounds of her coughs.

"Everything all right?" Stafford asked.

"Everything's fine," Orbits said, shutting down any further conversation.

Only it wasn't fine. He had just screwed up big time. He should have never told her he'd found the numbers. She could tell The Wolf right after he handed her over and he'd have to kiss whatever treasure she had hidden good-bye.

Dammit, dammit, dammit!

He would have to do something to rectify the situation. At the very least, drug the girl so she wouldn't wake up for a day or two. Of course, The Wolf wouldn't be pleased by that. Maybe she'd even refuse to authorize the final payment.

Son.

Of.

A.

Bitch.

AS THEY NEARED Kansas City, Quinn thought the others would be exiting the interstate soon, but the ambulance passed right through the center of the city and headed west into Kansas.

"Where the hell are they going?" Nate asked.

"We've got Lawrence and Topeka coming up," Quinn said, after a quick check of the map. "After that it's a long haul through farm country to Denver."

"If we keep going much longer, you're going to have to take over."

Quinn looked at his partner. "You need me to drive now?"

There was no missing the exhaustion in Nate's eyes. "I'm good for a little while longer."

"Pull over."

"I'm okay."

"Pull over."

With a resigned nod, Nate eased the car onto the shoulder. By the time they were on the road again, the ambulance was nearly a mile ahead.

They passed through Lawrence and soon after were driving through Topeka. By that point Nate was more asleep than awake, so when Quinn's phone vibrated in his partner's hand, Nate jerked and nearly dropped it.

"Sorry, sorry," he said. "It's, um, Orlando."

"Speaker."

As Nate hit the button, Quinn increased their speed to be back in sight of the ambulance in a few minutes.

"Don't tell me you're still following them," she said.

"Driving through Topeka, Kansas, right now," Quinn told her.

"If you're lucky, maybe they'll come all the way to California."

"I'm not sure I'd call that luck," Nate said, trying to stifle a yawn.

"How's Helen?" Quinn asked. He'd been less than pleased earlier when Orlando told him about the rescue, but begrudgingly had to admit she, Daeng, and Ananke had done the right thing.

"Haven't heard from her since she got back to San Francisco."

"What have you guys been doing, then?"

"Sleeping mostly. Nate, just an FYI. Ananke is using your bed so you might want to burn it."

"Noted," Nate said.

"The others are still asleep?" Quinn asked.

"Yeah."

"Why aren't you?"

"I had a few hours but I'm awake now. Thought I'd see what was going on with you."

Quinn frowned. "Is everything all right?"

"Of course everything's all right. Why wouldn't it be all right?" She paused. "Oh, unless you mean the baby. I delivered a few hours ago. Should I have called you?"

"Hilarious," he said. "Seriously, though, how are you feeling?"

"Annoyed that you keep asking me that every time we talk."

The city was beginning to fall away, leaving only the great plains in front of them. Quinn eased around a big rig, thinking they should now be able to pick out the distinctive taillights of the ambulance. But while he could see lights of trucks and passenger cars, he didn't see the ambulance.

Orlando was in the middle of saying something when Quinn blurted out, "Hang on." He glanced at Nate. "Check their location."

Nate put Orlando on hold and switched to the tracking app. A short pause, then, "They turned off."

"Where?" Quinn asked.

"Back in Topeka."

Quinn made a fast U-turn through the grass-covered center meridian and raced into the eastbound lanes.

"They're in the north part of the city, across the Kansas River," Nate said.

"Still moving?"

"Yes."

"Where do I exit?"

"Checking." Nate studied the screen for a moment. "First Avenue. It's about three miles ahead."

"Put Orlando back on."

Nate took her off hold.

"What's going on?" she said.

"Our friends left the interstate in Topeka."

"Stopping?"

"Unclear."

"Tell me as soon as you know."

"I will."

LOS ANGELES

ORLANDO HUNG UP and stared out the large window that overlooked the Los Angeles basin. The city lay before her like a brightly glowing carpet but she saw none of it, her thoughts focused on Quinn and Nate.

Though both men were extremely competent, there were only two of them. That would have been fine if they just had to worry about the men in the ambulance, but the auction meant others would likely soon be showing up.

Despite those odds, she knew Quinn would still try to rescue Dani .

She phoned her Los Angeles transportation contact. Once arrangements were made, she went downstairs and woke Daeng and Ananke.

EASTERN KANSAS

BY THE TIME Quinn took the First Avenue off-ramp, the ambulance was already out of town, continuing north on

Highway 4. The road was a single lane in each direction, but traffic was light. Quinn pushed their speed a bit above the limit.

"They're slowing," Nate said.

"Where?"

"Three and a half miles ahead. Yeah, they're definitely stopping."

THOUGH ORBITS NEEDED to find someplace to hold the exchange before calling it a night, there was no way he would be able to sleep until he made a stop at Danielle Chad's mysterious location. What he didn't want, however, was for Stafford and Parnell to come along.

To that end, he had them drop him off near a small neighborhood so he could score his own ride, telling them he'd call when he was ready for them to pick him up. It wasn't the perfect location to steal a car, but it was the best they'd seen so far.

The first house had a couple of trucks and an old Dodge Charger. The second, a minivan and another pickup. But the third had exactly what he needed, a late-model Ford C-Max hybrid. It barely made a sound when he started it up and pulled into the road.

As he neared the intersection with the highway, he saw the lights of a car heading his way from the south. It slowed, making him think it was going to turn onto his road, but then it increased its speed again and continued past his position, passing under the street lamp at the corner.

He stared after it in disbelief. The man behind the wheel was Quinn, and the place where he had slowed was the exact same place Orbits had been dropped off.

How did that son of a bitch end up here? Unless…

Clearly, he was the one who had bugged the girl, and given that he was still on Orbits's tail, he must have put more than one tracker on her.

Orbits put the battery back in his phone and dialed Stafford as he pulled onto the highway.

"That was quick," Stafford said. "You want us to pick you—"

"Listen," Orbits said. "You need to get a new vehicle *right* now. You're being followed."

"Are you sure?"

"Hell, yes, I'm sure. The girl must have another homing beacon on her. Leave everything she's got on in the ambulance. If you get caught, none of us gets paid. Understand?"

———

QUINN SLOWED AS they approached the spot where the others had paused.

"Are you sure this is it?" he asked.

"Positive," Nate said.

There were several houses ahead on the other side of the highway, but that was it. Nothing obvious to explain why they'd stopped.

Quinn increased their speed again and continued down the highway.

"They're turning," Nate said a few moments later. "Heading east on Eighty-sixth Street."

Eighty-sixth turned out to be dirt, the surface creating a rhythmic rattle throughout the car, forcing Quinn to slow.

"What could possibly be out here?" Nate asked. "Safe house?"

"That's as good a guess as any," Quinn replied.

"Turning south again. On Butler Road." Nate paused, then added, "They're speeding up."

Quinn resisted the urge to do the same until after they turned onto Butler. Even then, he only managed an extra few miles an hour, until they crossed a concrete bridge and found the road on the other side paved again. He slammed the pedal to the floor, but by that point the ambulance had already made several more turns through the nearby small town of Meriden.

"They've stopped again," Nate said. "Take your next right."

Nate guided him past another farm and into the town.

"How much father?" Quinn asked a couple minutes later.

"Almost there. Two more turns."

"They haven't moved?"

"No."

They ripped around the first turn, then slowed to a more neighborhood-appropriate speed as they took the second. The ambulance was parked at the side of the road next to a dirt lot filled with school buses.

"No one in front," Nate said as they drove past. "Can't tell about the back, but there are no lights on."

A sinking feeling tugged at Quinn's stomach as he swung back around to make a second pass. Still seeing no signs of life, he pulled in behind the ambulance.

They waited a moment for a reaction, and then climbed out, guns drawn.

The ambulance's back door was not only unlocked but not even fully closed. Quinn pointed his SIG at it and nodded at Nate, who quickly pulled it open. His gun tracking his gaze, Quinn scanned the interior. The back area was deserted.

The second he climbed inside, his dread increased at the sight of Dani's clothes piled against the wheels of the gurney. He searched for clues as to what might have happened, but there were none. He moved into the cab and retrieved Nate's phone.

When he jumped out the back door, he tossed the cell to his partner and said, "Let's go. They can't have gone far."

35

THE GPS COORDINATES led Orbits off the highway and onto a dirt road, then another, and finally a third that he almost didn't see. The entrance was nearly grown over, and had NO TRESSPASSING signs posted on each side.

It turned out to be more path than road, barely wide enough for a single car. From the way it was overgrown, he was sure no one had driven on it for years.

For the first few minutes, he caught glimpses of open fields through the trees, but then the brush began to thicken, making it feel like he was driving through a dark tunnel. It wasn't long after this that the road deteriorated even more, until finally he could go no farther.

According to the coordinates, the location wasn't too far ahead, so he decided to go the rest of the way on foot. The brush continued to crowd in, officially turning the road into a trail. The trees, too, grew thick above him, cutting off most of the sky.

He almost walked right into the barbed wire. He'd been shining his flashlight at the ground to watch his step, and had to stop abruptly when the beam lit up the lowest wire. There were six strands in all, each approximately a foot apart, and running off as far as he could see to either side. Mounted to one of the nearby poles was another NO TRESSPASSING sign.

The wire was rusty and had long ago lost some of its tension, making it easy for Orbits to pull two of the strands wide enough apart for him to slip through.

On the other side, the dense cover continued for another thirty yards, and then stopped entirely at the edge of the meadow he'd seen in the satellite photo. Though no X marked the spot, he did pick out the white objects hidden in the grass he'd seen in the satellite image. They turned out to be concrete squares that were part of two longer pieces running parallel to each another, just above ground level.

He moved between them to give himself a different view. As he took his second step, he felt the ground give a little. He jumped back, thinking he was about to be sucked into some kind of sinkhole. But the ground remained unchanged.

He knelt down on one of the concrete strips and put his fingers into the dirt near where he'd been standing. It was easier than it should have been to work his fingers through it. About five inches down, he hit something solid.

He pulled away grass and dirt until he had a palm-sized hole dug to the obstruction. Shining his light into it, he saw that the unmovable object was a flat piece of metal.

He removed the dirt between the strips, and in ten minutes uncovered a metal door.

Yeah, baby. This is what I'm talking about!

Built into the door was a handle, and next to the handle, protected from the dirt by a piece of scratched Plexiglas, was a row of eight tumblers, each showing the number 1.

He tried the handle first but the door didn't move.

The hinge connecting the Plexi to the metal surface had not fared as well as the rest. It took a considerable amount of force to break through the rust to get at the tumblers.

It was a lock, each dial containing digits from 0 to 9. He tried a few random combinations but, as he expected, none of them worked. The girl was the key. She had the coordinates to this place, so she had to have the combination, too.

Good thing he hadn't killed her.

He wondered what was down there. Gold? Cash?

Whatever the case, he figured he'd have at least a day before The Wolf showed up here. Maybe even two, depending on how Danielle reacted to the drug he'd give her before the handoff. Plenty of time to grab what he wanted.

Fifty million *and* whatever was beyond the door.

Hot damn.

HAVING NO IDEA which direction Orbits and his men had taken Dani, Quinn played a hunch and headed back toward Topeka. At one point, he and Nate caught sight of a pair of taillights in the distance, but before they could close the gap, the other vehicle disappeared.

As they approached the on-ramp to Highway 24 at the northern edge of the city, Quinn pulled to the side of the road.

"They could be thirty miles away by now," Nate said.

"Then why did they come up *this* way?" Quinn asked.

"They were trying to lose us," Nate said.

Quinn shook his head. "No. That didn't happen until they started making all those turns. Think about it. We had driven past the exit they'd taken and were almost out of Topeka before we realized they weren't there. When you checked, they were already heading north, but were they racing away?"

"No," Nate admitted.

"Were they employing any tactics to lose a tail?"

Nate shook his head. "They were heading down the highway at normal speed."

"Exactly. They had no idea we were still behind them."

"Maybe not then, but they did later."

"Something tipped them off, but not until *after* we neared them again." He fell silent for a moment. "No, they're in this area for a reason."

"Hold on," Nate said. "They could be just driving through and heading farther north."

"That wouldn't make sense." Quinn brought up a map of the area on his phone. "Look. Highway 4 connects to the same road we came across Missouri on. If Orbits wanted to go someplace to the north, he would have stayed on that and not dipped down to Kansas City. Whatever he's interested in, it's somewhere in this area." He circled a ten-mile length of Highway 4. "It's got to be."

Nate started to say something, but stopped.

"What?" Quinn asked.

"I was thinking—he's supposed to hand Dani off in about eight hours. This seems like kind of an odd place to do that, don't you think?"

It was a good point. A city would be considerably better for this kind of transfer—more location choices, not to mention plenty of options for getting away if things went south. But perhaps there were other circumstances dictating where it needed to take place. Something Roger Platt—Edmondson's partner—said echoed in Quinn's mind.

Sam wanted to get the location from her first.

The location.

The reason everyone was interested in Dani.

"I don't think the handoff is the reason Orbits came here," Quinn said.

"Then what is?"

He shared his thoughts with Nate.

"Whoa," Nate said. "Getting paid *and* taking whatever everyone's looking for—that's major double-dipping. If it's true, Orbits's got some balls. There are so many ways that could get messy."

The only problems now were, they didn't know where Orbits was or where the handoff would take place. Quinn called Orlando.

"Did you find them?" she asked.

He told her what had happened, and his theory about why Orbits had brought Dani here. "We could hunt around all night and not find them," he said. "The one thing we do know is that they'll be at a specific place at nine a.m., and there *is* a way to find out where that'll be."

She said nothing for a moment, then, "The Wolf."

"Exactly. There can't be too many chartered jets flying from Minneapolis to somewhere in eastern Kansas at just after seven in the morning."

"No, there shouldn't be. I'll let you know as soon as I find out where she's headed."

Now that he wasn't focused on telling her what he needed, he realized he could hear a background hum over the line. "Are you in a car?"

"Maybe."

"Where are you going?"

"Are you trying to keep tabs on me?"

"No, I was just—"

"Nate doesn't keep a lot of food in his house. I'm hungry, okay?" Her tone dared him to question her.

"Okay. Sorry. I didn't mean anything."

Softer now, she said, "I know. I love you. I'll talk to you in the morning."

"I love you, too." He hung up and said to Nate, "Let's find someplace to get some sleep."

LOS ANGELES

ORLANDO COULD FEEL Ananke staring at the back of her head as she put her phone away. "Go on. Say it."

"Say what?" Ananke asked.

"What you're thinking. That I just lied to him."

"Did you? I hadn't noticed."

"Because I'm not lying," Orlando said. "I'm starving. We'll stop on the way."

From the driver's seat, Daeng said, "Riggo's taco stand or In-N-Out?"

"In-N-Out, please. A double-double and fries, animal style."

36

EASTERN KANSAS

ORBITS AND HIS men camped out in a shuttered café along the road, north of Meriden.

In anticipation of the coming day's events, Orbits only slept in fits and starts, and was up and dressed at six fifteen. He checked the girl first. She was still asleep, the ill-fitting T-shirt Parnell had given her twisted around her chest, exposing her belly.

Careful not to disturb anyone, Orbits made his way out to the field behind the building and relieved himself. After zipping back up, he scanned the horizon. There were a few scattered clouds to the east, but otherwise the sky was clear.

A beautiful day. He took that as a good omen.

At precisely seven a.m., he reinstalled the battery in his phone and called The Wolf.

"Topeka, Kansas," he said without preamble. "If you have a good pilot, you should make it there by eight thirty without a problem. I'll call you then with further instructions. Oh, you should arrange for a car."

"Just tell me where to meet," she said. "There's no need for—"

"I'll call you in an hour and a half."

He hung up and removed the battery again."

MINNEAPOLIS

"DO YOU HAVE him?" The Wolf asked.

The man sitting across the aisle looked up from his computer and grimaced. "His signal's scrambled. About the best I can say is that he's in the Kansas-Missouri-Oklahoma area."

"That's a huge help," she said, unsmiling.

"I'll, uh, go over the data again. Maybe I can fine-tune it."

"You do that."

She turned her attention to the hunter in the seat in front of him. "Bianca," she said. "Would you mind telling the pilot that our destination is Topeka, Kansas?"

EASTERN KANSAS

A THROWBACK TO a bygone era of families in station wagons on cross-country journeys to take in the wonders of America, the motel at the north end of Topeka had one story with two wings forming an L around a parking area, and the prerequisite fenced-in swimming pool.

Quinn had woken the night clerk at two a.m. to get a room. Theirs was at the very end of the back portion of the L, farthest from the road. By the time six a.m. rolled around, he and Nate were both up, showered, and dressed.

Nate made a quick trip to pick them up some coffee, then, while they waited for Orlando's call, they silently went over their gear, cleaning weapons and making sure everything was ready if needed.

"It's seven," Nate said a little while later.

Somewhere nearby Orbits was telling The Wolf where the meeting was to take place. At most, Quinn figured it would be another ten or fifteen minutes before Orlando could pin down The Wolf's destination.

At fourteen minutes after seven, someone knocked on their door.

"Get rid of them," Quinn told Nate.

His partner walked over to the door, opened it a few inches, and turned back to Quinn. "We, um, have a visitor."

As Nate swung the door the rest of the way open, Quinn pulled his gun from his shoulder holster.

"Not exactly the greeting I was expecting," Orlando said.

"What in God's name are you doing here?" Quinn asked.

She stepped inside so Nate could close the door again. "What do you think I'm doing here? You and boy wonder need help."

"I never said that."

"You never not said that."

He frowned. "I actually did."

"Must be the hormones. I don't recall that."

"You could have just sent Daeng."

"I brought him with me. He's in our room."

"Your room?"

"We landed a couple hours ago, tracked your phone here, and figured we'd get a room to freshen up. He and Ananke should be here in a minute."

"You're unbelievable."

"Thank you."

"I didn't mean it as a compliment."

"But I'm taking it that way. Now, would you mind?" she asked, pointing at his hand.

He slipped his gun back into its holster, walked over, and pulled her into his arms. He couldn't lie to himself. It did feel good to have her here.

When they separated, Orlando said, "So, do you want to know where The Wolf is headed or not?"

THE CAR STAFFORD and Parnell had stolen was a gray Honda Accord. Though it wasn't that much larger than the C-Max, it was considerably more generic and had less chance of being ID'd as stolen by a local.

Orbits told his men to take their gear out to the car and wait while he prepped the girl for the exchange. As soon as they were gone, he made a big show of filling a syringe with a sedative.

"Before I give this to you," he said to the woman, "we have one last matter to discuss. I found the door."

No reaction.

"You know," he said, "the door those numbers under your tongue lead to. We're actually only a few miles from it."

"I don't believe you."

"I went and took a look at it last night. It was buried under some dirt so it took a little work to clean it off. You know what I found when I did?"

She didn't answer.

"That door of yours is locked. It needs an eight-number combination to open it."

Her eyes flared.

"See, here's the deal," he said. "Your secret's not so secret anymore. Whatever's down there, either I'm going to get it, or The Wolf is. That's what my dad would have called a foregone conclusion. Not a damn thing you can do about it. The only thing you have control over is which of us it's going to be.

"You're lucky with me. I found the numbers without having to work you over any. That's not going to be true with The Wolf. Whatever she tries to do to you, I can guarantee it will not be pleasant. My proposal is this. I know you have the combination. You give that to me, and I'll make sure The Wolf never gets ahold of you. The offer's time sensitive, though. In about…"—he checked his watch—"one hour, I'm supposed to hand you over. At that point, there'll be nothing I can do. For you, anyway. For me, I guess I'll just have to use a little explosive. That should bust the door in."

She laughed. "Go ahead and try. It's six inches thick. You set off a charge and you're liable to damage the automated supports that lift it. Then you'll never get it open."

"Then you should just give me the combo so I don't wreck anything."

"Never going to happen."

He stared at her for a moment before returning the syringe to its hard plastic container. "I'll tell you what. We'll take a ride first and give you some time to reconsider. I think you'll come around to seeing that I'm your best option."

"Don't count on it."

"THERE," ORLANDO SAID. She handed Quinn the binoculars and pointed.

He adjusted the focus, bringing the tiny shape of a private jet into view. "You're sure?"

"You have to ask?"

The plane landed at Topeka Regional Airport four minutes later, at 8:21 a.m. Bypassing the public terminal, it taxied over to one of the buildings to the north. Quinn and Orlando relocated to the edge of the public lot to get a direct view of the now stopped aircraft. After a few moments, the door opened and the steps were lowered. Four men exited first, and then two women.

"The last one matches Helen's description of The Wolf," Orlando said. "See, I do know what I'm doing."

It was the other woman who caught Quinn's attention.

"The blonde," he said. "She's the motorcycle rider who shot all the men at the helicopter."

"Well, then, I guess the gang's all here."

Quinn took his comm mic off mute. "Nate?"

"Go for Nate."

Nate, Daeng, and Ananke were near the private vehicle entrance, in the car he and Quinn had driven from Illinois.

"We've got visual confirmation on The Wolf," Quinn said. "Stand by."

"Copy."

A woman hurried out of the building and jogged over to The Wolf's party. A short conversation ensued before she led them over to two waiting SUVs. She handed them what Quinn assumed were keys and headed back to the building.

The Wolf and her team conferred for a moment before three of the men climbed into one of the vehicles, and the fourth man and the two women got into the other.

"They're in the two dark blue Explorers," Quinn told Nate. "Leaving now."

"Copy. We're on it."

NATE WAITED UNTIL the gate started to open before he pulled forward, his car a foot over the center line. Pretending he was arguing with Ananke, who sat up front with him, he slammed on the brakes when he "noticed" he was blocking the Explorer. Holding up a hand in apology, he reversed his car into his own lane, but left it hanging over just enough so that the SUV had to pass slowly.

As the second SUV did the same, Daeng crept out from where he'd been hiding behind the wall the gate shut against, and slipped a magnetic-backed tracking chip under the vehicle's license plate.

"All set," he said as the Explorer rushed off to catch its partner.

TIME WAS RUNNING out. With only twenty minutes until the meeting, Orbits needed to get the combo out of the girl now, or give up any dreams of finding out what was under that door.

Ahead, a copse of trees separated two farms. He pointed it out to Stafford. "Stop there for a minute."

When they were at the side of the road, he opened his door and grabbed the girl by the arm.

"Come with me."

DANI STUMBLED AS her captor pushed her deeper into the grove of trees, her bare feet feeling every twig and pebble.

"Careful," he grunted.

Once they could no longer see the car, he stopped and pushed her against a tree.

"All right, here it is. You know what I want. You tell me now, and I'll untie your wrists and let you go."

He was a good actor. His face was very I'm-doing-you-a-favor-against-my-better-judgment. But she knew he would give her to her father's old partner no matter what.

"In thirty seconds that option is off the table."

"You'll let me go," she said, playing along.

"That's the deal."

She made a show of thinking it over. "All right, I'll tell you."

"Now we're talking." He pulled out his phone and poised his thumb over his keypad. "Let's have it."

"Zero-nine-seven-six-four-three-one-zero."

He stopped entering it halfway through. "Give it to me again."

"Nine-eight-six-five-three-two-zero-nine."

He glared at her, his face reddening in anger.

"Again?" she asked. Though she did know the number, she was never going to give it to this asshole. "Eight-seven-five-four-two-one-nine-eight."

He slapped her hard.

"Looks like The Wolf will be the one to get it out of you," he said. "I wish you luck."

From his pocket, he removed the hard plastic case she'd seen him put the syringe into earlier.

As he pulled the needle out, she braced herself against the tree. When he turned to her, she kicked out, her bare foot whacking into his hand and sending the syringe flying.

ORBITS YELLED IN surprise. "You bitch!" he said, shoving her to the ground. "Don't move."

He didn't see where the syringe had landed and had to hunt around, stepping carefully. When he finally spotted it, he could see the plunger had twisted and allowed the drug to leak out. Cursing loudly, he picked it up and hurled it at a tree near the girl.

That sealed it, then. His claim on whatever was below the door in the meadow was null and void. He couldn't even risk a quick visit after the handoff. Maybe the girl wouldn't immediately tell The Wolf that Orbits knew where it was, but he had to assume she would.

He yanked her up by the arm. "So this is the way you want it, huh?" he said. "I could have been your friend. A little cooperation and you would have been free by now." A lie, but that wasn't important. "Walk." He pushed her in front of him. "It's time to meet your new owner."

37

"YOU CALLED IT," Orlando said.

She'd been guiding Quinn through Topeka based on the tracking information she was receiving from The Wolf's vehicle, but he'd known all along they'd end up heading north out of town on Highway 4.

He flicked on his comm mic. "Nate, status check."

"No change," Nate replied.

While Quinn and Orlando were on the road a minute in front of the SUVs, their friends were following a minute behind.

A few silent miles passed, with Quinn dividing his gaze between the road ahead and his mirrors. Approximately four and a half miles past the point where the 4 separated from US 24, he looked into the rearview mirror and shot a glance at Orlando.

"Did they speed up?" he asked.

She looked at her phone. "No. Why?"

"I've got an SUV that looks very much like one of the Explorers coming up fast."

Orlando angled herself to use the side mirror. "I see it."

Quinn glanced at the rearview mirror. The SUV he'd spotted was now a hundred yards behind them, still closing.

"That's got to be the lead vehicle," Orlando said.

Quinn informed the others.

Just as he finished, Orlando said, "Here they come."

The Explorer was close enough now for them to confirm that the men in front were two of those they'd seen getting out of the plane. For a couple seconds the vehicle looked as though it would ram into them, but when it was less than two car lengths back, it pulled into the next lane and shot past.

"What's their other one doing?" Quinn asked.

Checking the tracking app again, Orlando said, "Still hanging back."

"Scout mission," he said, thinking the lead SUV must have been sent to scope out the exchange location.

"Makes sense to me."

Forty-five seconds later, he spotted the Explorer again, this time pulled to the side of the road, its occupants climbing out. Quinn continued on without slowing. Though there was nothing but a few trees and bushes where the others had stopped, another three hundred yards down on the west side of the road was a sprawling service station called Karl's K-4. Three cars were at the pumps and several others were parked next to the main building. One of the doors to the large garage at the back of the property was open, revealing a truck inside with its hood up. Just to the south was a busy café. At least a dozen cars sat in its lot, and most of the tables visible through the windows were full.

There were basically two types of hostage exchange. The first involved two parties unworried that the other would try to take advantage of the situation. These were often held in quiet, out-of-the-way spots: a dark bar, a remote cabin, a deserted building. In the second kind, at least one of the parties would have serious doubts about the other's true intent, and insist the meeting occur at a location where civilians could get hurt if things turned ugly— the assumption being that neither group would risk that.

Someplace like Karl's K-4.

Less than a quarter mile past the station, Quinn turned onto a dirt road, pulled a U, and parked on the shoulder in front of the stop sign.

"The other Explorer's getting close to where their friends stopped," Orlando said, and then studied her screen for a moment. "They're stopping, too."

Quinn tapped his comm. "Nate, pull over."

"Copy."

Quinn checked his watch. It was eleven minutes until nine a.m. If Karl's K-4 wasn't the handoff location, then The Wolf and her people were going to be late.

"Nate, do you think you can close in some without being seen?" Quinn asked.

"Definitely."

"Do it."

"Copy."

Quinn looked at Orlando as he grabbed his door handle. "Keep me posted on any movements."

"Where are you going?" she asked.

"Where do you think?"

When he walked around the car a moment later, she glared at him through her closed window.

"Roll it down," he said. The glass remained where it was. "You want to hike to the gas station with me? If you can keep up, be my guest."

After a couple seconds, the window descended.

"I promise, after the baby, you can come with me every time."

He leaned through the window and kissed her.

"Try not to get shot," she said.

"My number one rule."

He'd apparently forgotten to turn off his mic, because Nate said, "See, I told you. You've got like a hundred number-one rules."

ORLANDO WATCHED QUINN run south along the shoulder of the highway. When she was sure he wouldn't turn around, she gave in to the pain of yet another false contraction. It was the second one she'd had that morning.

After it passed, she exited the car and moved around to the driver's seat.

"How about we have a nice, relaxing day," she said, rubbing her belly. "Mommy's got a little work to do."

ORBITS WAS CERTAIN The Wolf would have a manpower advantage, so he had to even the odds somehow. That meant stationing Parnell among the trees at the southwest corner of the lot where he could keep an eye on the road. Stafford and the girl were in the car, a mile north on the highway, waiting to be called in. Orbits was sitting at a window table in the café.

He checked his watch—8:56. *Almost.*

"Freshen up that coffee?" his waitress asked.

"Yes, please."

As she poured, she said, "Your omelet should be up in just a few minutes."

"Thank you." He had known when he ordered that there would be no time to eat. It was simply the rental price of the table.

As she walked away, he looked back out the window.

"Come on, come on, come on," he whispered. "Let's get this over with."

NATE STOPPED THE car the moment he caught sight of the two Explorers. Using his binoculars, he watched three of The Wolf's men cross the road and disappear into the field on the other side.

He radioed it in to Quinn.

"Can you follow unseen?" Quinn asked.

Nate studied the terrain. Running parallel to the highway on the other side was a brush-filled gully with trees lining the opposite bank.

"Shouldn't be a problem," Nate said.

"Do it."

Nate and Daeng retrieved their backpacks from the trunk.

As Nate was donning his, Ananke said, "Be a dear," and held out her weapon.

He slipped her SIG into his pack.

"Thanks, sweetie." She eyed both men as they finished getting ready. "Maybe after all of this is done, the three of us could go out and celebrate. We could have a lot of fun."

Putting on his most innocent voice, Nate said, "Great idea! We should include Quinn and Orlando."

She frowned. "Party killer."

THE WOLF SAT patiently in the backseat of the Explorer, Bianca beside her.

It would have been nice if Ricky Orbits had chosen a more cosmopolitan location. She much preferred cityscapes to open countryside like this. She figured he'd chosen it because he was familiar with the area, but no matter how well he knew it, it wasn't going to do him any good. She would have Danielle Hayes soon, and despite what Orbits might think, it would cost The Wolf nothing.

"Yeah, I'm here," her driver said into his ear-mounted radio. "Okay...got it." He twisted around and looked at The Wolf. "Point team reports visual confirmation of Orbits inside the café next door to the meeting point. There's also someone hiding in some trees nearby they presume is with him. The rest of the area appears clear."

"No sign of the girl?"

"No, ma'am."

She checked her watch—8:57. "Have them move into position to deal with the watcher, but not to engage until the meeting begins. Once you've done that, you can take us in."

"Yes, ma'am."

QUINN PAUSED AMONGST the trees at the north end of the gas station. He glanced at his watch. Two minutes until the meeting.

Needing to get closer, he sneaked to the back corner of the lot and scooted behind the long, rectangular garage.

"The SUV's on the move," Orlando reported.

"Nate, status," Quinn said as he continued down the back of the building.

No answer.

"Nate, status."

A mic click. Nate was there but couldn't talk.

"Do you need backup?"

Double click. *No.*

"Are you in position?"

A long pause, then a whispered, "Almost."

THE PARKING AREA for the café was only a hundred feet away when Nate's hand shot up, stopping his friends. Squatting down, he pointed ahead at the person he'd just seen. He motioned for them to stay where they were and began creeping forward.

The man was hiding in some trees, his gaze focused on the highway. As Nate's view of him improved, he saw that the guy fit the description of one those Quinn had seen with Orbits.

Nate was about to move in a little closer when he spotted two other men, twenty feet behind the first, these belonging to The Wolf.

He motioned for Daeng and Ananke to join him. Together, they watched The Wolf's duo move up another ten feet and stop.

Nate considered the options and then gestured to Daeng and Ananke what he wanted to do.

Ananke raised an eyebrow and grinned.

Quietly they moved forward, just settling into position when Quinn radioed to check their status.

AT 8:59 AND 56 seconds, a dark blue Ford Explorer pulled into the gas station.

Damn well better be her, Orbits thought.

He dropped a twenty-dollar bill on the table and got up, his omelet untouched.

38

ORBITS'S INSTRUCTIONS HAD been for The Wolf to park her vehicle on the north side of the gas station's main building, opposite the café, so her driver did exactly that.

After a moment, the man touched his headset and announced, "Mr. Orbits is leaving the café."

"Still alone?" The Wolf asked.

"Yes, ma'am."

"Bianca, be a darling and move into the front, if you don't mind."

"Of course."

Bianca switched to the front passenger seat, limping only slightly.

"He just reached the gas station," the driver reported.

QUINN LOOKED AROUND the southern end of the garage. From this new position, he could see the back of the café, but the gas station was hidden from view. He crept to the front corner where he had a view of both. What he didn't see, though, was the Explorer.

"Do you have a position on The Wolf?" Quinn asked Orlando.

"She's parked on the north side of the gas station."

The side he couldn't see. "Got it. Thanks."

He sneaked over to the main building, and moved along the back until he neared the north end. Crouching, he used his phone technique again to see the other side.

The Explorer was there, all right. He could even see the silhouettes of the people inside. They seemed to be just sitting there, doing nothing.

He was beginning to wonder if something had gone wrong when Orbits stepped around the front corner of the building.

THE SECOND THE Wolf saw Ricky Orbits, she said to her driver, "You can have the watcher dealt with now." She then pushed the button that rolled down her window and smiled. "Mr. Orbits. Good to see you. Why don't you join me?"

THE TWO-MAN team moved again.

When Nate was sure The Wolf's men were going to take down Orbits's guy, he, Daeng, and Ananke moved in behind them.

Orbits's man apparently sensed at the last moment that something was up, because he turned right before The Wolf's team got to him. A couple seconds earlier and maybe he could have escaped, but the best he could manage now was to get in a couple of hits before they subdued him.

He was barely on the ground when Nate, Daeng, and Ananke grabbed his attackers and rendered them unconscious.

They zip-tied everyone and gagged them with their own shirts.

"Three neutralized," Nate reported.

"Three?" Orlando said.

"One of the guys with Orbits and two with The Wolf."

"How did you….You know what? Never mind. Quinn's over at the gas station. The meeting's about to start. North side."

"Copy that."

ORBITS DIDN'T LIKE the idea of getting in the woman's car, but until he gave her the girl, he knew she wouldn't try anything.

He climbed into the backseat. In front, there was a man behind the wheel and a woman in the passenger seat, staring at him. She was a looker, the kind he might actually keep around for more than one night. She was sizing him up like he was a meal. It seemed as if at any moment she would start licking her lips. He kind of liked it.

"Pleasure to meet you in person," the woman beside him said, holding out her hand. "I'm The Wolf."

"Yeah, swell," he said, making a quick job of shaking. "How about we get the transfer done and get you your merchandise."

A chuckle. "You seem to forget the parameters of our agreement, Mr. Orbits. No money until I see the girl."

"And no girl until you at least free up the initial twenty-five million."

"Did it not go through?" she asked, feigning surprise. "Bianca, could you pass that bag back?"

The other woman, Bianca, handed The Wolf a thin, leather briefcase from which the Wolf removed a laptop. After she started it up, she spent a few moments navigating to where she wanted, and then said, "You're absolutely right. I am so sorry. I must have clicked the wrong box."

Right, he thought. *The wrong box.*

She tapped the keys a few more times and then turned the screen toward him. On it was the bank page for the escrow account with the initial payment. "My apologies again, but I've removed the hold so you can transfer it out at any time." She held the computer out to him. "You can use this if you'd like."

"I don't think so." He pulled out his phone and used it to initiate the transfer into his account. After he verified it was in process, he said, "Now, about the second twenty-five."

"For that, I will need to see the girl."

"Give me a moment."

As he reached for the door, she touched his arm.

"I'm sure you understand, but I must insist you remain here with me until I see her," she said.

Orbits turned, intending to tell her she could insist all she wanted but it wasn't going to happen, except the gun Bianca was pointing at him kept the words from leaving his mouth.

"All right, I get it. I can play it this way." He settled back in his seat. "I tell you, though, it would be easier if I'm not wondering if her finger might accidentally twitch."

With a nod from The Wolf, Bianca moved her weapon out of sight.

"Thanks," Orbits said, and then called Stafford. "Bring her in."

A SOFT CRUNCH. Dirt on asphalt.

Quinn whirled around to see one of The Wolf's men rushing at him. No way to stand up in time, he dove, hitting the man in the gut and knocking them both to the ground.

The guy shoved Quinn away and tried to push himself up, but Quinn got to his feet first and jammed a knee into the guy's head, sending the attacker back to the asphalt. Dropping onto him, Quinn slammed the butt of his palm into the side of the man's head. Two more slugs and the guy was out.

"Well done."

Quinn twisted around, ready to take on a new attacker, but found Nate, Daeng, and Ananke.

"Have I mentioned what a pleasure it is to watch you work?" Ananke whispered.

"Ananke, shut up," Nate whispered.

With Nate's and Daeng's help, Quinn moved the guy behind a Dumpster and secured him.

Three of The Wolf's men were now out of commission. The woman's team had been reduced to the guy driving her SUV and the motorcyclist. Orbits was in even worse shape. One man down had cut his team in half.

Quinn used his camera to check on the meeting. Nothing appeared to have changed—Orbits was still inside the SUV with The Wolf.

"Nate, Ananke, go around front and hold at the corner," Quinn said.

They headed off the long way around.

Quinn watched the phone's screen, knowing something had to happen soon. The wait ended two minutes later when a sedan turned off the highway and pulled into the spot next to the Explorer.

"Nate, do you have eyes on the sedan?" he asked.

"Yeah," Nate whispered.

"How many inside?"

"I can only see one. It's the guy who was driving the ambulance."

"No Dani?"

"I don't see...wait." A pause. "He's looking into the backseat area and talking. She must be there." Another beat. "The door to the Explorer is opening."

Quinn looked at his phone again, but the door in question was on the other side and he couldn't see much of anything.

"Orbits is getting out," Nate continued. "So is the driver of the sedan. They're talking...okay, Orbits is opening the back door. The Wolf is getting out now...she's looking into the sedan."

Quinn was starting to get frustrated about not having a direct line of sight, but then the front passenger door of the Explorer opened. The motorcyclist slipped out quietly and moved around the back of the SUV.

"Nate, be ready," Quinn said. "Daeng, follow me."

"HERE WE GO," Orbits said as Stafford pulled the sedan beside The Wolf's vehicle. He reached for the door but stopped and looked back, first at Bianca and then at The Wolf. "I'm going to get out. Don't shoot me."

The Wolf gestured at his door. "Please."

He exited and motioned for Stafford to do the same. Once the other man was out, he asked in a hushed voice, "Any problems?"

"All good," Stafford responded.

"Has Parnell seen anything?"

"I haven't heard from him."

No news was good news.

"Mr. Orbits? Is everything all right?" The Wolf called from inside the SUV.

"Just fine," he said.

He opened the sedan's back door. Danielle Chad lay across the rear seat, her head at the other end. Stafford had tied a cloth around her mouth so apparently it hadn't been *all* good.

"It's showtime, baby," he said. He looked back at the SUV. "If you want to see the merchandise, now's your chance."

After exiting her vehicle, The Wolf bent down and looked into the sedan.

"Well, well. Miss Hayes. It's been a long time."

Hayes? Orbits hadn't heard that name before, but it obviously meant something to the girl, because the defiance she'd been wearing as a second skin was showing cracks.

"Okay, you've seen her," he said. "Authorize the final payment and she's all yours."

The Wolf straightened back up. "Good idea. I'll need my

computer." She climbed back into the Explorer, but instead of grabbing her laptop, she shut the door.

STAYING LOW, QUINN and Daeng moved over to the SUV. Quinn gestured for his friend to remain near the front end, where Daeng could watch the driver, and then headed to the back. The motorcyclist stood at the other corner, gun in hand, peering at Orbits and The Wolf.

Quinn could hear the two talking on the other side, something about payment and computer. A moment later, the Explorer rocked slightly, followed by the door slamming shut.

Taking this as her cue, the motorcyclist moved around the corner toward Orbits.

ORBITS TWISTED AROUND to find a smiling Bianca pointing her gun at him.

His own weapon was still under his jacket. He might've been able to pull it out, but he'd never get a shot off. So he threw himself into the sedan on top of Danielle. From outside, he heard the spit of Bianca's weapon, the bullet sailing through the spot he'd been.

He grabbed his pistol but the barrel caught on his jacket. The weapon slipped from his hands and slid under the front seat. He felt around for it but couldn't find it.

Two more shots went off, one from Bianca's direction, the other coming from where Orbits had last seen Stafford.

Giving up on the gun, Orbits threw himself into the front seat as more shots were fired. When he started the engine, Stafford fell against the hood, his face covered with blood.

Son of a bitch!

Certain that Bianca was only a step away from putting a bullet in the back of his own head, Orbits shoved the car into reverse and slammed the gas pedal to the floor.

BEFORE QUINN COULD get to the other side, he heard two sound-suppressed gunshots. As he sneaked a look around the corner, he saw Orbits's other man pop up from the other side of the sedan and fire his weapon. The motorcyclist returned the favor, her aim a lot better than his.

Quinn rushed in behind her and placed his gun against her back. "Drop it."

She froze.

"Last warning."

As the pistol fell from her hand, the sedan shot backward, the open rear door smacking into the motorcyclist and shoving her against Quinn. Together they whacked into the Explorer and tumbled to the ground.

The woman tried to grab his gun but he was having none of it. So she spun around until she spotted her own weapon several feet away and dove for it. Her fingers had just touched the hilt when—

"Not a good idea," Nate said.

Nate's gun was pointed at the woman, while Ananke and Daeng had their weapons trained on two people still inside the SUV.

Quinn jumped up and yanked open the Explorer's back door.

"Out." He grabbed The Wolf's arm and jerked her out, then pressed his gun against the base of the driver's neck. "You, too."

The driver did not resist.

While Quinn picked up the dropped weapons, Nate and Ananke quickly patted down the driver and the women, confiscating a Glock 9mm from the man but finding nothing on the women. Daeng zip-tied their hands and ankles.

"Let's go," Quinn said, and climbed behind the wheel of the Explorer. He smiled at The Wolf. "Thanks for the ride."

When the others were inside, he whipped the Explorer backward and raced away from Karl's K-4.

"Nate, call the cops," he said. "Have them pick up The Wolf and her friends." He checked to make sure his comm mic was on. "Orlando, Orbits is heading your way."

No response.

"Orlando?"

39

ORLANDO STARED IN the direction of the unseen gas station, trying to visualize what was going on from the less than descriptive conversation coming over the comm. Something had gone down, that's for sure. It sounded like her friends had gotten the upper hand.

She was starting to think maybe it was all over and they could get back to their lives when she spotted a gray sedan heading north at an unusually fast speed. She watched it approach. It appeared to have only one occupant.

It wasn't until the car passed by that she was able to get a good look at the driver.

Ricky Orbits.

She started the car and pulled onto Highway 4, a couple hundred feet behind him.

FOR THE FIRST thirty seconds after Orbits sped away from Karl's K-4, he watched his rearview mirror more than he watched the road ahead. He was sure The Wolf's Explorer would be right on his tail, but so far, it didn't appear to have even left the station.

At some point, though, they would come. And this piece-of-crap sedan would never be able to outrun them. He needed a place to hide, somewhere they would never look.

The abandoned café they'd used the night before was coming up in a few miles, but it was right off the highway and seemed too exposed.

Hold on.

There was one place that only Orbits knew about, and it was definitely not just off the highway.

Feeling like he might have a chance, he continued north until he reached the unmarked dirt road.

———————

ORLANDO PICKED UP the call after the third ring.

"Nate?" she said, her voice coming out of the speaker.

"It's all of us," Nate told her.

"What happened back there?"

"Later," Quinn said. "Right now you need to keep an eye out for—"

"Orbits?" she asked.

Quinn paused. "Yeah."

"He buzzed by me a few minutes ago. I'm following him now."

That explained why her comm wasn't working. She'd driven out of range.

"Does he know you're behind him?" Quinn asked.

"I don't think so. He's flying down the road, but not any faster than when I first saw him. Please tell me that you got Danielle so I can back off."

"We didn't. He still has her."

She swore under her breath. "What happened?"

"It's complicated."

"What about The Wolf?"

"Left her and her people tied up at the gas station and called the cops. We've got her Explorer."

"You weren't kidding about complicated."

"Where are you?"

"We blew past Meriden about a minute ago," she said. "If we're lucky, the highway patrol will pull him over."

"That puts us about three minutes behind you. We'll try to—"

"Hold on, he's slowing," she said. "Dammit, I'm going to have to drive by him or he'll suspect something." She said nothing for a few seconds. "He's turning down a dirt road." She gave a quick description of where the road began. "Okay, he's out of sight. I'm going to double back."

"Just wait at the turnoff until we get there," Quinn said.

No response.

"Orlando?"

"She hung up," Nate said.

"Get her back."

Nate called her again but was sent straight to voice mail.

Quinn squeezed the steering wheel.

Dammit!

ORLANDO HEARD WHAT Quinn wanted her to do, but screw that. Who knew where the dirt road went? Orbits could be out of reach by the time the others reached her.

"Orlan—"

She turned her phone off and circled back to the turnoff for the dirt road. Orbits's sedan had kicked up a small cloud of dust obscuring much of her view, but if she was having a hard time seeing him, he'd have the same problem with her.

She turned across the highway and headed down the road.

Not quite a mile in, she came to a T-bone intersection. Once again, it was dust that gave Orbits away. She followed for at least another mile until the dirt cloud disappeared. Ahead, the road was empty.

Had Orbits hidden while she drove by? She twisted around as far as her body would allow, but she could see she was alone.

She backtracked to the point where she estimated his dust trail had ended, but there was nowhere for him to go. It was as if he had vanished.

She killed her engine and climbed out of the car. After a few seconds she heard a motor somewhere in the wilderness on the east side of the road.

She walked down the shoulder, trying to judge exactly where it was coming from. About thirty yards back, she spotted an opening in the brush, just wide enough for a car. On the ground were two wheel ruts, overgrown with grass, and nailed to old fence posts on either side, half hidden by the brush, were faded NO TRESPASSING signs.

She had no idea what could be back there, but Orbits must have known. He'd headed directly here.

She hurried back to her car.

ORBITS PARKED IN the same spot he had the night before. It was different here in the daylight, not quite as eerie.

He opened the back door and felt around under the front seat until he found his gun. After he put it back in his holster, he cut the ties holding the girl's feet together and pulled her out. "Recognize this place?"

If she did, she showed no sign of it.

Grabbing her arm, he said, "This way," and pushed her into the woods.

After a few minutes of walking, they came to the barbed-wire fence.

"Sit," Orbits commanded her.

Once she was down, Orbits looked around until he found a

couple of suitable branches of similar size and used them to separate two of the wire strands, creating a hole wide enough to duck through. As soon as he was sure the braces would hold, he made the girl go through first before following.

When they had reached the door in the middle of the clearing, the girl looked at it with a sort of awe, which made him think maybe this *was* her first time here.

He moved her over to where the tumblers were, pushed her to her knees, and flipped open the Plexiglas lid. "Open it," he said.

Through her gag, she said, "Go to hell."

"We don't have time to mess around. Open it!"

She stared at him, unmoving.

He pulled his gun out and placed it against the side of her head. "You either put in the combination or I pull the trigger. That's a promise."

When she didn't respond, he fired a bullet into the ground next to her leg and then aimed the gun at her head again. "Open it now."

DANI AND MARIANNE had never discussed this possibility. The assumption was that the location would never be found. That was their job, to keep it out of the hands of others.

She remembered once asking Marianne why they couldn't just forget where it was and have it be forever lost? But she already knew the answer. The promise they'd made in memory of their mother and to each other. The promise to, if not balance the scales, then tip them a little bit in that direction. It was their duty, their familial penance.

If her captor were not alone, she would have chosen death rather than let him inside, knowing she wouldn't have a chance of escape. But no one else was here and the man was clearly agitated. He'd likely make mistakes she could take advantage of.

Live, Marianne whispered. *Finish our work.*

Dani leaned over the tumblers and, with her hands still tied, turned them one by one until she'd input the full combination.

From below the steel rose a soft hum.

Dani jumped back as the hydraulic hinges began lifting the door open.

"Nice!" the man shouted.

When the door was out of the way, he and Dani looked in. A set of footholds were cut into the concrete wall below the door, running down like a ladder to a wide landing about eight feet down. On the left side of the landing was a door.

"What's down there?" the man asked.

Dani said nothing.

"There's gotta be some lights."

She pointed at a junction box that could be accessed once they were on the landing.

"You sure?"

She shrugged.

Hell, yes, she was sure. Though she had never been here, she knew every inch of this place. Marianne had drilled it into her.

He studied the inside for a moment longer, and then said, "Here's how we're going to do this. I go first, but you come right after me. I'll be holding on to you, so don't even think about trying anything."

A hand around her ankle, he lowered himself through the opening until only his upper body was still outside.

"Now you," he said, giving her a yank.

She moved her leg through the opening until her foot found the uppermost cutout.

The man switched his hand from her ankle to the waist of her pants and gave it a tug. "Other leg." When both her feet were on the cutout, he said, "How do we close this thing?"

She made a sound to remind him she still had a gag in her mouth. The man reached up, untied the cloth, and let it drop to the landing.

"Controls are there," she said, pointing at three gray buttons just below the lip where the door would nestle.

He reached toward them.

"Wait," she said. "It's been a while since it was last opened. The door can come down pretty quick." She didn't know if the last was true or not, but an idea had begun to grow in her mind, and for it to work she needed to be the one who pushed the button. "Unless you want to get knocked the rest of the way down, we should get below door level first."

He pondered this for a moment before saying, "Fine. Let's move it."

Once Dani's head was lower than the door frame, she pushed the middle button, hoping she was remembering correctly.

The first to open. The second to close. The third to lock.

The third would turn the dials back to zero, and the combination would have to be entered again into the matching set of tumblers on the underside of the door, increasing the time it would take the exit to open again. She didn't want that.

Her plan was to sneak away when he was preoccupied and escape out the top. After she shut the metal door again, that's when she would scramble the tumblers and lock him inside. Wait a month and he'd be dead for sure. She could then return and do the work she'd come back to the States to do.

As the door swung down above her, she shot a quick glance at the tumblers to make sure they hadn't reset to 1. With relief, she saw the combo was still in place.

"Hurry up," the man said, pulling on her belt loop.

She continued down.

THE ROAD WAS so rough at times that Orlando was sure, despite her condition, she could have walked it faster. Though she tried avoiding the worst of it, the bumps and dips still banged at the undercarriage, threatening to rip the axles off. It became so bad that she had to focus all her attention on the tire ruts immediately in front of her, and didn't notice Orbits's car until it was right in front of her.

She slammed on the brakes, ready to throw the car into reverse, but the other vehicle appeared empty and a scan revealed no one standing around. She retrieved her gun and stuffed an extra mag in her pocket before climbing out. In her head, she could hear Quinn telling her to stay in the car, but she knew the others might not arrive in time to help Dani.

Keeping an eye on the woods in case Orbits was still around, she moved over to his car and double-checked inside. It was empty.

A quick search of the area revealed fresh tracks leading to the northeast along what was left of the road. Orlando followed them to a barbed-wire fence, where a couple pieces of wood had been braced between two strands, creating a pass-through. She eased her way between them, and congratulated herself when she reached the other side without cutting herself or falling on her butt.

Her celebration was short lived, however, as she was hit with another false contraction. This one was the most intense so far. About the only good thing was that it didn't last too long, and soon she was moving again. The trail continued through the trees to the edge of a meadow.

She stopped and looked around. Unless Orbits and Dani were lying in the grass, they weren't in the meadow. She did see something odd. In the center, near two blocks of concrete that peeked up above the grass, was a pile of dirt that looked dark and rich, like it had recently been turned.

She stepped out from the protection of the trees and cautiously approached the pile. What she found was certainly not what she'd expected. A metal door lay between a concrete frame, the dirt clearly having covered it until very recently. She was able to lift it about half an inch, but it was too heavy to move any further.

Clearly it was unlocked, but it must have some sort of assist mechanism to get it open.

Maybe she needed to reenter the combination to trigger the opening mechanism.

After smoothing out part of the dirt pile, she wrote in it the numbers showing on the tumblers and then turned the dials, mixing them up. When she was done, she reinput the sequence.

When she input the final number, she heard something hum inside.

"THAT'S GOTTA BE wrong," Quinn said.

"No," Nate told him. He was looking at the phone locator app on his cell. Even though Orlando's phone was off, she hadn't pulled her SIM card and they could still track it. Nate pointed out the window. "She went right through there and is about a half mile back."

"Is it just me," Ananke said, leaning over Daeng so she could see out his window, "or does that look like a road someone would take at the beginning of a bad horror film?"

Quinn didn't like the looks of it, either. Orlando should have waited for them.

He switched the Explorer into four-wheel drive and turned down the road.

"Do you hear them?" Ananke asked.

"Hear who?" Daeng said.

"Everyone in the theater yelling, 'Don't go that way! Don't go that way!'"

Quinn pushed the SUV, not worrying about what damage he might be doing to the suspension. Even then, the going was slow, and it took nearly five minutes before Orlando's sedan came into sight.

"There's another car in front of hers," Nate said. "Looks like Orbits's."

The Explorer skidded to a stop. Quinn jumped out, gun drawn, and rushed over to Orlando's car.

Empty.

He circled the sedan, looking for any signs of struggle or gunfire, but there were none.

Orbits's vehicle was also deserted.

"I've got tracks over here," Daeng yelled. He had moved down the road beyond the two cars.

They all converged on his location.

Nate looked at his cell. "That's the direction her phone's in, too."

Without a word, they headed deeper into the woods.

40

THE SPIRAL STAIRS had walls on both sides, preventing Orbits from getting any sense of what they had entered.

An old mine? Was there anything to dig for in this part of Kansas? He didn't know. The last time he'd been in the state was on a road trip with his parents when he was thirteen. All he remembered from back then was that the place seemed like one giant farm.

"This had better open up into something," he said.

Walking a few steps in front of him, the girl remained silent.

Round and round they went, each section looking exactly like the last. At one point he heard a faint noise coming from behind them. He'd made Danielle stop while he listened, but after several seconds of quiet, he told her to get moving again.

Finally, the stairs ended at another landing. It, too, had a door, though this one was on the wall they'd been circling.

As Danielle reached for the handle, Orbits said, "Wait." He grabbed the back of her shirt. "Okay, open it. *Slowly*."

The door opened inward, so Danielle had to step over the threshold as she pushed it. Orbits dashed in behind her.

"Where's the lights?" he asked.

Except for the light spilling in from the stairwell, the space was dark.

Danielle stepped over to a box on the wall near the door, identical to the one on the upper landing, and flipped on the switches inside.

For a moment, nothing happened. Then high above them a vapor light flickered to life, and then another and another and another. It took several seconds for them to come to full strength, but even before they reached that point, Orbits could see he and the girl were inside a giant tube, with pipes and steel grating hugging the sides all the way up. The entire floor was clear, though there were scars in the concrete where things had been anchored. Equipment, perhaps?

He almost asked what the hell this place was when it dawned on him.

Frowning, he said, "This is what all the fuss is about? Some damn empty missile silo? I got news for you. You can buy one of these off the Internet for a couple hundred grand. Why would someone want to pay fifty million so you could guide them here?"

FOR A FEW seconds, Dani forgot she'd been brought here against her will. She stared upward into the vast space above them as the lights came on, hardly believing she was finally seeing it with her own eyes.

There, just like Marianne had described them, were the gantries that would be lowered when a missile was in place for technicians to work on. Next to them, the conduits that carried the wires controlling the concrete doors at the very top, now buried under several feet of dirt. Off to the right, near the floor, was the hatch covering the service tunnel. And there, straight ahead, was the unassuming door behind which was her father's unwanted legacy.

When her captor started talking, reality came crashing back.

"Why would someone want to pay fifty million so you could guide them here?"

She'd been so conditioned to protect the secret that her arm felt like it weighed a ton as she lifted it and pointed at the door across the room.

The man's gaze followed the motion. "Yeah? So? It's a door. What about it?"

Her throat had never felt so dry, and she was sure she wouldn't be able to answer, but her only hope lay in getting him into the other side of the facility. She swallowed. "It's what you came for," she said, forcing out the words.

He grimaced, his expression turning annoyed. "And what exactly would that be?"

"It's easier if…if I show you."

She started toward the door, hoping he would follow. After a brief hesitation, he did.

KNOWING THAT BEING underground would interfere with the ability to track her phone, Orlando set her cell on top of one of the concrete blocks and climbed down the hole, leaving the door open. Descending the built-in ladder was not fun. If there were any more like it, she wouldn't be going far. At least the baby hadn't taken that moment to remind her it was almost time.

On the other side of the landing door, she found a spiral staircase.

Okay, she thought. *This, I can do.*

As she moved downward, she detected the echo of footsteps ahead. How far away was hard to tell. It wasn't long before they went silent.

Around a hundred steps down, she stopped for a breather.

Quinn's voice in her head was even louder now, repeatedly telling her this was a bad idea.

Bad or not, she wasn't going to turn around now. She just prayed there was an elevator she could take back to the top.

ORBITS ONCE MORE made Danielle open the door.

A hallway, circular like a pipe, but made from corrugated metal. More a drainage pipe than sewer, Orbits thought.

About thirty feet in, it bent to the left. After they rounded it, they walked about the same distance before coming to another door.

"This had better be it," he said, his patience all but gone.

Without looking back at him, she said, "It is."

Danielle opened the door and turned on the lights.

"There are three more floors like this," she said.

The room was full of stacked wooden crates of varying sizes, all in tidy rows.

"What do we have here?" he asked.

"See for yourself."

He walked over to a stack of boxes that were three times as long as they were thick.

"How am I supposed to open this?" he asked.

"I have no idea," Danielle.

He considered it for a moment longer, and then said, "Screw it."

It took two shoves to move it far enough for gravity to send it crashing to the floor. Though the top didn't come all the way off, it ripped from two of the sides, creating a gap through which he could see the barrel end of a rifle. He worked the weapon out the hole.

An M16A2. Not the latest version but still an excellent model. This one had been prepped for long-term storage and clearly never used. He examined it, liking the feel of it in his hands. His gaze drifted to the boxes nearest him.

"All these contain weapons?" he asked, and looked over at Danielle.

Only she wasn't there.

———

QUINN REACHED THE meadow first and spotted the rectangular metal plate standing on end. When the others joined him, they spread out to approach it in a widely spaced line in case of ambush.

The plate turned out to be a door that had covered a hole in the ground. Quinn scanned the interior and saw it was empty.

"Orlando's phone," Nate said, picking it up off a concrete block. "At least she wanted us to find her."

Ananke peeked into the hole. "I hate to repeat myself but *horror film*."

Quinn lowered himself over the edge.

"Am I the only one who remembers what we found the last time we went below ground?" she asked.

"Stay up there if you want," he said as he reached the landing. "We need someone to watch the entrance anyway."

"Oh, no," she said. "I don't want that responsibility. I'm going with you."

As she moved onto the ladder, Daeng said, "I'll stay."

Once Ananke was out of the way, Nate came down.

"Cover the door," Quinn told them.

Moving as far to the side as he could, he opened the door on the landing.

"Clear," Nate whispered.

They headed down the spiral staircase, moving as quickly as they dared. Just shy of the hundred and fiftieth step, they heard a distant, muffled gunshot.

———

WHILE ORBITS PUSHED on the wooden crate, Dani inched toward the still-open door. She made her escape when the box started to fall.

Holding her cuffed hands high so she could run as fast as possible, she raced down the tunnel. If she could make it across the silo and into the stairwell, he probably wouldn't be able to catch her before she exited the top and locked him inside.

She was almost to the silo entrance when she heard Orbits enter the other end of the hall. She looked back, but he was still out of sight around the bend.

As she twisted forward and reached for the door handle, she realized it was already moving on its own.

ORLANDO KNEW WHAT kind of place she was in before she even passed through the door at the bottom of the stairs.

Kansas countryside. A massively fortified underground facility. It had Cold War missile-launch facility written all over it.

Walking into the empty silo confirmed it.

As she leaned against the wall and caught her breath again, she took a look around. Directly across from the stairwell was the only other door. She would have liked to rest there for a little while longer, but knew there was no time to waste. She pushed herself off the wall and headed across the room.

She felt a twinge of discomfort as she neared the door, and paused for a moment. When it didn't get worse, she grabbed the handle and pulled the door open.

Less than three feet away, and coming at her fast, was Dani, eyes wide.

Orlando barely had time to turn her head before the woman knocked into her.

Orlando staggered backward, smarting from Dani's shoulder connecting with her cheek. The collision had knocked Dani off balance and sent her down to a knee.

"That's far enough!" Orbits yelled from beyond the door.

Dani shot a look at the open door, and then sprang to her feet and ran toward the stairwell entrance.

A bullet ripped out from the hallway, missing Orlando by a few feet. She ducked to the side and pressed herself against the wall next to the door. Three more shots, growing louder and louder, the man's suppressor losing its effectiveness.

Across the room, Dani had nearly reached the other door when one of the bullets smacked into the door frame. The girl dropped to the floor and skittered out of Orbits's direct line of sight. Another shot boomed, this time the bullet piercing the stairwell door itself.

As the sound of the shot subsided, Orlando could hear Orbits running down the hallway toward them. Without looking, she pointed her gun around the opening and let off three quick shots.

Orbits fired again, his bullet hitting the jamb, inches from her muzzle. She shot twice more and then moved her gun back.

She glanced over to check on Dani. The girl was moving along the wall, heading away from the stairwell door. Orlando heard a soft scrape from the hallway, closer than before, Orbits trying to sneak up. She sent another shot inside and heard him scurry backward.

She was about to shoot again when she grabbed her belly.

Oh, crap. Not now.

The cramp threatened to bring her to her knees, but she pressed against the wall and willed herself to remain standing. She looked back at Dani and saw that she was pulling at something embedded into the concrete.

Doing her best to ignore her pain, Orlando sent another shot into the hall. When she glanced back across the room, Dani had disappeared.

BY THE TIME Dani saw the woman, it was too late to stop. She crashed into her and stumbled to the ground. But hearing Orbits's voice was all she needed to push back to her feet.

She sprinted across the silo, her eyes locked on the door to the stairwell.

When the first bullet flew past her, she looked back, thinking the woman had tried to shoot her. But instead, the woman was firing *into* the hallway to keep Orbits back.

Several more bullets sailed into the silo. She'd almost reached the door when one ripped into the frame less than a foot from her head. As she dove for the floor and moved to the side, another bullet punched into the door.

Orbits had the stairwell entrance covered. There was no way she was getting out.

She huddled next to the wall, frozen by panic.

Remember, Marianne whispered. *Remember.*

Dani almost said out loud, "Remember what?" Then she realized she knew what her sister meant.

The details.

The sequence to open the top hatch. The exact number of spiral steps to the silo floor. The metal-lined tunnel to the storage area. The four floors packed with weapons procured by their illegal-arms-dealing father. The four special items contained in the secret level below the others, where also waited the true treasure, the one she had come to retrieve.

There were other details. Lights and wiring and plumbing and…

The service tunnel.

She had noted its entrance when she initially entered the silo, but had thought no more of it. Until now.

It was her only chance.

After jumping to her feet, she ran along the wall, bent at the waist. When she finally reached the hatch, she knelt down and pulled up on the long lever that would unlock it. For a moment, it seemed stuck in place, but it finally gave way and the hatch swung open.

She climbed in and took one last look back. The woman was shooting into the hall again. For the first time, Dani sensed something odd about her beyond the fact she was there in the first place, but there was no time to think about it.

She closed herself in and began crawling through the darkness.

ORLANDO MOVED BACKWARD through the silo, toward the spot where Dani disappeared. Twice, she fired at the hallway, the angle only allowing the bullets to hit the wall a few feet in.

When she reached the metal plate, she sent off two more shots, one making it through the doorway, and the other hitting the wall right outside it.

She saw now that Dani had been pulling on a long handle mounted to a hatch. She moved the handle up and yanked the hatch open. On the other side was a dark tunnel, large enough for a person, but only if on all fours.

She fired off the remaining bullets in her mag and then moved into the tunnel, closing the hatch behind her.

Using her penlight, she looked for a way to lock the door but found none.

After replacing the empty magazine in her pistol, she shone the light down the tunnel. No sign of Dani, but there was only one way she could have gone. With her belly just an inch above the floor, Orlando began to crawl.

WHO THE HELL *is out there?* Orbits wondered.

It couldn't be The Wolf's people. She would have needed to be right behind him all the way from the gas station, and he knew for a fact that had not been the case.

It also wasn't Danielle. He'd seen her running across the silo just a moment before another bullet had flown his way, and besides, the way the shots were angled, the shooter had to be somewhere outside to his left.

The first time he tried to get in closer, he was forced to retreat by a shot that had almost clipped his shoulder. When the shooting died down, he tried again.

He heard two more shots, but held his ground as one of the bullets hit the right wall three feet from the door, and the other seemed to have missed the hallway completely.

He was about to move all the way to the opening when several shots rang out. He pressed himself to the floor, wanting the shooter to pull his trigger again so Orbits could get a better idea of the person's location.

Ten seconds passed. Twenty. Thirty.

Maybe the asshole needs a nudge.

Orbits aimed as far left as he could and fired into the room.

There was no return shot.

He slid along the wall until he was right at the door, and fired again.

Still nothing.

He peeked into the silo.

No Danielle. No shooter.

He'd had a view of the stairwell door the whole time, so how was that even possible?

As he stepped through the doorway to take a better look, he heard the pounding of feet approaching the stairwell door from the other side. He jumped back and pulled the hallway door shut just as the other one opened.

For a moment, he panicked.

But then he remembered. He had a whole arsenal at the other end of the hall.

QUINN YANKED OPEN the door at the bottom of the stairs just as the only other door in the room beyond slammed shut with a loud *thunk*. He took a second to scan his new surroundings before sprinting across the circular room toward the other exit.

Pressing himself against the wall, he cracked the door open an inch. Someone was running but the steps were distant. Quinn motioned for Nate and Ananke to cover the door, and then he pushed it all the way open.

The moment Nate whispered, "Clear," Quinn swung around the jamb and raced into what turned out to be a tunnel, his friends following. There was another *thunk* from farther down. They ran around a bend and down to the door at the far end. Once more, Nate and Ananke covered it while Quinn pulled on the handle, but it didn't move.

"It's jammed," he said. "Give me a hand."

Nate grabbed the handle and pulled with Quinn. It wouldn't move at first, but then there was a pop from the other side and the handle gave way. Nate stepped back as Quinn pushed the door open.

The room on the other side appeared to be a storage area. Wooden crates were stacked in rows on either side of the door. More were straight ahead on the other side of a central aisle. No one in sight, though.

Quinn and Nate crept out, each sticking close to one of the rows. With each step they could see more of the room.

"All clear that way," Nate whispered when they reached the end.

Though Quinn didn't see anyone in the direction he was looking, either, something did catch his attention. "Cover me," he said.

He moved into the central aisle and over to a crate that had fallen on the floor and broken open. He pulled one of the sides back.

Rifles.

M16s.

Nearby were other crates, exactly the same size. More rifles, he assumed. Several of the stacks were identical.

From deeper in the room came a crash.

THE GIRL HAD said there were three other floors just like this one. If Orbits could get to one of them, he'd have more time to search for additional weapons.

He found the way up at the other end of the room. A freight elevator, more than large enough to carry multiple crates between levels. As he took a step toward it, he heard a voice coming from back toward the tunnel and realized his pursuers were already in the room.

Hoping to slow them down, he rocked a stack of boxes back and forth until they tumbled into the aisle and blocked the way. He ran into the elevator and pulled down the vertical door.

Looking at the controls, he saw he was on level one, and that the other three levels were above him. There was also a fifth button off to the side with no markings, just a slot for a key next to it.

He pushed the button for level four, and the elevator began moving. When he arrived, he looked for the emergency stop button to keep the car there but the panel didn't have one. It wasn't all bad, though. When the car started moving again, it would alert him that trouble was on the way.

He ran out of the elevator and headed out among the boxes.

A GENTLE BREEZE blew across the meadow but did little to dampen the morning heat. Daeng had been born in a part of the world where it was hot year round and he was used to sweating, but he wasn't stupid enough to stay in direct sunlight. Which was why he was sitting in the shade created by the open metal door when he heard the distant sound of a car in the woods.

He stood up and turned his head toward the noise, but after only a few seconds, the motor cut out. He was able to determine it had come from the same direction in which they had arrived. He sprinted across the meadow to the woods and crept between the trees, slipping between the strains of the barbed-wire fence and sneaking up on the spot where the cars had been left.

A small sedan had joined the three vehicles already there. He moved around until he could get a good look at it and saw it was empty. He studied the area for movement, but saw nothing. The new arrivals could have gone to only one place.

Moving quickly but without making noise, he retraced his path to the meadow. He was still a dozen feet from the edge of the trees when he spotted three people at the hatch. No, four, he realized, catching sight of a woman's head right before she disappeared into the bunker. Two men followed her down. When the final person—a woman—followed, she turned just enough for him to see her face.

The Wolf.

There was no time to worry about how they had gotten free.

He raced across the meadow toward the hatch.

41

I T WAS AS if the departure of the SUV from Karl's K-4 was some kind of signal, because all of a sudden people began running from the gas station, and the cars that had been at the pumps raced away.

"Somebody get these things off me!" The Wolf yelled, holding up her bound hands.

Bianca rolled over to the man she'd killed when Orbits got away. Though the others had taken his gun, they hadn't patted him down. Like most competent field agents, he was carrying a knife. After Bianca cut the zip-ties from the hands and ankles of The Wolf and the driver, The Wolf told the man to find them a ride and then freed her hunter.

Rubbing her wrists, Bianca said, "Well, that didn't go as planned."

The Wolf shot her a look. "You should have killed them."

"The day's not over yet."

Something banged over and over from behind the building. Bianca motioned for her boss to stay where she was before moving around the back corner to check it out. When she returned, she had one of The Wolf's other men with her.

"Where the hell have you been?" The Wolf demanded.

Bianca said, "He was tied up behind a Dumpster."

"How did that—" The Wolf stopped mid-question as the driver raced up in a small sedan.

Once they were on the highway, The Wolf pulled out her phone. When the tech answered, she described the car Orbits had been using and said, "Find it!"

Two minutes passed before he called back. "Got him on satellite. He headed off the highway and disappeared into some woods."

Following the directions he gave them, they made it to the little used road and found not only Orbits's sedan, but The Wolf's Explorer *and* a third vehicle. Five minutes later they reached the meadow. When The Wolf saw the rectangular object sticking up near the middle, she started to get a bad feeling. And when they looked down into the hole and saw the space below, she knew her instinct had been right.

That damn Ricky Orbits had gotten Danielle to tell him where the goods were located. The bastard had probably planned to hand the girl over and then empty the place of the weapons that rightfully belonged to her. She admired his audacity and vowed to tell him that right before she had him killed.

"What do you want to do?" the driver asked.

"What do you mean, what do I want to do? We go down."

THE CRAMPED TUNNEL was *not* designed with pregnant women in mind, Orlando concluded. It was hard enough crawling on her hands and knees, but when she came to a ninety-degree turn, she almost gave up. Forcing herself to continue, she squeezed around the corner and shined her light ahead. At the farthest reaches of her light, she caught sight of Dani's shoes as the girl rushed away.

"Wait!" Orlando said. "I'm not going to hurt you. I'm here to help."

Dani didn't stop.

Groaning in frustration, Orlando yelled, "Come on, Dani! Please. I'm Quinn's partner! My name's Orlando. You might've heard him talk—"

QUINN'S PARTNER?

Dani stopped crawling and called back, "You're lying."

"I'm not. We were trying to rescue you at the gas station."

Dani had heard Quinn's voice when the handoff went awry, and had even hoped he would get her out.

"If you're his partner, you're something else, too," she said, remembering the conversations she'd overheard.

"You mean girlfriend? Yeah, that, too." The woman paused, breathing deeply. "If I was here to hurt you, wouldn't I have been shooting at you instead of at that jerk who took you?"

"People don't want to hurt me. They want what I have."

"Yeah, I have a feeling the cat's out of the bag on that one. I mean, this place, right? It's your big secret."

Dani held her tongue. The silo was only *part* of the secret.

Beyond the light, Orlando groaned.

"Are you okay?" Dani asked. "Did you get shot?"

"What? No, um, just…give me a moment."

Dani thought she heard another groan, but it was very low.

"How much farther does this thing go?" Orlando asked a few seconds later.

Dani hesitated. "I'm not exactly sure. Not too far, I think. There should be another exit up here."

"Into what?"

"One of the storage levels."

"Will you wait for me?" Orlando asked. "Please."

Dani chewed the inside of her lip, not knowing if that was a good idea or not, but in the end said, "Okay."

The woman's light began moving again. Soon Dani could see

the woman behind it. That's when she realized why she'd noted something odd about Orlando earlier.

"You're pregnant," she said, as if Orlando might not be aware of it.

"Not for much longer."

Dani's eyes widened. "What does that mean?"

"Nothing you need to worry about." She nodded at Dani's hands. "Here, let me cut those off you."

QUINN, NATE, AND Ananke climbed over the fallen boxes and reached the elevator just as the motor switched off. Nate was able to work the door open and take a peek up the shaft.

"Looks like it's three floors up," he said.

"Anyone spot a stairwell on our way here?" Quinn asked.

Nate and Ananke shook their heads.

"We could crawl up the shaft," Nate suggested. "There are plenty of things in there we can use for handholds. The only problem is, we wouldn't be able to get around the bottom of the car."

"Not if all three of us go," Quinn said. "But if two of us climb up onto the floor below him, and whoever stays down here calls the elevator, we climb up once it passes us." He looked at Ananke. "You know him. You should come with me."

"I'd really rather not," she said, a sour look on her face.

Quinn stared at her.

After a moment, she closed her eyes and let out a disgusted huff. "All right, I'll go. But I won't be held responsible if I accidentally shoot him."

"Our number one priorities are Dani and Orlando," Quinn said. "If he's standing in our way, I'm not going to question anything."

"That sounds fair to me," she said.

Nate lifted the door and held it open while Quinn and Ananke transitioned into the shaft. There appeared to be one floor beneath them and at least the three above. As Nate had promised, they had plenty of things to grab on to, and in less than a minute, they were prying open the door for the level right below the elevator car.

When they were out of the shaft, Quinn waved to Nate.

THE WOLF AND her people had already exited the upper landing when Daeng reached the entrance. He climbed down and eased into the stairwell.

Staying tight to the inner wall, he moved along the steps until the man at the very back came into sight. Daeng allowed himself a brief smile. They had strung out in a line just like he'd hoped they would.

Once he'd moved in right behind the last man, he placed the end of his suppressor against the guy's head and wrapped an arm around his neck, stopping him in his tracks.

"One word and I pull the trigger," Daeng whispered into the man's ear.

The man stayed quiet.

As the others continued walking away, Daeng squeezed his arm tight. As soon as the man lost consciousness, Daeng laid him on the steps, secured his hands and feet, and continued his pursuit.

Next in line was the other man, only things didn't go quite as smoothly. Daeng was able to quietly grab him, but while he was cutting off the blood flow to the man's brain, the guy began to struggle and his feet scraped loudly on the steps.

Before Daeng could finish the job, the blonde woman came back up the steps far enough to see what was going on. Daeng aimed his gun at her, but she ran out of sight before he could pull the trigger. He laid the man on the steps and secured him, then went after her, already several seconds behind.

Ahead, he could hear the two women taking the stairs, their pace as fast as his. Then came the sound of a door opening and all went quiet.

He hit the bottom landing and shoved open the door as the women were passing through another doorway on the far side of the room beyond.

Not stopping, Daeng touched his comm. "Daeng for Quinn." Nothing.

"Daeng for Nate, for anyone, can you hear me?"

"Daeng?" Nate said. "Where...ou?"

"The Wolf's back. I took out two of her men, but she and that other—"

"Can't hear...what...you..."

"Hostiles," Daeng said. "The Wolf and the blonde woman. I've followed them down."

He reached the door and pulled it open. There was a tunnel on the other side, but no sign of the women.

"I...catch..."

Daeng repeated what he'd said, but if Nate responded, he didn't hear it.

He took the bend in the tunnel at full speed. That turned out to be a mistake.

The blonde was waiting against the wall on the other side, and launched at him. They slammed against the corrugated siding, Daeng's gun flying out of his hand. As they slid down the curved surface, she punched him in the ribs twice and jammed her knee into his hip.

Daeng rolled when they hit bottom and pulled her under him. At the edge of his vision he spotted his gun on the floor by her head. He grabbed for it, but before he could reach it she shoved him in the chest, throwing him onto the floor beside her.

In a mad scramble they both lunged for the gun. The woman got there first, but as she wrapped her fingers around the grip, Daeng grabbed the barrel and twisted the weapon until it popped out of both of their hands.

He dove after it. His hand was only a few inches from the gun when the woman kicked it out from under him, sending it sailing down the tunnel, straight at The Wolf.

Realizing he'd never get it now, Daeng knocked his attacker to the side, jumped to his feet, and ran. He'd just rounded the bend when he heard the *thup* of his gun and the smack of the bullet hitting the wall behind him.

He sprinted out of the tunnel and slammed the door shut.

"Daeng for Nate or Quinn," he said.

No response.

"Can anyone hear me?"

Nothing.

"If you can hear me, The Wolf's inside, and she's armed!"

THE ELEVATOR MOTOR whined to life a moment before the car began to descend.

Though Orbits had been expecting it, he would have liked a little more time. So far he'd found crates of riflescopes, combat knives, and flare cartridges but no flare guns.

He scanned for boxes that looked like they might contain something with more firepower than his pistol. Near the back of the room, he spotted a stack of small boxes marked 5.56 x 45mm.

M16 ammo.

He cursed at himself for not taking one of the rifles from downstairs, but then, just beyond the bullets, he saw a stack of long boxes exactly like the ones the rifles had been in. He smiled.

Please let me be lucky.

QUINN WATCHED THE elevator pass level three, and then nodded at Ananke.

They climbed up to either side of the shaft until they were in position beside the entrance to level four. Quinn grabbed the lip of the door and pushed it up a few inches so Ananke could take a look at the other side.

"Clear," she mouthed.

He pushed it up until it was wide enough for her to pass through. She then held it in place for him and quietly closed it again.

They heard grunts off to the left, followed by a crash on the floor. Using the stacks as cover, they moved closer.

The groan of a nail being pulled out of wood told Quinn Orbits was trying to open a box. After a moment, there was the *pop* of a board breaking. Some shuffling around, and then—

"Dammit!" Orbits yelled.

Quinn crept to the very edge of a stack, no more than twenty feet from Orbits, and peeked around the corner. Orbits threw a piece of wood on the ground and cursed again. As he was turning, his gaze fell on Quinn.

"Oh, shit!" he said, and dropped out of sight.

Quinn said, "No one needs to get hurt. We just want—"

A bullet whacked into the crate right in front of him.

"You don't want to do that," Quinn yelled. "You'll never win a shooting match. We've got you outnumbered."

"IS THAT RIGHT?" Orbits replied. "Well, the box full of M16s I have here says differently."

If only that were true. The box Orbits had thought held more rifles turned out to contain a disassembled grenade launcher. And, in keeping with his string of luck, there were no grenades.

"Just give us the women," the man said. "There's no reason for them to be in the middle of this."

Women? Was there someone around other than Danielle? Screw it. The only important thing at that moment was getting out alive.

"I don't care what you want. Unless you leave right now, the only thing you'll get from me is death."

"Dear God. Did you really just say that?"

Orbits's brow furrowed. It hadn't been the man who'd spoken, but an annoyed-sounding woman. A very *familiar* annoyed-sounding woman.

"Ricky, you stupid son of a bitch, get the hell out here. Now!"

"Kitty-kat?"

AS THE ELEVATOR descended, Nate tried reaching Daeng again. He'd caught enough of his friend's message to know something was wrong, but had been unable to discern anything else.

"Nate for Daeng," he said again.

The radio remained silent.

Behind him, the elevator came to a stop.

"Daeng, are you there?"

He heard a low thunk, not from the radio but from the other end of the room.

Pulling out his gun, he stepped lightly over to the crates lining the walkway to the elevator. He moved up to the central aisle.

The room was quiet so he moved around the corner and crept over to the pile of boxes Orbits had created. Using a gap in the debris, he looked toward the other end of the room. Though he didn't see anything unusual, his senses told him something was wrong. He stared down the aisle, waiting. Half a minute later, his patience paid off.

First the motorcyclist and then The Wolf appeared around the crates near the tunnel entrance. Every few seconds they glanced back the way they'd come, as if expecting someone else to join them. Their appearance was unexpected, but Nate was even more surprised when The Wolf handed the other woman a gun. They should have been unarmed.

Behind him, the elevator came to life again. The women heard it, too, and ducked behind a stack, out of sight.

Nate frowned. *Just when I thought it was going to be easy.*

"I TOLD YOU not to call me that," Ananke yelled at Orbits.

"Don't rile him up," Quinn whispered. "Just get him in the open."

"What are you doing over there, kitten? I, um, mean Annie," Orbits said.

"Annie's not my name, either," she yelled. "What the hell's wrong with you?"

"I'm sorry," he replied defensively.

"Ricky, if you don't want to get hurt, get out here!"

"Oh, yeah? Well, I'm not the one who's going to get hurt!"

"All right, then. Prove to us you have an M16. Fire off a round." She paused. "Go ahead. Any time now." Another pause. "We're waiting." Still nothing.

As Quinn had suspected—and apparently Ananke had, too—Orbits had lied about the rifle.

"If I come out there, you'll shoot me," Orbits said.

"If I was going to shoot you, I'd have done it years ago. God knows I probably should have. But you know why I won't?"

"Why?"

"Because you can't help that you're an idiot."

"Hey, that's not—"

"Ricky!"

"Fine, maybe you won't shoot me, but your friend will."

With a roll of her eyes, she said loudly enough for Ricky to hear, "Quinn, are you going to shoot him?"

"Not if he cooperates," Quinn replied, his volume matching hers.

"See, no one's going to shoot you. Now, last chance or I'm coming over there myself and putting you out of our misery!"

"Fine, fine. I'm coming out. But I swear, if you shoot me…"

"What?" Ananke asked. "If we shoot you, what are you going to do, Ricky?"

"Why are you so pissed off at me?"

Quinn edged around the crate, pointing his gun toward Orbits's voice, while Ananke positioned herself beside him so she could see, too. "Any time now," Quinn said.

"I'm coming, all right? Calm down."

Orbits appeared from behind the boxes, his hands shoulder high. In his right was his gun.

"Toss the weapon this way," Quinn ordered.

"Now why would I—"

Ananke fired a bullet past his head.

"Okay," Orbits said. "It's all yours."

He lobbed the gun into the aisle with enough force that when it hit the concrete, it skidded past Quinn and Ananke's position with no sign of stopping.

"Happy?" Orbits asked.

Quinn and Ananke stepped out from their hiding place.

"Where are the women?" Quinn asked.

"I don't know anything about any *women*," Orbits said. "Wait, that didn't come out right."

"Where are Dani and Orlando?"

"If by Dani you mean Danielle, that little…"

Quinn raised his gun a few inches.

Orbits said, "…*princess* ran off right before you two started chasing me."

"She's not with you?" Ananke asked.

"Not anymore."

"Where did she go?" Quinn said.

"Well, you should know. You were the ones shooting at me while she got away."

"We weren't the ones shooting at you."

Orbits looked confused. "You weren't?"

"Orlando," Ananke said to Quinn.

"Who's this Orlando?"

Quinn motioned toward the elevator. "Come on."

"Where are we going?" Orbits asked.

"Out."

"I'm not go—"

"Ricky, move!" Ananke ordered.

They started down the aisle, Ricky in front with Quinn and Ananke right behind him.

"Just so we're clear," Orbits said, "I've got dibs on this place."

NATE SNEAKED OVER to the wall and slipped sideways through the gap at the end of the row. He repeated the move at the next two stacks, stopping when he reached the crates that separated him from where he'd last seen the women.

He heard the elevator stop at the top for a few seconds and then descend again. Wanting to neutralize the problem before Quinn and the others arrived, he slid into the final gap and inched forward, pausing just short of the corner.

No sounds. Had they moved on?

He inched forward again, easing his head out of the stack for a quick look.

"Hi, there."

The motorcyclist stood four feet away, her gun pointed between his eyes.

QUINN MADE RICKY open the elevator door when they reached the first level. Stepping out, he expected to find Nate waiting for them, but his partner wasn't there.

"Nate?" he said. When no response came, he flicked on his mic and repeated his friend's name.

Ananke looked at him, alarmed.

"What's going on?" Orbits asked.

"Shut up," she whispered.

Quinn cautiously approached the central aisle, but before he could reach it Nate came around the corner, the motorcyclist holding a gun to the back of his head. As Quinn and Ananke jerked their weapons up, The Wolf stepped out behind the motorcyclist, also armed.

"Well, isn't this convenient?" The Wolf said. "All the people I've been…" She stopped. "Hold on. Where's Danielle?"

"Drop your weapons," Quinn said.

The Wolf laughed. "I don't think so. You drop yours."

"Not going to happen."

"Then we have a problem," she said. "But one we can easily solve. I want to know what happened to the girl. Did you kill her now that you found this place? It's what I would have done."

"Let my friend go," Quinn said.

"Or do you have her tied up somewhere? I hope so. I've so been looking forward to reminiscing with her about her father."

"I said, let him go."

"Answer my question and maybe we will. If you don't, I *will* have Bianca kill him."

Quinn drew in a breath. "We both know that won't happen. If she kills him, then we kill you."

"Well, isn't this exciting?" Orbits said. "Four guns, two on each side. I kind of feel left out. I probably should just—"

"Don't move," Ananke said, her eyes not leaving The Wolf. "Or you will be the first one hit."

Orbits froze.

"Let him go now," Quinn said to The Wolf, "and we'll leave this place to you."

"It's that easy, is it? Why do I have the feeling that when we finally leave, the police and FBI would be waiting for us up top?"

"I promise, there won't be any police."

"That's comforting. How about we do this?"

AFTER PAUSING TWICE more so Orlando could rest, she and Dani finally reached the door at the end of the emergency tunnel.

"What's on the other side?" Orlando asked.

"Level one."

"And what's there?"

"Storage."

"Storing what?"

Dani was silent for a moment, and then seemed to come to some kind of decision. "Weapons."

"What kinds of weapons?"

"Military grade, mostly. Rifles, guns, ammunition, explosives, different things like that."

"Why?"

Another pause. "Do you know who Charles Hayes was?"

Orlando stared at her. "The arms dealer?"

Dani nodded. "This was his secret hoard."

Hayes had been the kind of man who sold weapons to both sides of a conflict to keep the flow of cash coming. No wonder The Wolf was involved. She'd been his partner and had been crippled when their business collapsed after his death.

"How do you know about this place?" Orlando asked.

"He was my father."

That was even more stunning.

"Please tell me you're not here to lay claim to all of it."

"God, no. I've been trying to keep it secret so no one would ever find it."

Orlando believed her. There was so much more she wanted to ask, but that could wait until they were safe.

"Switch places with me," she said.

It took some coordination to squeeze past each other, but soon Orlando was at the door with Dani behind her. She pulled down on the lever and was relieved when it didn't stick.

Of course, just when she cracked the door open, another

contraction hit. She leaned against the wall as the pain shot through her.

"Are you all right?" Dani whispered.

No, she wasn't all right, but even if Orlando had wanted to admit it, she couldn't at that moment because she'd temporarily lost her command of words. She held up a finger, hoping that would be enough to answer Dani.

She couldn't deny it anymore. The contractions hadn't been false at all. She was officially in labor. She tried to remember how long it had been since the last contraction. Fifteen minutes ago? Less?

Finally, her muscles started to relax again. She took a deep but quiet breath. As soon as she could manage it, she smiled at Dani. "I'm fine," she whispered.

"Are you about to have—"

"Don't," Orlando said. "Don't even say it."

She turned back to the door. When she'd cracked it a few minutes earlier, she hadn't remembered hearing any voices, but she could definitely hear them now. Quinn's voice, and a woman's. She opened the door farther, saw she wasn't in direct sight of anyone, and crawled out.

Free of the tunnel's confines, she could now hear every word being spoken. She motioned for Dani to stay where she was, and then worked her way along a row of crates until she could have a visual on the situation.

"I'M SURE THERE'S a room here we can lock you all in," The Wolf said. "You can spend your last few days starving to death. No messy bullets. It's a good offer."

"Some might say generous," Quinn said.

The Wolf smiled. "Very true."

"I'm not one of them."

She sighed. "I'm afraid it's the best I can do."

"You're not getting out of this," he said. "Drop your weapons and we'll—"

With a suddenness that surprised everyone, Orlando slipped out from the stack directly behind the women and whipped the barrel of her gun into Bianca's head. As the hunter staggered, Orlando yanked the woman's gun from her hand. She then pointed one of her weapons at The Wolf and the other at Bianca.

"What was the plan here, folks?" she asked. "Were you all going to talk each other to death?"

As The Wolf started to move her gun around, Orlando took a quick sidestep and shoved the muzzle of her gun into the woman's ear.

"Go ahead and test me," she said. "I am *not* in a good mood."

The woman lowered her gun hand.

"Drop it."

The Wolf let the pistol clatter to the floor.

Orbits, apparently seeing an opportunity, ran past Orlando and down the central aisle toward the exit.

"Please tell me I'm supposed to shoot him," Orlando said.

"I'll get him," Ananke said.

As the assassin ran off, Quinn and Nate took over watching The Wolf and Bianca.

"Where were you?" Quinn asked Orlando.

"Service tunnel." She made a vague gesture across the room.

"Have you seen Dani?"

"How do you think I found the damn thing?" Raising her voice, she said, "Dani, it's okay. Come on out."

After a moment, Dani stepped into the aisle.

ANANKE RACED AFTER Orbits.

"Ricky! Stop!" she yelled to no avail.

He turned down the short aisle to the exit and disappeared

into the tunnel. She entered just in time to see him go around the bend. She then heard a cry of surprise and a thud.

She slowed as she came to the corner and raised her gun before moving around it.

"I think I may have hit him too hard," Daeng said.

He was kneeling next to Orbits, who lay on the floor, unconscious.

Ananke lowered her weapon. "I doubt it."

42

THEY PUT THE Wolf and Bianca in an empty maintenance closet and tied them up.

"You know I'll be free again in no time," The Wolf said. "I know people in very important positions. I'll never see the inside of a prison."

"Perhaps not a typical prison," Quinn said. "But I'm sure Helen will find someplace nice to put you."

"Helen? Do you mean Helen Cho? I hate to break it to you but Helen won't be doing anything anymore."

"And why is that?" Orlando asked.

"Let's just say I never worry about the dead."

"Oh, right," Orlando said. "You're under the impression your people killed her at the Imperial Theater." She shook her head sympathetically. "Sorry, but she got out yesterday, very much alive. And I know she's going to be pleased to learn that you're our guest."

For the first time, The Wolf looked uncertain. Her eyes flicked past Quinn and Orlando to Dani standing just outside the room. "You're not going to let them do this to me, are you? I was your father's friend. I used to play with you when you were a baby. We're practically family."

Dani stared at her, and then stepped into the doorway. Without taking her eyes off The Wolf, she swung around the hand she'd been holding behind her back. In it was a gun, pointed at The Wolf.

"Hold on, Dani," Quinn said. "Think about what you're doing."

"My father?" Dani said to The Wolf. "You think I care about your relationship to him? I hate him for who he was, for the harm he did. My real family—my mother and sister—are dead because of him. You were his partner so you are just as responsible." She pushed the muzzle against The Wolf's cheek.

"Dani," Orlando whispered calmly.

"How many hundreds of thousands of lives are you responsible for taking already?" Dani asked as if no one else but The Wolf was there. With her free hand, she gestured behind her. "And how many more would you be responsible for after you took everything my father had stashed here?" She pressed the gun deeper into The Wolf's skin.

Quinn tentatively placed a hand on her shoulder. "Dani, you don't want to do this."

She shot him a quick look and then focused back on The Wolf. "Tell me one reason why she doesn't deserve to die."

He took a step forward and put a hand over the gun. "Even if there isn't one, you're not an executioner."

He pulled gently on the barrel, her resistance holding it in place for another second before she relaxed.

The Wolf smiled. "I guess you're not your father's daughter after all."

"That's probably the nicest thing you could have said to her," Orlando said, before she smacked the grip of her gun into The Wolf's cheek.

ORBITS CAME TO as they finished zip-tying him to one of the pipes running up the side of the silo.

"Are you going to leave me here to die?" he asked.

"I wish," Ananke said.

"Then what's going to happen to me?"

"That'll be up to our client," Quinn said.

"Your client? No, no, no. There's no reason you can't just let me go now. You've got The Wolf, man. Your client will be more than happy with her. And don't worry about me. I'll strike this place from my memory."

Ananke looked at him as if he were a child. "Ricky, you auctioned off a human being."

"Well, okay, sure, but ultimately I didn't. In fact, if anyone should be in trouble for that, it should be The Wolf for stiffing me."

"I'm sure she will be aptly punished," Quinn said.

Looking less than satisfied with the answer, Orbits said, "That won't get me my money, though, will it?"

After the two men Daeng had taken care of on the stairs had been carried into the room with The Wolf, Quinn had everyone gather back in the level-one storage area.

"So…what now?" Ananke said. "We call Helen and let her deal with everything?"

"Soon enough," Quinn said. He looked at Dani. "We're going to have to tell our client, you realize that, right?"

"What will she do with everything?"

"See that it doesn't fall into the wrong hands."

"Who decides whose hands are right and whose are wrong?"

He paused for a moment, and then said, "I can only tell you that I trust her."

Dani nodded. "I guess that's the best I can hope for."

"Can I ask a question?" he said.

Dani looked at him.

"When you were, um, talking to The Wolf, you mentioned your father. Who was he?"

She looked at Orlando and back at Quinn. "Charles Hayes. He was an arms dealer."

Quinn had heard the name before but it had been years. "And The Wolf was his partner?"

"Yeah."

"So all this," Nate said, looking around, "was what? A shipment that didn't get delivered?"

"Backup supply. He'd skim a bit off other jobs and deposit it here. He once told my sister it was his retirement plan."

"You were trying to get here when Edmondson caught you, weren't you?" Orlando asked.

A nod. "I thought...I thought there'd been enough time. I thought everyone would have forgotten."

"What do you mean?" Nate asked.

"I'd stayed out of the country for ten years, living under a false name. For the first few years, people tried to find me. There were rumors, you know, about my father's 'treasure.' After a while, they stopped searching. I promised myself I'd wait a full ten years. I guess it wasn't enough."

"But why come back at all?" he asked.

"Because I had to."

No one said anything, all waiting for her to go on.

"My mom didn't know what my dad really did until after my sister and I were born. When she found out, it scared her to death. She wanted to leave him, but she was afraid he'd take us from her. So she stayed, and secretly brought us up to hate everything he stood for. Marianne and I were scared of him, too, and it wasn't hard hiding from him how we really felt.

"When Marianne turned sixteen, he said it was time to start showing her the business. I was ten then. The idea that he would expose Marianne to his world finally set off my mom. They argued for nearly two weeks, night and day. Then one morning Mom was gone. Our father said she was visiting a friend or something like that, I don't remember exactly. But she never came back."

"He killed her?" Nate said.

"There was never a body, but, yes, I'm sure he did. Marianne told me not to worry. That she would take care of me. She let our father teach her the business. He showed her everything, even this place. She acted interested but she became even more revolted by what he was. We would sit up nights and sometimes think of ways to destroy him, but it was all just wishful thinking.

"That was until I turned fifteen, and he said it was almost time for me to join the business. Marianne had no intention of letting that happen. She told me she had a plan. She laid it out and then taught me my part, going over and over every detail for months, including the backup plan in case things went wrong. Turned out the main part of the plan was just a smoke screen, and the emergency plan was what she'd intended for me to carry out all along. A month shy of my sixteenth birthday, she killed him in his office. Later that night she died in a one-car accident that wasn't an accident at all. My father's people were responsible."

"The Wolf?" Orlando asked.

"It wouldn't surprise me," Dani said. "I think Marianne knew she wasn't going to get away with it. That's why she worked so hard to prepare me. She'd even arranged it so that immediately following the funerals, I was sent to a boarding school in London. The day after I arrived in England, a friend of Marianne's took me to France and helped me disappear."

"There's something I still don't understand," Quinn said. "The gear here has got to be worth hundreds of millions, but it's older stuff. On top of that, getting it out of here without attracting attention won't be easy, not to mention getting it out of the country. Transportation costs, bribes—even if we ignore The Wolf's fifty-million-dollar bid for you, the next highest was in the upper forties. That's too much for this."

"That's because everything you've seen is just the icing," Dani said.

Without another word, she led them to the elevator. Even though the car was sitting there and the door was open, she stepped over to the call button and ran her fingers along the edge of its metal faceplate.

"Ah, there," she said with a grin as the plate swung out.

In addition to the wires leading from the button, a key sat in a small space at the bottom.

"Who's coming with me?" she asked as she stepped onto the elevator.

"Daeng, Ananke, if you don't mind staying here and keeping an eye on things?" Quinn said.

"Of course," Daeng said.

"You can stay," Ananke said, "but I'm not going to miss this."

Quinn was about to argue, but Daeng held up a hand. "It's okay. I can handle things."

As Orlando moved toward the elevator, Dani looked at her stomach.

"You should probably stay up here, too," Dani said.

Orlando stopped. "Why?"

"Just a precaution."

"A precaution from what?"

"It's okay," Quinn said. "Keep Daeng company. If I think it's safe, I'll come get you."

Orlando did not look happy at all, but only said, "Don't be long."

"Nate, do you mind shutting the doors?" Dani asked.

While he did this, she stuck the key into the hole next to the orphaned button on the control panel. When she turned it, the button lit up and the elevator began descending.

The trip was a short one. Nate opened the inner gate when they stopped, only to find a set of closed doors on the other side, split down the middle top to bottom. Embedded in the door was a meter with a range from green to red, the needle resting comfortably in the former.

"What's that for?" Nate asked.

"Just a safety precaution. Green is good," Dani replied.

When she turned the key again, the doors slid apart and lights came on in the space beyond.

Though Quinn was sure the size of the room was no different than that of the levels above them, it appeared considerably larger since there were no stacks of crates filling it. The only unusual feature was a boxed-off room of some kind protruding from the wall on the other side. Quinn wasn't surprised when Dani began walking toward it.

Halfway there, they passed another meter, this one mounted to a structural post. It, too, was registering in the green zone.

The walls of the separate room were unpainted concrete. Near the only door—also made of concrete—were two more meters, a monitor, and a control panel. The needle on one of the meters was in the green, but the other one was sitting a bit past the point where green started fading into yellow.

"What is this?" Quinn asked.

"You wanted to know why people were willing to spend so much?" Dani said. "This is it."

She fiddled with the control panel until the monitor came to life, revealing a shot of what was presumably the room's interior. Four trunks sat side by side, approximately two feet apart from each other. All were black with gold-colored metal trim and had what looked like thick leather handles. The feed could have easily been of a photograph because the image was completely still.

The back of Quinn's neck began to tingle. A bunker full of weapons. An isolation room. Strategically placed meters. "Please tell me those aren't what I think they are."

"They are."

Nate looked at Quinn and then the monitor again. "Nukes?"

"What?" Ananke said, moving several steps backward. "Are you saying those are nukes?"

Dani nodded. "According to Marianne, my father considered the trunks his greatest asset. But you don't have to worry. The room has a thick lead lining and three feet of concrete on the outside."

"Is that enough?" Ananke asked. She looked at the others. "Does anyone know? There could be a leak."

"No leak," Dani said. "The meters are all in the green."

Ananke did not look convinced.

Quinn said, "Unless there's something else, I think we should head back up."

Ananke turned and headed for the elevator.

"There is one thing I need to get first," Dani said. "Go on. I'll be right there."

Quinn eyed her for a moment. "You're not planning on going inside there, are you?"

"What? No. I don't have a death wish."

"Don't take too long," he said. "I don't think I can make Ananke stay down here much longer."

THE WALK TOWARD the corner of the room felt unreal, as if Dani were watching it on a movie screen instead of making the journey herself. How many times had she thought about this? How many times had Marianne gone over the details so Dani wouldn't forget?

Go to the corner left of the chamber.

Run a finger up the south wall and feel for the thin line cut into the surface.

Three inches up, push.

The concrete cracked under the pressure of her hand and fell in small chunks to the floor, revealing a black door no larger than a postcard. She slipped a finger into a depression and pulled the door open.

As she'd been told to expect, in the box was only one thing—a small Moleskine notebook. Though the other bidders would have been interested in the rumored bombs her father had hidden away, Dani knew this notebook was what The Wolf had really been after. She put it in her pocket, not bothering to open it. Either the information was there, or it wasn't.

"All set?" Quinn asked as she entered the elevator.

"All set." She turned the key and started their ascent.

"You going to tell us what that was all about?" Nate asked.

"No," she said.

THOUGH ORLANDO HAD been less than pleased when Dani suggested she remain behind, it turned out to be a good thing. The others had not been gone for more than a few minutes when another round of contractions hit.

Daeng had gone off to check on the prisoners and by the time he returned, she was in control enough to hide her discomfort.

She had to get out of there soon, though. The interval between contractions was already down to ten minutes—probably a little less. With Garrett, labor had been a slow and steady process, but this time it felt like Orlando had suddenly caught a brakeless express train to Delivery City.

Several minutes later, the elevator motor kicked in and the car returned.

"Well?" Orlando asked as everyone piled out.

"Be thankful you stayed here," Ananke said, looking unnerved.

"What happened?" Orlando asked Quinn.

Quinn told her about the four portable nukes, then said, "There's no reason we need to hang around here any longer. I'll call Helen. This place is her problem, not ours." He glanced at Dani. "Unless you have any objections."

She shook her head.

The discussion turned to whether or not they should leave the prisoners there, but Orlando heard only bits and pieces as her contractions ramped up once more.

"Helen should make that call," Quinn said. "We'll leave them down—" He looked at Orlando. "Are you okay?"

She gave up all attempts to conceal her pain and grabbed Daeng's arm to keep from falling. "Not exactly," she said, her fingers digging into her friend's flesh.

Quinn rushed over and put an arm around her to help support her. "What's wrong?"

She looked at him as if he were insane. "What do you think is wrong?"

Ananke, calm and clinical, asked, "How far apart are your contractions?"

Orlando blew out a breath. "I think about eight minutes that time." She closed her eyes and clenched her teeth, riding out another wave of pain before continuing.

"She's having the baby?" Nate asked. "Now? Here?"

"Just breathe, sweetie," Quinn said. "Breathe."

"What the hell do you think I'm doing?" Orlando said.

"I-I'm sorry," he stammered. "I didn't mean—"

"I *know* you didn't mean anything!" Orlando shouted.

"Maybe you should sit down," Nate suggested. "Shouldn't she sit down?"

"Do you want some water?" Dani asked. "I'm sure I can find some."

Ananke slammed her palm against one of the nearby crates. "Hey, everyone. Eyes on me!"

All conversation ceased.

Looking at Quinn, she said, "Unless you want your baby born in a missile silo, I suggest we concentrate on getting her out of here!"

ANANKE AND DANI led the way up with Nate and Daeng coming next, carrying Orlando in the cradle of their clasped arms. Quinn was immediately behind them.

Not knowing what else to do, he alternated between giving Orlando words of encouragement and updates on their progress. Whether she was listening to him or not, he didn't know, but he couldn't stop talking even if he wanted to.

When they stopped for a quick rest around the three-quarters point, Quinn offered to switch with one of his friends.

"Absolutely not," Orlando said. "Look at you. You'll drop me."

He hadn't noticed until that moment that he was shaking.

Not long after they began walking again, Orlando's contractions returned. Ananke looked at her watch.

"How far apart?" Quinn asked.

Without looking back, Ananke said, "Let's just say the sooner we get out of here, the better."

THE BABY WAS born in the backseat of The Wolf's Explorer. Ananke, the only one with any birthing experience, acted as Orlando's midwife. After she made sure the child was breathing properly, she held the cord for Quinn to cut and handed him his daughter.

"Do you have a name picked out?" she asked.

If their child had been a boy, he would have been named David Abraham, in honor of Quinn's brother who'd died as a child, and Orlando's mentor who'd passed the previous winter. And if a girl—

"Claire," Orlando said, looking both exhausted and happy.

"Claire what?" Ananke asked.

"We haven't decided on a middle name yet," Quinn said.

"How about Ananke? It has a certain ring to it."

Orlando frowned. "I don't think so."

"Correct me if I'm wrong, but I did just help you deliver her."

Orlando's expression softened. "You did. Thank you. I...I'm glad you were here."

Ananke looked at her for a moment, as if waiting for a punch line. When one didn't come, she said, "I didn't have anywhere else to be."

THOUGH TAKING THE Explorer would have been preferable, the police would be looking for it and the car Orbits had fled in. So the only safe vehicle for Quinn and his team to leave in was the sedan Orlando had been driving. Everyone was able to fit in only by having Orlando lie across Quinn's, Daeng's, and Ananke's laps.

A phone call to the Mole secured the services of a doctor in Topeka who wouldn't ask questions. They arrived at his home twenty minutes later, and soon after Orlando and Claire were both asleep in the doctor's guest room.

"Quinn?"

Dani was standing just outside the guest-room doorway. Quinn quietly walked into the hall and shut the door.

"I need to get going," she said. "I have...things I need to take care of."

He knew it had something to do with whatever she took from the bottom storage level.

"I can leave, can't I?" she asked.

"Of course."

"What about your client? You're supposed to give me to her."

"My client will be more than happy with the silo. I can't guarantee others won't still be looking for you, though. It'll be a little while before word gets out that your father's stash is in the hands of the US government." He paused. "I might know someone who can help you."

"I don't need help."

"Have you not been paying attention the last couple of days? Because clearly you do," he said with a smile. "My friend can get you new identifications, arrange travel to wherever you want to go, and make sure you're not being followed."

"And then he tells you and you know where I am?"

"I have no interest in knowing where you are. I'll put you in contact with him and then I'm out. He's a little odd but you can trust him."

When she finally accepted his offer, he connected her to the Mole. An hour later, a car arrived at the doctor's house to pick her up.

Nate, Ananke, and Daeng said their good-byes before Quinn took his turn.

"In a few months you should be able to stop hiding."

"I'm not sure I know how to do that," she said.

"You'll figure it out."

She wrapped her arms around him. "Thank you. I'm glad you guys were the ones who found me."

"I am, too."

She planted a kiss on his cheek and then hurried to her car.

ANANKE LEFT THAT evening after spending some closed-door time with Orlando. With a wink and a "see you later, boys," she was gone.

"What were you two talking about?" Quinn asked Orlando later.

"Old stuff. Nothing you need worry about."

"Are you two friends now?"

"Did I say that?" she asked, but with none of the venom he would have expected.

Claire squirmed and opened her eyes.

"Can you hold her for a moment?" Orlando asked.

He lifted his daughter into his arms and stared into her eyes. "We did this?"

"Yeah, we did."

Claire wrinkled her brow in the exact same way he'd seen Orlando do a million times.

"She's perfect," he said, as he wondered if there could ever be a better moment than this.

43

FOR THE LAST several days, Helen Cho had embarked on a housecleaning mission. The first casualty was the overnight director on duty when she'd been kidnapped, who'd been recruited by The Wolf. It turned out he wasn't the only leak in the office. An assistant info tech had been feeding information to another branch of US Intelligence, and an agent doing the same with an independent, ultra-patriotic organization. All three were arrested and would soon be appearing in a secret court.

The acquisition of the silo was an unexpected bonus. With the weapons and the nuclear devices came the woman responsible for Helen's disappearance. Not wanting to chance losing her in the stateside system, Helen had The Wolf rendered to a secret base in eastern Europe, where the extraction of information about the woman's business dealings would be performed under less rigorous standards than in the States. As for Ricky Orbits, Helen decided a nice, ten-year stretch in a federal facility would be adequate.

NEW YORK, NEW YORK

THERE WAS NO official rebuke of Morse's actions in connection with the Charles Hayes matter. There were only citations and tributes in the wake of a "requested" early retirement. As for Lyle Clark, Morse's contact on the board of directors, some people were too powerful to be removed.

WASHINGTON, DC

VALOR, TOO, HAD to serve up a sacrificial lamb. Though Scott Bennett had been no more than a go-between, he was called upon to pay the price.

News services carried a story about rumors concerning a well-known lobbyist's connections to Mexican drug cartels. The connections would one day be proved as false, but the mere mention of the possibility was all that was needed to start the death spiral of his career, and the business he had worked so hard to build disappeared overnight.

Valor understood sacrifice, and appreciated Bennett playing his part. He would be required to live a quieter life, but money would continue to flow his way, and he was promised that one day he would achieve great success again.

BERLIN, GERMANY

ASSISTANT TRADE ATTACHÉ Komarov had a message waiting for him when he arrived at the embassy instructing him to destroy the codebook hidden behind his filing cabinet. He was further instructed to avoid all contact with Herr Schwartz.

He knew it had to do with the operation a week earlier, but what specifically he had no idea, and didn't want to find out.

It was over. That's all that was important. And he couldn't be happier.

LOS ANGELES, CALIFORNIA

THE CITY OF Angels was abuzz with the news of prominent businessman Thomas Rachett's arrest in connection with a secret sex club he had apparently been running. Each day more tidbits would leak out about other illegal dealings he'd supposedly been involved in, threatening to bring down not only Rachett but several well-known politicians.

GEORGE TOWN, CAYMAN ISLANDS

THE MOLE TURNED out to be even more helpful than Dani could have hoped. Within forty-eight hours of leaving Quinn, she had five sets of IDs, all with different names, and had crossed unmolested into Mexico.

Per the Mole's suggestion, she had taken a circuitous route to her primary destination, allowing him to ensure she didn't pick up any unwanted admirers. By the time she stepped off the plane in the Cayman Islands, a whole four days had passed since she had visited the silo.

She was up early that first morning, studying the appropriate page of her father's notebook. At nine a.m., she put the book away, showered, dressed, and walked the five blocks from her hotel in George Town to the bank where the first account was kept.

The bank president personally handled everything for her, but even with his help it took all morning to finalize the transfer. That afternoon she repeated the process at bank number two.

The next day she was able to fit in three different institutions. And on the seventh day after she left Kansas, she visited the final four.

One would never know from the modest dinner she had that evening that she was now worth nine hundred and forty-eight million dollars. But her wealth would only be temporary. The money wasn't really hers.

It belonged to the promise.

"There's a book he keeps in the bottom level," Marianne had explained. "Bank account numbers and passwords. His failsafe in case he needs to purge his digital copy. If I can't get it, you have to."

"I will," Dani had said, though at that time, she hadn't known how, if it came to it, she could possibly pull it off.

"And promise me you'll use the money to help whoever he's hurt. If I can't, you'll be the only one left."

"I promise."

Made in United States
North Haven, CT
01 August 2024